Praise for *Dial Em for Murder*

"Bates weaves a fast-paced, heart-in-throat thriller with characters who first skewer you with wit and then punch you in the feels. Start this one early, because you won't want to stop!"

—Mary Elizabeth Summer,
author of *Trust Me, I'm Lying* and *Trust Me, I'm Trouble*

"Marni Bates knows how to bring the suspense! *Dial Em for Murder* kept me up—with all the lights on—long past my bedtime."

—Tracy Deebs, author of *Doomed* and The Tempest series,
and coauthor of The Hero Agenda series

"Marni Bates's *Dial Em for Murder* has it all: quirky humor, pulse-quickening action, and a sassy heroine you'll love so much you won't know which of the two hot guys to root for. It's the perfect beach read!"

—Emily McKay, author of The Farm series

"*Dial Em for Murder* combines a feisty heroine with enough action, mystery, humor, and romance to keep readers flipping pages well into the night. The main characters are all endearing in their own ways, but I was never sure who I could trust. Each time I thought I had everything figured out, the story spun me for another loop. A funny and engaging read that will keep you guessing."

—Paula Stokes, author of *Liars, Inc.*

Dedication

This book is dedicated to every coffee-shop daydreamer.
Sometimes those fantasies really do come true.
(You're reading this right now! That's proof.)
I hope you never stop fighting for your dreams.

———

Acknowledgments

This book wouldn't exist without the tireless help and support of my agent, Shannon Hassan. You pushed me creatively, and I am so grateful that you did. Thank you. You are amazing. I also want to extend an enormous thank-you to my fabulous editor Jacquelyn Mitchard and her wonderful team at Merit for bringing this book to life! It means the world to me.

I'm incredibly lucky to have patient family members and friends. A special thanks to my mom for listening to every possible plot twist. My writing sprint partner, Alicia Thompson, for forcing me to face the blank page. Diana Wiener for a thousand and one supportive words and coffee-shop visits! Marina Adair for some truly incredible advice. Laura Fraley for laughing with me when I can't sleep because I'm too afraid of my own imaginary villains. I need to thank Tracy Wolff, Erica Cameron, MK Meredith, Cecily White, Hannah Jayne, Abigail Dock, Katrina Galka, Lisa Lin, Paula Stokes, Anja Johnson, Jen Maneja, Angela Bailey, and oh man, a few hundred other amazing people who have given me hugs/coffee/laughter/endless encouragement. You know how much I love ya!

Lastly, I want to thank my fans. You make me feel like the luckiest writer in the whole freaking world. Thank you for believing in me. Each of you is infinitely precious to me!

All my love,
Marni

DIAL EM
FOR
Murder

SHE WANTED TO WRITE A MYSTERY, NOT LIVE IT

— MARNI BATES —

MeritPress | fw

Published by
Merit Press
an imprint of F+W Media, Inc.
10151 Carver Road, Suite 200
Blue Ash, OH 45242. U.S.A.
www.meritpressbooks.com

ISBN 10: 1-4405-9585-2
ISBN 13: 978-1-4405-9585-1
eISBN 10: 1-4405-9586-0
eISBN 13: 978-1-4405-9586-8

Printed in the United States of America.

10 9 8 7 6 5 4 3 2 1

This is a work of fiction. Names, characters, corporations, institutions, organizations, events, or locales in this novel are either the product of the author's imagination or, if real, used fictitiously. The resemblance of any character to actual persons (living or dead) is entirely coincidental.

Many of the designations used by manufacturers and sellers to distinguish their products are claimed as trademarks. Where those designations appear in this book and F+W Media, Inc. was aware of a trademark claim, the designations have been printed with initial capital letters.

Cover design by Sylvia McArdle.
Cover images © iStockphoto.com/Peter Zelei, MartinaVaculikova.

This book is available at quantity discounts for bulk purchases.
For information, please call 1-800-289-0963.

CHAPTER 1

She sighed as he moved his lips more firmly across hers. "Oh Josh!" Christine moaned. "Take me with you! I'm not afraid of facing down a drug cartel if it means that we can stay together!"

Tapping one nail-bitten finger against the Starbucks table, I grimaced as I reread the words that I had just typed on the screen.

They sucked.

The characters were flat, the dialogue stilted, and the motivations felt awfully flimsy to me. I mean, any girl willing to *die* for some random guy—even if they did just share a night of blistering passion—was an airhead in my book.

Which was exactly why the whole thing belonged in the little trash icon at the bottom of the screen. So much for seeing my name, Emmy Danvers, gracing the cover of a book. At this rate, I'd be stuck with forty manuscripts hidden under my bed that would never see the light of day.

"Grande mocha Frappuccino for Emmy."

I shot one last frustrated look at the laptop screen before grabbing my bag and moving toward the counter. The only benefit to checking out the same ancient high school laptop every week, besides the obvious fact that I couldn't afford to buy one of my own, was that *nobody* would be even slightly tempted to steal it while my back was turned. I mentally began to flip through ways to describe my characters' intense attraction—a passion that wouldn't be diminished even by the evil drug lord determined to pull them asunder.

Her heart raced.

His pulse began to pound.

I reached for my drink, contemplating the subtle differences between gasping and panting, only to have a wrinkled, age-spotted hand snatch it away from me.

The old man was painfully thin with a sweater bagging loosely around his slight frame, white grizzled hair, and slightly rheumy ice blue eyes. I pointedly cleared my throat, but instead of catching his mistake and apologizing like a normal person, he *winked* at me as he sauntered toward his table as if this was all some big joke. As if he had every right to steal *my* drink without so much as a mumbled apology. As if he hadn't just taken my *caffeine*.

Still, I tried to keep it civil. "Um, sir? That's my drink."

"Sit down. We have much to discuss." His tone was cultured, the words precise and clipped.

"We don't have anything to discuss. If you'll just hand over my drink, I'll leave you alone. See, it says 'Em' right here and—"

A strange look crossed his face as if every muscle in his body tightened. It was like I'd tripped over a panic button and put a nuclear missile on standby alert. He grabbed my wrist with his one free hand in a painfully tight hold while I stared at him, too stunned to do anything more than instinctively lurch backwards.

I had no idea what was going on, but his grip *hurt*.

The pressure increased and the small part of my brain that was observing all of this with a detached sense of disbelief pointed out that his strength was pretty damn impressive for an old man who had probably been cashing in his senior citizen discount for over a decade. I tried to flag down a barista by flailing my free arm. But the four Starbucks employees were too focused on the long line of waiting customers to spare a glance for the good-natured old man they probably assumed was holding hands with his beloved great niece.

Nobody around me seemed to realize that something was seriously off.

"Em," he repeated my name roughly. "You need to listen to me. Pay attention, dammit! You're not safe."

No freaking kidding.

"You're hurting me, sir." I began mentally negotiating with whatever higher power that might be interested in getting me out of this situation. *If he lets go of my wrist, I'll make more of an effort in P.E. I'll stop doing those half-assed pushups with my knees on the ground. Hell, I'll even try to do a chin-up instead of just dangling from the iron bar.*

"Your father's in danger." The old man shook me like I was a piggy bank with a reluctant penny rattling around inside. "You're both in danger and I can't fix it. *Not anymore.*"

No drink was worth this kind of hassle.

"You've got the wrong girl," I said cautiously. "You need to let me go."

His eyes glassed over and his whole body trembled with the effort it took to remain latched onto my wrist.

"Morgan will know what to do, always was better with the details. And they're coming, girl. I'd stake my life on it. They're coming to kill me."

Well, okay.

That explained everything. He was certifiably insane—just like all the other New York City crazies who barged into Starbucks yelling about the Secret Service, Queen Elizabeth, Beyoncé, Jesus, and, on one very memorable occasion, Charlie Chaplin.

If he hadn't maintained his grip on my wrist, I would've grabbed my laptop and left without looking back. Okay, there would've been *one* backward glance, but only because the level of detail in my romance manuscripts needed work. I tended to skim over the small things; the way his breath smelled slightly of peppermint, the soft nubby texture of his sweater rubbing against my wrist, the surge of strength in his leathery fingers.

"Uh, I'm sure you're right, sir. Morgan will know how to help you."

Okay, so I was lying to a man who was a single outburst away from joining the cast of *One Flew Over the Cuckoo's Nest*. For starters, my dad's name wasn't Morgan. And if my dad had any interest in helping me, he would've been there for me back in third grade when I broke my arm on the playground. Considering that my trip to the hospital and nearly three months in a cast hadn't been enough to snag his attention, I doubted a delusional old man would have any better luck.

"So you'll warn him?" he croaked. "Do you really mean it?"

I nodded, my face solemn. "Sure. Any other messages you want me to give my dad? That 9/11 was an inside job, maybe? The details behind JFK's assassination?"

His grin was far more unsettling than his earlier glare. There was something wild and feral lingering at the edges of it. A crocodile smile.

"Oswald completely botched that job. There's a reason things went down the way they did, but we don't have time to discuss it." He shook his head slowly, but his lips tilted upward into a gentler smile. "Why don't you go play outside now, Gracie? Your uncle and I have business to discuss."

Gracie. Okay, so maybe he was suffering from Alzheimer's instead of straight-up insanity. Maybe my deception was only making his delusions worse. Guilt jabbed at me.

"Uh, it's Em, sir," I said gently. "Emmy Danvers."

I probably should have kept that information to myself. His face did that tightening thing again, but he finally released my wrist and I yanked it back to my chest. My skin felt raw and bruised, but it was the old man who looked pained.

"Right. Emmy Danvers," he repeated. "You can't trust anyone. Do you understand what I am telling you? *Trust nobody and stay alert.* You won't survive long in the business if you don't go for the jugular, girl. That's how I always did it."

I blinked and fought the urge to ask him to explain that *rationally*.

"I really just wanted my drink." I grabbed my drink and stumbled toward my laptop, pausing only when I stood well beyond grabbing range. I don't know what compelled me to swivel around and meet his gaze again. He probably wouldn't remember meeting me within the next handful of minutes. Those ice-blue eyes of his were already becoming shuttered once more.

"I hope you get the help you need."

I wasn't kidding.

Even knowing that the people trying to kill him were all in his head, well, that didn't make it feel any less real to *him*. So maybe the guy was a whack job—I still understood feeling powerless. I'd experienced the acidic taste that it leaves behind in your mouth, a mixture of fear and copper pennies, every time my mom brought home another one of her sketchy boyfriends. Every time she tried to convince us both that she was one audition away from stardom.

I wondered if Gracie was real. If it broke his daughter Gracie's heart every time the old man descended into twisted nightmares where killers lurked within well-lit coffee shops. If she was his daughter, frantically searching for him, trying to figure out where he could have wandered this time. Or if Gracie was nothing more than another one of his delusions.

I wished him luck because I wasn't sure which scenario was worse.

Big mistake.

He tackled me. Right there in Starbucks, in front of all the baristas and the caffeine addicts and the people who happened to glance through the windows as they strolled down Madison Avenue. The old guy leaped at me as if he were a defensive linebacker in the NFL and sent me sprawling across the tile flooring, knocking the air right out of me. The stupid mocha Frappuccino that started this whole mess exploded on impact, drenching me.

A painfully long silence rocked the room. Each second stretched into something longer, languid, ugly. Nobody spoke. Nobody moved. Nobody breathed.

Maybe if somebody had rushed to my aid, they would have heard him whisper, "Always a caveat. Guard this with your life or you'll be next. Tell . . . your dad sorry."

Maybe they would have seen him slip something into my coat pocket.

But nobody did.

Pinning me to the floor and coated with coffee, the old man shuddered, convulsed, and died.

CHAPTER 2

"He *died* on you? For real? Take-him-to-the-morgue-and-bury-him died?"

My two best friends, Audrey Weinstein and Ben Tucker, stared at me in disbelief. Correction: Audrey stared at me in disbelief; Ben flat out didn't believe me. He had also been snickering ever since I'd mentioned working on my latest romance novel. Even if I caved and started letting people read my manuscripts, I would *never* show them to him. He'd only start quoting the dialogue from *Kidnapped by Her Italian Billionaire Lover* whenever he was in the mood to mock me.

I didn't think that one was my worst attempt at a novel, either.

My reply stamped out all traces of his amusement. "Yeah, he dive-bombed on top of me right before he went to the great Starbucks in the sky."

The euphemism didn't make me feel any better. I had hoped it would create a false sense of distance in my mind. If I could make an empty joke out of it, then maybe I wouldn't be haunted by the way his body had tenuously clung to life before he had stilled. I'd mentally replayed it throughout the night, unable to stand even the familiar weight of my comforter. Not when it reminded me of his prone form draped on top of me. I could still hear that last breath rattling out of him, right into my ear, as he apologized.

To me or to someone else—I had no idea.

The only thing worse than feeling his final gust of air tickle my neck was being trapped beneath the weight of his corpse.

Ben's smile disappeared and I could feel him giving me a slow once-over that had nothing to do with attraction and everything to do with his overly developed protective instinct that was on full display whenever he looked after his little brother, Cameron.

"Wow." Audrey tucked a strand of her pitch-black hair behind her ear and then shot me a suspicious look. "Are you messing with us? If this is a new writing technique, I'm not okay with it."

I pointed to the redness rimming my green eyes from my sleepless night, wishing that my skin had the golden undertone that Audrey had inherited from her Japanese-American mother. Whenever I was sleep-deprived or stressed people tended to ask if I was seriously ill. "Does this look like I'm kidding? I've been freaking out ever since it happened!"

"Em's not that good an actress, either," Ben said in what I considered a failed attempt to lighten the mood. I shot him my best death-ray glare when he ruffled my hair.

"Why didn't you call us?" Audrey gestured behind us at all the students milling around the cafeteria, loading their trays with enough saturated fats to send someone into cardiac arrest. "New rule, Em: If someone *dies*, you don't wait until lunch to casually bring it up! That's not okay."

"What was I supposed to do? Call you and say, 'Hey an old dude just tackled me in Starbucks, but I'm fine. Mostly. I'm doing better than he is, which, y'know, isn't saying much since he's dead. He's very dead. And I've gotta hang up and give the police my statement now. Bye!'"

Actually, that's *exactly* what I should have done. Audrey and Ben would have bolted to the nearest subway station and kept right on talking to me until the reception in the tunnel disconnected us. They would have been there for me, without any hesitation. Except it was pretty damn obvious that Audrey wasn't entirely over the breakup with Nasir, her boyfriend of four weeks, and the last thing I wanted to do was dump any of my baggage in her lap. Andrey wasn't the type to verbally rehash a relationship. Once it was over all she wanted was plenty of personal space. Calling her mid-freak-out had seemed selfish.

And okay, that reasoning didn't exactly hold up with Ben, considering that his Thursday afternoons usually consisted of coaching his eight-year-old brother, Cameron, in the finer points of baseball and smiling at whichever girl happened to catch his eye. I didn't doubt for a second that if I had called in a panic, the two of them would've showed up, baseball bats at the ready. As far as Cam was concerned, I'd reached honorary big sister status years ago. Which was kind of disconcerting since I definitely didn't have any sisterly impulses when Ben grinned at me.

So, yes, I could've called him for moral support, but I didn't.

Instead, I'd done my best to answer routine questions for the cops without tripping over my own tongue. Tried and failed. Miserably. The transcript probably read something like this:

Witness: Emmy Danvers. Sixteen years old. Caucasian. 5' 7". Lanky build. Red hair. Green eyes. Painfully average. Slightly shell-shocked.

Officer McHaffrey: So, at what time did the altercation occur?

Emmy Danvers: Uh, I don't know? I was sort of busy concentrating on my romance novel. It's called Dangerously Undercover. My heroine gets roped into helping an undercover DEA agent. Although if you think about it, shouldn't they be called DE agents? Otherwise you're calling them Drug Enforcement Agent Agents.

Officer McHaffrey: Alright.

Emmy Danvers: Well, they take down a drug cartel.

Officer McHaffrey: I see.

Emmy Danvers: I doubt it. The plot is actually pretty complicated because her sister-in-law—

Officer McHaffrey: Let's try to stay on topic, miss. I heard someone say that he took your drink. Did you confront him about it?
Emmy Danvers: I told him I wanted it back. Does that count?
Officer McHaffrey: Yes, it does. And did he return it to you?
(Emmy Danvers points to her sopping wet shirt, stained with the remnants of a grande mocha Frappuccino.)
Emmy Danvers: Uh, I guess he did?

Somehow I segued from there back to my romance novel, describing every plot point, while Officer McHaffrey did his best to maneuver me back to our very own—very dead—John Doe.

Officer McHaffrey: Can you tell me anything about his state of mind?
Emmy Danvers: Well, he seemed confused. Really paranoid and Alzheimer-y.
Officer McHaffrey: Alzheimer-y?
Emmy Danvers: (shrugs) Yeah. I think that sums it up.

I didn't say another word, not because I *actually* believed the dead man was right and that I couldn't trust anyone ever again, but because if I mentioned the dead man's cryptic warning about my father, Officer McHaffrey would've been obligated to ask some pointed questions about my home life, and I didn't want to get personal. The last thing I wanted to discuss right after having a stranger's lifeless body rolled off me was my complete lack of a reliable father figure. It wasn't as if being raised by a single parent increased the likelihood of being attacked by a strange man in a coffee shop. Explaining that I'd never met my father, not even for something as insignificant as a pumpkin spice latte, *did* make it far more likely that I'd graduate from uncontrollable shaking with adrenaline to full-on ugly crying on the sidewalk outside the Starbucks.

I focused on delivering one-word answers and nodding my way through the rest of the interview. It was the only way to postpone the tears I could feel welling up inside me, threatening to spill out at any second. Officer McHaffrey had barely finished thanking me for my cooperation when I bolted.

My sneakers slapped the pavement in a steady beat that offered no real comfort, especially when my breathing became shallow and choked. I couldn't drown out the morbid whispers of onlookers, and their words continued ringing in my ears.

"He didn't look sick to me, until—"
"Are you kidding? He had one foot in the grave before he even pushed open the door!"
"I wonder if the police have already identified the body."

The tight knot of revulsion in my stomach only began to ease when I swiped my keycard into my apartment building, instantly smelling the familiar mix of mildew and detergent that lingered from the laundry room. Something about it steadied my pounding heart rate, helped clear my head. I needed to walk up the three flights of stairs to the cramped apartment I shared with my mom, change into my favorite pair of hole-ridden jeans and my baggiest sweater, before attempting to wash the coffee stains out of my clothes. Then I needed to pretend that nothing out of the ordinary had happened. That nobody had whispered a cryptic warning to me during their last moments on earth. That the storm had passed, the worst was over—insert reassuring cliché here—and that my life would now return to its regularly scheduled programming.

I might have even convinced myself, if I hadn't double-checked all my pockets to make sure they were empty before shoving the clothes into the washer. There was something weighing down my jacket. Something that most definitely hadn't been there before my run-in with a geriatric coffee thief. Fingers still trembling from shock and adrenaline and a dozen other emotions I didn't particularly want to name, I delved deeper inside. I should have felt the papery folds of a secondhand book about the Vietnam War or a pamphlet full of conspiracy theories, some weird manifesto I could toss in the dumpster without a second thought. Instead the pad of my thumb slid across a smooth glass screen that I nearly fumbled and dropped to the ground because, oh holy crap, this did not belong with me. An old man slipping a handful of butterscotch toffees into my coat? Okay, that would be strange but sort of understandable in that who-knows-why-old-people-do-what-they-do kind of way. But randomly giving me one of the most expensive tablets on the market? That went well beyond weird.

Slate Industries had produced the Ferrari of electronics and my sticky Frappuccino fingers had no business holding one of their masterpieces. Roughly the size of a large smartphone but thinner than three quarters stacked on top of each other, it had been lauded as the tablet/phone love child hybrid that nobody realized they needed until they felt it resting in the palm of their hands. Then it became the next generation of tech they couldn't live without. The Slate's superior memory, speed, privacy settings, battery life, durability, and general awesomeness came with a hefty price tag attached.

And yet now one of them belonged to *me*.

For some reason all I could think as my fingers skimmed across the smooth chrome exterior was that anyone who could afford a Slate should be buying their own damn Frappuccinos. My Starbucks Stranger didn't need to resort to theft to get his caffeine fix. But for some reason he'd claimed *my* drink, grabbed *my* wrist with his ridiculously strong fingers, and slid this outrageously beautiful machine into *my* pocket. So maybe keeping it was the right thing to do. Even to my own ears that rationalization sounded awfully thin. "Finders keepers, losers weepers" probably didn't apply to cases where the loser turned up *dead*. Then again, turning over the Slate to the cops wouldn't magically bring the old man back to life. Most likely, it would go mysteriously missing, and if an officer in the department happened to start using an identical Slate, well, none of the other cops would ask too many questions about where he got it. As far as I was concerned there was enough moral ambiguity to keep me on the safe side of karma. If I handed it over to the authorities, I would be denying a dying man's parting gift. That would be rude. Disrespectful. Downright dishonorable.

I was merely respecting his final wishes.

"*Earth to Emmy!*" Audrey waved her arms dramatically in front of my face. "Are you even listening to me? You should have called us!"

I nodded and then did a quick sweep of the cafeteria. Nobody seemed to be paying us any undue attention, but I couldn't shake the feeling that I was being watched. Probably leftover paranoia from the old man's creepy warnings. "I know, okay? I should have called. Can we move on already?"

Audrey and Ben traded looks. The problem with best friends is that sometimes they know you a little too well. They can tell when you are holding out on them. And they have absolutely no qualms about poking and prodding until you've spilled all your secrets.

"Em's just mad he interrupted her alone time with her fictional Prince Charming."

I glared at Ben as my cheeks heated with annoyance. Ever since he caught me with a big dopey smile plastered across my face as I finished the last paragraph of a romance novel, he'd started giving me crap about my personal life. Which was blatantly unfair, because did I criticize him for hooking up with random girls after baseball practice or outside the batting cages or on the subway or wherever the hell else he happened to meet them?

No, I did not.

Much.

But that wasn't the point.

Zzzzz! Zzzzz! Zzzzz!

The three of us stared in silence while my backpack jolted like the victim of an invisible stun gun.

Ben raised an eyebrow. "You going to answer that anytime soon?"

"It's nothing," I lied, grabbing my backpack off the chair and shoving it farther under the table. "Just ignore it."

Confusion radiated from Audrey's warm brown eyes. "I don't get it, Em. Why are you suddenly hiding stuff from *us*?"

Because I don't want you to tell me to do the right thing. Not yet.

Ben used his foot to snag the strap, and with one effortless movement he brought up the backpack and dumped all my possessions onto the lunch table. Textbooks, notebooks, my graphing calculator, a few cheap pens with the names of real estate offices on them, a special journal for all of my novel ideas, and the Slate I definitely should have left at home. I'd been uncomfortable with the idea of leaving it on my bedside dresser—or anywhere out of reach, really—which was stupid because I hadn't been brave enough to do more than flip the Slate over half a dozen times, examining every smooth inch. The possibility, no matter how remote, that my information might be listed in the dead man's contacts had scared me into inaction. Or maybe that had been the product of the shock finally catching up with me. Either way, I didn't mean for the Slate to become my very own show-and-tell exhibit.

The Slate writhed on the cafeteria table before I snatched it up and stuffed it into the crumpled sweatshirt. It buzzed one last time and then quieted, probably because the battery had died. I wasn't sure how I'd afford a charger, but that wasn't my most immediate problem. Not when my best friends were staring at me like I'd gone off the deep end.

"What," Ben asked with forced calmness, "is that?"

"You mean, beyond a total violation of my privacy?" I began shoveling all my belongings back into my bag. "My new Slate."

Audrey's jaw dropped open. "There's no way you could afford that unless you sold your kidney on the black market." I watched as comprehension dawned across her face. "The dead guy?"

"Can you keep your voice down?" I muttered. "This isn't something I want to advertise."

"You robbed a *dead guy?*"

"No! Of course I didn't. He gave it to me. Sort of."

"Yeah, nothing weird about that," Audrey scoffed.

"He gave it to me," I repeated. Neither of them looked impressed with the repetition of that particular point, so I quickly moved on. "That makes it mine. Case closed."

Ben sat up straighter as he quickly zipped my bag shut. "I doubt the cops see it that way, since they're headed right toward us."

CHAPTER 3

The two police officers weren't exactly chatty as they hustled me out of the cafeteria.

They wouldn't tell me why or where they were taking me. In fact, the cops barely spared me a glance. Instead, they flashed their badges at the lunch monitor, told him that they'd already cleared everything with our school principal, and assured him that this was merely a safety precaution. Officer Eva Thorton's exact words were, "We have a credible reason to believe this young woman's safety is at risk." Then she placed one hand on my shoulder and frog-marched me out the door and into a waiting squad car. Her partner, Andre Brown, stayed two steps ahead of us. His wide shoulders partially blocked my view of the growing crowd of students, but I could still see plenty of people staring at me with open-mouthed amazement. I could hear the rumors starting.

"Do you think she slept with the principal?"
"Oh, come on! Everyone knows that she robbed a convenience store."
"No way! If she had money, she wouldn't be wearing those ugly-ass sneakers."

On a normal day, being the center of attention would've freaked me out. I've never enjoyed being on stage or doing public speaking. Or public anything, really. So if an old man *hadn't* died on top of me less than twenty-four hours earlier, this would've been my worst nightmare.

Nothing like a quick brush with death to put life in perspective.

The popular girls like Beckie Miller could whisper whatever they wanted. I had much bigger concerns, like what kind of "credible threat" could have two well-armed police officers pulling me out of school.

Tell your dad sorry.

Yesterday I'd thought that apology was intended for someone who didn't exist. Now I couldn't help wondering if it really had been directed at me. If he'd been perfectly aware that he was adding this much chaos to my life the moment he stole my drink.

A little more context would've gone a long way toward clearing everything up, but my police escort seemed to be playing ambivalent cop, silent cop.

"Um, excuse me?" I said hesitantly, unable to take the silence any longer. "Can you tell me what's going on?"

The two officers exchanged a meaningful glance as we pulled up to the station.

"We're here to ensure your safety. A detective will be talking with you soon," Officer Thorton said brusquely as she pulled open the door. Even without the handcuffs, I felt like I'd already been marked as a criminal.

"Breathe, kid," Officer Brown said at last. "You'll be fine."

Five words might be a soliloquy by his standards, but they did nothing to reassure me.

"A *detective?*" I squeaked. "Um, what's wrong with the two of you?"

That didn't come out quite the way I intended.

"Nothing is wrong with us." Thorton hustled me forward with an air of complete confidence that I envied. She didn't look like she put up with crap from anyone, like she might play roller derby in her spare time because she loved the rush of physically knocking people out of her way.

"Then why—"

I lost my train of thought as they led me into the heart of the station. Everyone was scurrying around, barking orders, gulping down coffee, or glaring at their computers. I looked at Officer Brown and hoped my red-rimmed eyes would guilt-trip him into telling me *something* useful, but he just steered me into a room empty of furniture beyond a dinged-up table and two chairs. Then they left me alone to wait.

And wait.

And then wait some more.

By the time a stocky man with small dark eyes in a face that had the air of perpetual dissatisfaction stepped through the door, I had already plotted out a whole new romance novel. One that involved a plucky heroine, a very sexy district attorney, and a corrupt police station intent on covering up a prostitution ring.

"I'm Detective Luke O'Brian," he introduced himself easily before sinking into the chair on his side of the table. "You've gotten yourself into quite the mess, Miss Danvers."

Maybe it was knowing that the entire school would still be gossiping about me on Monday, or the fact that I *still* had no freaking idea why New York's finest had unceremoniously hauled me in only to make me sit alone for the better part of an hour, or that a dead man had pretty much warned me this might happen, but I completely lost it.

"*I've* gotten myself into a mess?" I repeated indignantly. "You might want to brush up on your detective work. *I* didn't start anything!"

He raised a single eyebrow, looking thoroughly unmoved. Probably because I was the least threatening person to ever take a seat in his interrogation room. "Why don't we—"

But I didn't give him a chance to finish.

"Tell me, is it normal for high school girls to be summoned here—or am I special?"

He smiled, but it didn't reach his dark brown eyes. "Most girls your age don't get tangled up in murder investigations. I'd say that makes you very special, Miss Danvers."

"*Murder?*" My knees weakened unexpectedly and I sank back into my chair. "What are you talking about? I was *there*, Detective. He tackled me and died. End of story."

"I'm going to play something for you, Miss Danvers. And then I suspect you'll be *dying* to change your statement."

A sardonic gleam flashed in his eyes and my stomach twisted painfully, as if I had been dared to eat a seafood quesadilla and was now deeply regretting it.

For some reason I couldn't even begin to fathom, he *wanted* to scare me.

That's when I should've pulled the Slate out of my backpack. I should've slid it across the table and said, *Here you go. Enjoy. Now please keep me out of this. All of this.*

Except I couldn't help mentally replaying the old man's warnings, even as the detective flicked open the briefcase to reveal a laptop inside.

They're coming to kill me.
Trust nobody.
You won't survive long if you don't go for the jugular, girl.

It had been so easy to dismiss those words in the coffee shop as the meaningless ramblings of a senile man. But he didn't sound crazy now. Not when the police were willing to drag me to the precinct for questioning in a *murder* investigation.

If my coffee thief was right, if someone really had been out to get him, then maybe he wasn't mistaken about the other stuff, either. Although that kind of thinking was exactly how psychics reeled in their customers. The psychic would say something vaguely cryptic, the client would search for a meaning in their own lives, and come up with *something* that linked the two together. And anything that didn't fit the story? That tended to be ignored. Just because the old man had been close to death didn't automatically mean anyone else was in danger.

Detective O'Brian spun the computer around so that I could view the screen. "Maybe this will jog your memory."

One click later and I saw myself as a grayish figure sitting at one of the window tables, courtesy of what had to be the Starbucks' security camera. It felt so weird watching onscreen-Emmy glare in frustration at the loaner laptop before moving toward the counter, and—

O'Brian froze the video just as the old man snatched my drink. "Anything yet?"

I shook my head so he let the security feed keep playing, although this time he kept up a running commentary. "He's holding on to your arm for quite a while there. You say this is the first time you ever met him?"

"That's right."

"And yet the two of you are looking awfully chummy."

I didn't think that particular statement merited a response, so I took a page out of Officer Brown's playbook and pressed my lips tightly together. The detective pointed to the Emmy onscreen who had just reclaimed her drink.

"Now here's where it gets interesting. Watch what happens as you move toward your table."

My pixelated figure slowly began to walk across the room while I braced myself for the inevitable tackle that would send me hurtling to the ground. Even knowing *exactly* what was coming, the scene disturbed me. I flinched instinctively as the old man flew through the air with all the grace of a professional baseball player diving for home base. I focused my attention on the placement of his hands and tried to resign myself to the reality of the situation.

There was no way Detective O'Brian would overlook the Slate that was slipped into my pocket. Not when he already seemed intent on proving that the two of us shared some kind of past. The dead man's fingers dipped into his coat and my breath caught in my throat. Any second now and I'd see a silvery flash of chrome caught on camera.

The detective was right; I did need to amend my statement.

I'm sorry I didn't come forward about this earlier, but—

My jaw dropped open in surprise as I watched his body release its tentative hold on life. Two empty age-spotted hands sprawled across the sticky floor. He hadn't given me a thing.

At least not as far as the security footage was concerned.

Two businessmen in suits had moved forward when the old man lunged for me, then hesitated in a painfully long moment of indecision, obscuring the old man's right side from view. They were probably unsure if it would be more dangerous to move him before the ambulance arrived. I did my best not to exhale in relief.

The police didn't know about the Slate. Yet.

I scooted the laptop so that it faced away from me and gave the detective my best disinterested glare. The one I usually reserved for anyone trying to shove a pamphlet or a flier into my hands.

"Fascinating. What's your point?"

"Why don't you try watching it again," he advised. "This time pay attention to the man in the hat behind you."

While the old man refused to surrender my drink onscreen, my gaze locked on the relatively wiry build of yet another stranger. The blurry man in the dark blue baseball cap held something a lot more lethal than a Starbucks Doubleshot in his hand. I couldn't begin to speculate on the make or model, but even I could tell it was some kind of gun.

And he was aiming it right at *me*.

I watched in horror as the old man lunged forward, knocking me to the ground and absorbing the hit without flinching.

My stomach rolled over and my fingers gripped the edge of the desk tightly, as if I were gripping the safety bar on a rollercoaster ride. "I-I thought it was a heart attack. Everyone said he had a heart attack!"

"Oh, it was," O'Brian replied easily, as he returned the laptop to the briefcase. "Our medical examiner confirmed it. According to the toxicology report the heart attack just wasn't due to natural causes."

"So you think the old man died for *me*?"

"It would appear that way." He leaned forward so that I couldn't look away from the chill in his dark brown eyes. "Now you can either start talking or wait for the killer to take another swing at the job. So let's try this again. Why does that man want you dead?"

I blurted out the truth, knowing that it was the one thing he would never believe.

"*I have no freaking idea!*"

CHAPTER 4

Detective O'Brian didn't seem to find my denial particularly convincing.

Then again, I doubted I could've said anything to him to prove either my innocence or my ignorance. The man was too busy trying to make me crack under the pressure of his withering glare to actually hear me out. In his eyes, I wasn't a teenage girl who had chosen to write a romance novel at the wrong time in the wrong coffee shop.

Nope, one conversation with a dead man and I was a potential suspect in a murder investigation.

I had no trouble picturing Detective O'Brian practicing his Serious Cop Face every night in the mirror, but that didn't make it any less effective. My hands had started shaking all over again and this time I couldn't run off the worst of my panic. It felt like the oxygen was being sucked out of the small interrogation room. I couldn't think clearly.

Or maybe I was simply trying too hard to make sense out of something that defied all logic.

Somebody wanted me *dead*.

Me.

The situation had driven beyond strange, past absurd, and taken a hard left down batshit crazy lane. There was no way to prove that I didn't deserve to be grilled by a detective. A *homicide* detective, I realized belatedly. If this were a romance novel, Detective Luke O'Brian would be the jaded cop who had spent years uncovering the darkest, most brutal acts people could commit. He would growl and glower and snap at anyone who dared get in his way.

Funny how I'd always enjoyed those kinds of theatrics on cop shows until I found myself seated in an interrogation room.

If I thought for even half a second that he might believe me, I would have spilled the truth about everything. As it was, I didn't want to give him a reason to blame me for a crime that I didn't commit. A crime that I didn't understand.

"Shouldn't you be questioning the killer instead of me? That seems like a much better use of your time." My cheeks reddened under the intensity of his glare. "I'm trying to be helpful here!"

"Try harder," Detective O'Brian suggested. "We don't have your friend in the baseball cap in police custody yet. Which means that I have all the time in the world to talk to you."

I felt lightheaded. The few bites of lunch I'd eaten earlier churned uneasily in my stomach. "Let me get this straight: you're grilling *me* instead of looking for *him*? And by 'him' I mean *the guy who tried to kill me*?"

"I'm not grilling you, Miss Danvers. You've got this all turned around. I'm the one keeping you nice and safe. Now why don't you try your best to be helpful?"

I sure as hell didn't feel safe. Not in the police station and *definitely* not with him. I couldn't tell if Detective O'Brian really thought that I was involved with the guilty party or if he was simply trying to scare me into letting something slip. Either way, I was catching a strong whiff of bait. And it wasn't coming from the only other person sitting in the room.

The dead guy was right once again; I couldn't trust anyone.

"I don't know anything, Detective!" The words felt as if they were being ripped out of my chest. "I can't think of *anyone* who would want to hurt me. I don't have any vengeful former lovers. I don't make a habit of chatting with known felons. I don't even own a fake ID!"

The detective leaned toward me. "Then why were you talking to a stranger in Starbucks?"

"Because he stole my drink!" I stumbled to my feet. "I've told you all of this. Multiple times. So either charge me with a crime or let me go."

I'm not sure what I expected him to say. I seriously doubted that threatening a walkout would make the detective any more forthcoming. Still, I wasn't prepared for him to open the door and usher me out of the interrogation room.

"After you," he said smoothly. "You might want to tell your friends to walk three paces behind you. When you consider that the last man to stand in front of you was murdered, well, no use dwelling on that, right? Have a lovely afternoon, Miss Danvers."

I twisted in the doorway and couldn't keep my voice from trembling. "What do you *want* from me?"

"Why don't you sit in the waiting area and we'll talk more when your mom shows up. That'll give you some time to contemplate all your options. And, hey, let me know if the killer pays you another visit. Although come to think of it, you probably won't be in a position to do much talking." Detective O'Brian shrugged as if he didn't care either way. My legs went numb as he propelled me forward. "Just give a holler if you happen to remember anything."

Then with only the barest of nods for the officer manning the front desk, Detective O'Brian sauntered back into the heart of the station, leaving me with the unenviable task of finding the best place to sit with all of the other people who desperately wanted to be anywhere else. A Hispanic woman with a swelling black eye appeared to be battling tears as she filled out a form. Four seats away from her, a lean man with a long goatee was ranting about the unfairness of his jaywalking ticket loudly enough to be receiving the lion's share of attention.

I'd already reached my quota of crazy interactions with strangers for a lifetime, so I purposefully walked to the calmest corner of the room. There was a boy sitting three spaces down from me, but he had headphones in and appeared immersed in a battered copy of *The Catcher in the Rye*, his head bent low over the dog-eared pages. Even slouching in his chair, he looked out of place with his perfectly pressed slacks, a button-down shirt, and an overcoat with a price tag that would probably set my mom back a month in rent.

He wore wealth with the kind of confidence that only comes from familiarity with it. Luxury that was such an everyday occurrence that he dismissed it as commonplace. He was probably there to file a complaint for his daddy. Maybe his Lexus had been taken to the impound lot and he couldn't handle taking the family Porsche for more than two days in a row.

A nicer person wouldn't feel the need to take mental potshots at a rich kid just to distract herself from the biggest crapfest of her life. I sank into my seat and shrugged, chalking it up to my writer's temperament as I searched for a good way to describe the unruly mass of hair that fell across his forehead. Crows-wing black sounded (a) pretentious and (b) inaccurate. It was more of a dark chocolate brown than a pure black. If someone tried to dye their hair that color it would probably have some ridiculous name on the package, like "espresso roast" or "midnight mahogany."

Not that it mattered since no self-respecting hero would *ever* look in the mirror and think to himself, "Why yes, my thick head of midnight mahogany hair *is* looking particularly good tonight," before sauntering off into the darkness.

"What did you tell the cops?"

My leg jerked as if he'd tested my reflexes with one of those little hammers that pediatricians always have within easy reach. There might not be an official rule against talking, but the front entrance of a police precinct isn't the kind of place where it's socially acceptable to chat with strangers. Not that the rich kid appeared to care about breaking social norms. He also didn't bother setting down the book that was probably more of a prop than anything else. I had to admit, he was doing an impressive job of hiding his face with it. This boy seemed to know exactly how far to tilt his forehead, how to position his neck, how wide to open the paperback, and how to utilize the shadows cast by his disheveled hair to make anything above the unsmiling lines of his lips difficult to see. When it came to knowing his angles, this guy could probably give even the most devoted selfie enthusiast a few pointers.

"Um, what?" I said profoundly.

"What. Did. You. Tell. The. Cops?" He repeated the question slowly as if he honestly thought the problem was that I hadn't heard him right the first time. It was hard to tell when he enunciated each word, but I thought there was something vaguely familiar about his voice. It was like catching the end of a commercial and knowing that the actor explaining why you should buy this revolutionary new ergonomic something-or-other was a supporting character in a movie you watched years ago but couldn't identify now.

I crossed my arms and briefly considered moving to a different seat. Just because we were the only high school–age kids in the place didn't mean we needed to pretend that this was a bizarre remake of *The Breakfast Club* with a significantly smaller cast.

"I told them the truth." I tried to keep my voice steady, but the slight quiver I couldn't control made it sound like a lie.

The boy snorted in disgust. "Oh yeah? And how did that work out for you?"

Not particularly well. Detective O'Brian hadn't believed a single word I'd said, making it sound like he arrested painfully boring sixteen-year-old girls like me all the time. As if it made perfect sense for me to have gun-wielding archenemies despite the fact that up until yesterday my biggest adversaries were the manspreaders who somehow took up three seats on the subway with their legs.

"I'm not in handcuffs," I pointed out, right before my curiosity got the better of me. It was a bad idea to make small talk in a police precinct, because either something terrible had just happened to them or they'd done something terrible to somebody else. Either way, not the best time to practice making casual conversation, but I couldn't seem to stop myself. "What, uh, brings you here?"

The boy stretched out his long legs and I wondered somewhat inanely whether he played sports. If he was accustomed to deflecting soccer balls with his ridiculously strong jaw. The segment of his nose that I could see appeared unbroken, but for all I knew there was a gigantic bump right between his eyes and that's why he was so self-conscious about showing his face. Although it wasn't as if he could spend his entire life hiding behind a paperback.

"I thought that was obvious. I'm your 'Get Out of Jail Free' card, Emmy." He lowered the book, and if his first words had been a shock, the recognition that filled me as I met his piercing blue eyes and got a good look at the full picture of his face was a cattle prod to the stomach.

Sebastian St. James.

If there was one person I never *ever* wanted to see again, it was the Starbucks killer in the baseball cap. But if I was allowed to add another name to the list, I would have scrawled Sebastian St. James on the second line without any hesitation. Sebastian even beat out my mom's current jackass boyfriend, Viktor, for that highly coveted spot, which was pretty impressive considering that I had only met him once roughly two months ago. To my way of thinking, our three-minute conversation in a poorly lit room had lasted three minutes too long.

"Don't tell me you've forgotten me, *bestie*." Sebastian sounded darkly amused. We both knew that he was a lot of things, but unmemorable wasn't one of them. Apparently I'd made an impression of my own. Although that was probably because most girls don't duck away from their best friend in the midst of a huge party at a fancy private residence that was within the gated walls of some exclusive prep school, which seemed weird to me on a whole bunch of levels, but whatever. Rich people made strange life decisions all the time. My plan was to blend in with the wallpaper, keeping the volume on my phone cranked all the way up in case Audrey needed me. She was the only reason I had agreed to go in the first place. And since she seemed to be handling the horde of unfamiliar faces fine without me, I decided to do a little exploring on my own—only to stumble upon a burglary in progress. A leanly built dark-haired boy calmly put away his lock-picking set and pulled out a bottle of amber liquid from a heavy oak desk. He didn't appear overly concerned about being caught in the act. He lifted an eyebrow in a silent challenge, as if daring me to call him out. A smart girl probably would have kept her mouth shut. Minded heir own business. Returned to the party as if nothing had happened.

Instead, I texted Audrey, *Tell your boyfriend that I caught someone breaking into the liquor cabinet.* Then just to ensure that they actually found me in the enormous private residence, I added, *I'm in the first floor study. With the thief. And I think there might be a candlestick.*

Audrey and Nasir had rushed into the room, only to find me blocking the exit while the strange boy with the lock-pick set relaxed in an enormous leather chair with his glass of amber liquor.

Nasir couldn't hide his amusement as he explained that my thief was the owner's grandson.

That it was basically his place and *definitely* his party.

Yeah, nobody makes an idiot of themselves quite as spectacularly as me.

My cheeks heated with embarrassment at the memory. "So does this mean you were finally busted for stealing? Let me guess, this time you were caught with something a lot more expensive than alcohol."

He smiled, the expression one of pure smugness. "First of all, I *allegedly* stole a thirty-year-old bottle of Glenlivet scotch, not some cheap beer on tap. Show some respect, please. Secondly, you're the one who probably needs a drink. It'll make it a lot easier for you to accept that I'm the best ally you've got."

An odd squeak emerged from my throat that sounded like the demented cousin of my normal laugh. "Let me see if I've got this straight: *You* want to help *me*. Out of the goodness of your nonexistent heart. Because that's the kind of favor you like to do for your best friend's ex-girlfriend's best friend. Sure. That makes sense." I gritted out the last part, but instead of returning my scowl, Sebastian's grin flashed a set of perfectly straight white teeth.

I hoped that smile had cost him a fortune.

"A word of advice. When someone is throwing you a lifeline, it's best not to make them want to rescind the offer."

I looked at Sebastian in disbelief. "The only reason you would ever throw me a lifeline is if you wanted to watch me hang myself with it."

"As tempting as that image is right now, I'm going to fill you in on how the next few hours are going to play out. Someone is going to burst through those doors," he pointed to the front of the police station, "and demand to know what their precious little girl is doing sitting here instead of in school. That's when some jackass is going to suggest the Witness Protection Program, which we both know you can't accept without screwing up your agenda. That's why I'm going to make you my offer first." He extended a hand, and I found myself shaking it before my brain caught up with my body. "Welcome to Emptor Academy. Your first lesson starts today."

CHAPTER 5

"What agenda are you talking about?! And what makes you think I'd want to attend your snobby school, Sebastian? Their students haven't exactly impressed me with their winning personalities." There was definitely something intimidating about him, though. I'd be willing to bet that everything he owned—right down to his silk boxers with mother-of-pearl buttons—had been designed specifically for him.

It was the kind of detail I would include for a sexy billionaire sheik and his virgin secretary-turned-mistress, but so *not* an image I wanted associated with Sebastian St. James.

He didn't appear even remotely offended. If anything, his smirk only deepened, his eyes sparking with mocking amusement. "Emptor Academy has a state-of-the-art security system, classes taught by some of the world's most brilliant minds, and political connections that make the Ivy League green with jealousy. I'm sure there are benefits to the public school system." He tapped his chin thoughtfully. "You have plenty of time to prepare yourself for a future of staggering mediocrity."

I hated him.

More than anything, I wanted to come up with a clever put-down. Something so deliciously snarky it would wipe that smile right off his face. Except I wasn't sure what to say. My high school *did* suck. The classes were packed past capacity and the teachers could barely keep their heads above water. Still, it was *my* shitty education.

But I didn't say a word as the full impact of my conversation with Detective O'Brian finally sank in.

Somebody wanted me dead and the cops appeared more intent on dangling me as bait than, y'know, protecting and serving. Given that Emptor Academy housed the children of diplomats and rock stars, they probably had an impeccable security system in place. Something that would keep the Starbucks Killers of the world far, far away from me.

"I can't afford it," I mumbled, hating to admit the truth. Breakfast, lunch, and dinner were all probably served on fine china and prepared by master chefs. Any one of those meals would decimate my nearly nonexistent college fund. I didn't want to guess how much they charged for residency in their fancy dorms. The answer would only depress me.

"We happen to have an excellent scholarship program." Sebastian leaned back in his chair as if he offered tuition to girls sitting in police precincts all the time.

Heyyy, wanna transfer to my prep school? I'll pick up the tab, girl. No worries.

I nearly snorted out loud. No worries. That was a good one.

"What do you get out of this?"

This whole conversation was giving me flashbacks of my eighth birthday when my mom's unemployed boyfriend du jour, Pierre, had handed her twenty bucks and suggested a girls-only burger dinner. My mom and I had searched her closet for the most ridiculously colorful outfits we could find. She'd paired a floor-length gown with dozens of beaded necklaces, sneakers, and hot pink lipstick. I remember thinking she was the most beautiful woman in the whole world as she took my hand and shared a conspiratorial smile with me. As if the two of us were playing an elaborate joke on everyone who gave us funny looks. We had strolled into a tiny diner and giggled together over our milkshake and fries—only to come home to a burglarized apartment. Pierre had hocked our television, toaster, everything that wasn't nailed down before making his exit. My mom had quietly surveyed the damage before walking straight into the bathroom and scrubbed at her face until every last speck of makeup had been removed. She didn't leave her bedroom for any reason except work over the next two days. I sat cross-legged where the couch had been only a few hours earlier, scrunched my eyes shut, and wished that my mom would stop dating losers. I wished that she'd give up on men and be happy with me. Only me.

It hadn't happened.

That was the day I'd learned never to trust someone who acts out of character. Especially when that someone has nothing to gain by this seemingly random act of generosity. A lesson that made it impossible for me to simply accept Sebastian's offer at face value.

"I'm bored. I might as well see how this plays out," Sebastian replied slowly, too casually, and I knew that he was hiding something. Something big that involved *me*.

"You don't offer favors, Sebastian. That's even harder to believe than the 'goodness of your heart' bullshit."

His lips quirked up into a smile. "Interesting. So you *do* have some instincts. Given your crappy taste in friends I assumed you were that stupid about everyone. I'm feeling more entertained already."

"Let's say, hypothetically, that I do accept the scholarship. What happens next?"

Sebastian smirked, as if he hadn't expected any other response. People probably didn't say no to him often.

"Then you'll go home, pack your things, and a car will arrive for you at precisely nine o'clock."

"What are the living arrangements?" I asked.

My stomach lurched at the thought of transferring schools, no matter how temporary the move. *Ben.* I wouldn't be able to see him, or Audrey, for that matter, if I was stuck keeping a low profile at Empty Academy while the cops *hopefully* shifted their focus back to the killer with the baseball cap. And okay, if I was being totally honest with myself, the thought of increasing my distance from Ben seriously freaked me out. Things had been *off* with our dynamic for a while, even though I couldn't quite put my finger on when or why it had shifted. Ben and I still teased and bickered and spent time alone together. I helped explain multiplying fractions to his little brother, Cameron. I even shared my suspicion that his former lab partner, Shelby Thomas, wanted to conduct more than chemistry experiments with him. Nothing had changed. Except now the air between us felt heavily charged with anticipation, as if we were both bracing ourselves for something momentous. But the reason I'd never acted on the impulse to rise up on tip-toes and sneak attack him with a kiss was because it was, well, *Ben*.

He was the one guy I had always been able to count on. My rock. Whenever my mom went through one of her frantic dating spree phases, determined to find The One she believed was somewhere out there searching for her on whatever new dating app just hit the market, I could always hide out at his place until I was ready to face an empty apartment. It happened frequently enough that his mom considered finding me eating cereal in her kitchen a normal event on a Saturday morning. Ben had been there for me through the Pierre years, the Dimitri era, the Hans episode, and he hadn't so much as flinched when I told him about my mom's current flame, Viktor. He had just tugged playfully on the end of my ponytail and said, "I'll make omelets in the morning with pepper jack cheese."

Because he knew that was my favorite.

Ben was my escape hatch and Audrey was my seatbelt. I *needed* them.

If that wasn't incentive enough to stay put, there was also the fact that my mom needed me. I was in charge of cooking and cleaning every time she got her heart broken and resisted climbing out of bed. It was my job to repeat over and over that she was a great mom, that she was going to be fine, that we would both be fine, every time she became withdrawn and secretive.

I couldn't do any of that from Emptor Academy. I didn't care if the dorm rooms there came equipped with four-poster beds and enormous clawfoot bathtubs. It was only a matter of time before my mom was completely suckered in by her boyfriend. Again.

Ben might think I was a hopeless romantic, but I knew better. I loved my romance novels because the hero *never* robbed the heroine on her daughter's birthday. There was safety in a happily ever after ending. You could trust your heart in the pages of a romance novel.

Watching my mom date loser after loser had dulled my own optimism.

"Emptor Academy provides communal living at its finest," Sebastian said, unaware that I'd already considered and rejected his offer. "You'll be sharing a room with Kayla. She's very clean. She'll make you feel right at home."

I was momentarily distracted by the mental image of a faceless girl who obsessively wiped down windowsills. She probably wore Prada while she sprayed the doorknob with disinfectant.

"And you would know this how?" I asked disdainfully.

He leaned in closer and I caught a heady whiff of male arrogance, which should have been repulsive but somehow wasn't.

"Because—as previously established—I know everything."

It felt good to scoff at him, even as a small part of me wondered what kind of access he had to private information. Money talks, and with a few well-placed bills and a smile, he could probably gain access to nuclear launch codes.

He had tracked me to the police station.

That much I did know. I forced myself to take a moment and break down the components of our conversation into easily digested chunks. Sebastian had tracked me down. He wanted something from me. He thought *I* had a secret agenda, probably because he had one of his own.

I shook my head and tried to make it even simpler.

Sebastian St. James had the funds to make nearly any problem solvable and there was a mystery in my life that no police officers would eagerly agree to help me answer. The Case of the Absentee Dad. My pulse began speeding up. According to my mom, they had met and fallen in love when she was playing the small, but critical, role of Waitress #3 on a big-budget action movie in Los Angeles. He had been everything she'd always looked for in a man. Funny, warm-hearted, with a genuine smile that made her knees go weak. He left supportive little notes on napkins next to the coffeepot each morning. Held her in his arms as she fell asleep each night. My mom's eyes tended to go dreamy when she reached that part of the story. For three blissful months they'd been inseparable—right up until the day she'd woken up to find him gone. No note. No explanation. After two weeks of waiting for him to return, she took a pregnancy test that put everything in perspective real fast.

My mom liked to say that she left Hollywood with the only Emmy that truly mattered.

That my dad would always be the one that got away.

The man that my mom described became my ultimate fantasy father. Endearingly nervous about meeting me for the first time and full of regret for all the years that he'd already missed, I pictured him standing at the steps of my school with an enormous bouquet of flowers and an explanation for everything. It was easy to imagine because I'd always known it was pure fantasy. That I would never be able to find him on my own.

Morgan will know what to do, always was better with the details. And they're coming, girl. I'd stake my life on it.

42

Ben would tell me to hand in the Slate and be done with the whole thing. To do my civic duty and get the hell out. To accept whichever deal the police offered that would keep me the safest.

Except if the dead man was right and my father—my actual biological *dad*—was in danger and his Slate could help me track him down? I wasn't sure I could walk away from that possibility without regretting it for the rest of my life. If he was even half as wonderful as my mom claimed, then maybe he really could keep her happy. Maybe he'd be able to prevent the headlong collision course she appeared to be on with every lowlife creep within a fifteen-mile radius.

"What if I change my mind?" I shoved back the wisps of auburn hair that had slipped free from my ponytail because I needed to do something with my hands. If I didn't keep them in motion Sebastian might notice that they were still trembling slightly. "What if I get to Empty Academy and decide that I want out?"

Sebastian laughed the low chuckle of someone assured of their own victory.

"You'd be the first."

It looked like I'd be setting all sorts of new precedents, because I had no intention of settling in, staying put, or sticking around. I just needed to buy myself a little more alone time with the Slate.

So I met his stormy blue eyes straight on and hoped that he couldn't tell I was bluffing.

"I'm in."

CHAPTER 6

Sebastian didn't stick around to watch my mom make her big entrance. Instead, he pressed a business card into my palm and left without so much as pausing to say goodbye or good luck or whatever it was you should say to someone when they are stuck sitting in a police precinct for their mom to arrive. I glanced down at the card, unsure what to expect.

Sebastian St. James
Certified Bad Boy

He was the kind of guy who could get away with putting a warning label on his own business card. Then again, maybe being the kind of a seventeen-year-old who *carried* business cards was its own kind of warning. My fingers instinctively rubbed the thick cardstock, and as much as I hated to admit it, the velvety texture felt good.

I flipped it over and in the left hand corner it gave the address and contact information of a Manhattan law firm where he must have one of the senior partners on retainer. For a boy who got his kicks using lock picks to steal whiskey from his own home, the ability to hand over his lawyer's number had probably gotten him out of more than a few tight spots.

Detective O'Brian poked his head into the waiting room and said, "Still breathing? That's good. Try to keep that up, will ya?" before returning to his desk in the inner sanctum. Leaving me to sit there, twirling the business card in clumsy circles as I tried to distract myself by creating a best-case scenario. My mom would be thrilled to learn that I'd been accepted as a student in an elite private school. She'd break things off with Viktor and decide to learn how to be happy on her own. We'd go home and she might attempt some ridiculously complicated recipe from Hungary or Romania or some other Eastern European country, blasting Latin music from our crappy speakers until Mrs. Sampson in apartment 36 yelled at us to quiet down.

I wouldn't miss that old lady. Not in the slightest. She was the kind of woman you expect to end up splashed across the news as the Trick or Treat Killer who slips razor blades into homemade Halloween cookies. The first time she saw Ben walking toward the apartment with me she had said disdainfully, "Like mother, like daughter, I suppose. Try not to get knocked up. You'll only regret it."

Ben had draped an arm across my shoulder and leered at me with mock interest.

"I dunno, I think we would make great parents. I'm thinking Victory Cabbage if it's a girl, but I'm open to other suggestions." He had grinned down at me, waiting for my speechlessness to give way to laughter, as if he'd known that arguing with him over ridiculous baby names would soon drive away Mrs. Sampson's vicious words. Transform it into one big joke.

The memory hit my stomach so painfully that it cramped. Ben could find a way to make me smile through just about anything. Without him, without *Audrey*, I wouldn't have enjoyed a single day at our public high school. Starting over at a new high school without them? It felt as unthinkable as chopping off my own limb to survive. Part of me couldn't believe that the situation could really be this dire. That Sebastian's offer could truly be my best option. Even if I transferred to Emptor Academy, I'd still be the only student eating lunch by herself. It wouldn't exactly be hard for an assassin to pick me out of the crowd.

I was so royally screwed.

My phone chirped at me to signal that I had incoming texts.

Ben: You okay?
Audrey: What's going on? Did they take the Slate? CALL ME!

I fought the urge to reexamine the Slate that had landed me in this mess. The last thing I wanted was for Detective O'Brian to have any more questionable video footage of me. I didn't know what to believe, but staring at a battery-dead tablet wasn't going to solve anything. And after being informed that someone was out to kill me, texting anything about the Slate seemed like a particularly bad idea. So instead I sent a quick message back and tried not to flinch every time the door to the precinct opened.

Em: Fine here. Fill you in later.

I should've been prepared to see my mom striding toward me, but somehow I wasn't. Maybe it was the panic glazing her brown eyes that had me rattled. She looked sweaty and scared and absolutely panic-stricken. An unwanted pang of guilt tugged at me as she swept me into a fiercely protective hug. I'd done that to her. I'd scared her speechless.

Someone at the front desk must have paged Detective O'Brian because he sauntered into the waiting room like he owned the place. Judging by the appraising gleam in Detective O'Brian eyes after giving my mom a prolonged once-over, he didn't see anything wrong with her looks. My already queasy stomach twisted in disgust. Detective Luke O'Brian had no moral qualms preventing him from scaring the living daylights out of a sixteen-year-old girl, which meant he was a complete jerk.

In other words, he was exactly her type.

"Sorry to keep you waiting, Mrs. Danvers," he said smoothly.

"It's Ms. Danvers, actually, but you can call me Vera." She released me from the tight clasp of her arms, but couldn't seem to resist resting a hand on my shoulder blade. I must not have inherited my shaking hands from my mom, because her grip remained steady as she focused her attention on the jackass in front of us.

"Well, Vera, I'm *Homicide* Detective Luke O'Brian." His chest puffed out as he lingered on the *homicide* part as if it were possible my mom might fail to understand the gravity of the job unless he spelled it out for her.

My mom blanched as she pulled me closer. "Is it Viktor?" she demanded. "Did he do something?"

Oh god.

I didn't know how to feel. Part of me was pissed off that she even had to ask if her boyfriend was involved in something deadly. Furious that she would invite someone into our lives if some small part of her wondered if he might be dangerous. Another part of me was already sick of being forced to explain the events of yesterday, *again*, knowing full well that none of it would make any more sense now than it did when I'd spoken to Officer McHaffrey.

Except this time I'd also have to put up with Detective Dumbass checking himself out in every reflective surface as he continued hitting on my mom. He'd also be waiting for me to slip up. To reveal some discrepancy between this explanation and what I said in the interrogation room.

So I decided to keep the whole thing as straightforward as possible.

"Remember how I told you I was going to be writing in Starbucks yesterday?" My mom nodded so I pressed on. "Well, Detective O'Brian here—" I forced myself to spit out the title, "believes that someone in a baseball cap tried to kill me."

My mom's immediate hug was so tight that she effectively cut off any further explanation. There was no way I could speak when I could barely manage a tight wheeze.

"Listen Vera—"

But whatever Detective Dumbass said next fell on deaf ears, because my mom was running her hands over me, as if searching for invisible bullet holes or battle wounds. It was like she thought that the press of her hands would magically heal whatever pain might linger beneath the surface of my skin.

"Emmy?" My name on her lips sounded so fragile. It felt wrong, like I had broken something soft inside her. She stared at me with her heart in her eyes, fear dilating her pupils until the amber brown of her irises were a thin ring of color around a bottomless pool of black.

"Yeah, Mom. I'm okay." I raised my arms skyward to show that there wasn't even a scratch on me. "No harm, no foul."

Okay, so *that* was the biggest lie I'd ever told.

Detective Dumbass snorted behind me. "Ms. Danvers, your daughter isn't being entirely truthful with you."

My mom clenched her hand tightly into the fabric at the back of my shirt, but otherwise appeared totally calm. She was in her acting mode, which meant that she would control every single facial tic until we were home and she could decompress. It was like watching a master gambler put on a poker face after being dealt a particularly crappy hand.

"I thought we agreed you'd call me Vera."

I wanted to puke. *This* was the reason I preferred the dialogue in my romance novels to the real world. Nothing that my mom said mattered; it was all about the way she leaned toward the detective, effortlessly displaying a teasing hint of cleavage, as she widened her eyes.

Put my mom within five feet of an asshole and suddenly there was hair twirling and slow, sly smiles. I wasn't sure if she even realized how much of her time she spent acting without a paycheck.

"We believe that Emmy is withholding valuable information about the killer," the detective's voice dropped an octave to make it sound conspiratorial. "Information that is essential for her continued safety."

"Emmy?" My mom's grip tightened and I tried not to wince as her fingers clamped down and pinched some skin. "Is this true?"

"I don't know why anyone would've wanted to hurt me, Mom." At least that much I could say honestly. I skipped over the whole I-was-handed-a-valuable-piece-of-technology thing. It wasn't like I'd entered the coffee shop with the intention of walking off with someone else's personal property.

"I did some thinking in the lobby, though, and—"

"Oh, this should be good," Detective Dumbass interrupted, crossing his arms and giving my mom a look that was a cross between arrogant self-satisfaction and sympathy that she had to put up with me on a regular basis. "I'm glad the precinct waiting room knocked some sense into you. Are you ready to tell us what really happened in that Starbucks?"

I refused to acknowledge his question. Instead, I kept my eyes trained on my mom's face. "I'm going to Emptor Academy."

My mom looked surprised, but I wasn't entirely sure if it was because of what I'd said or because Detective Dumbass decided to punctuate that announcement with a whole string of profanity that ended on the worst curse of them all: "Sebastian St. James."

Apparently I wasn't the only teenager on Detective Luke O'Brian's shit list.

CHAPTER 7

Detective Dumbass clammed up right after that, maybe because swearing in front of a minor and her mother was generally frowned upon in law enforcement circles. Then again, maybe he was afraid that he'd accidentally let something slip. Something even bigger than his own mysterious connection to Sebastian St. James.

Given that I had known within seconds of my first encounter with Sebastian that he was a rich entitled punk, it wasn't surprising that he'd also rubbed the detective the wrong way.

What *did* surprise me was how quickly the defective detective made the connection between Emptor Academy and the wolf in saint's clothing.

"You know Sebastian?" I asked, mentally picturing Sebastian handing the detective one of his business cards before strolling out of the precinct. Free and clear of any charges.

Detective Dumbass grimaced. "Just met him today. He's one very creepy kid. I told him that his grandpa was dead and he *smiled* at me. I've never had that reaction before. Not from a kid, at any rate." He turned to me and his own expression darkened. "You sure that's who you want to go to school with, Miss Danvers? I wouldn't pick him to watch my back unless I was *trying* to get stabbed."

My mom audibly sucked in a breath at the same time I said, "Sebastian's grandfather died?"

He hadn't seemed broken up over anything in the waiting room. He'd been irritable and impatient, as if I were holding him up from something far more interesting, but not as if he'd recently learned of a death in the family. I wracked my brain as I tried to remember if Audrey had told me anything about Sebastian right before we had gone to his stupid party six weeks ago. Mostly she'd emphasized that he was Nasir's best friend, making it painfully obvious that I had been invited in case all of his friends inexplicably decided to hate her. Sebastian's penchant for lock picking I had discovered all on my own.

Detective Luke O'Brian folded his arms. "No need to pretend to be so surprised. After all, you were the one to provide a blow-by-blow account of his grandpa's death."

My stomach dropped and I struggled to process all of it. Sebastian St. James's grandfather was the man I met in Starbucks. Sebastian's *grandfather* was *my* Coffee Thief.

He was the man who had risked his life to save mine.

In this case, I was willing to say that the apple fell far from the tree, then rolled down a hill, plopped into a river and floated for a few miles, before bobbing off into a freaking ocean. No way would Sebastian ever consider doing something that selfless for anyone.

The only similarity I could see between them were those stormy light blue eyes that seemed to look right through a person. Well, that and the way they both radiated a sense of assurance that the rest of the world (like oh, I dunno, *me*) would just fall in line at the snap of their fingers.

I kept all of that to myself.

"Sebastian's not a killer," I said, the silence that settled between my mom and the detective unnerving me.

"Who is this, Emmy?" My mom's voice held a note of frustration. "And why is this the first time I'm hearing of him?"

Well, gee, Mom. I've only met him once when he was breaking into the liquor cabinet at his own party. So I know for sure that he's a thief, but the jury is still out on the whole murder thing.

Not exactly the best way to reassure her.

"He's a friend of Audrey's." I tried to meet her gaze and not look past her toward the police precinct waiting room, but my eyes still flitted to the exit. A clear sign that I was lying. Ben said it wasn't fair to play poker against me, considering that the more innocent I tried to look the more obvious my bluff. Even Ben's little brother Cameron had been thoroughly disgusted with me during our rounds of Go Fish. I just hoped that even if my mom realized something was amiss she wouldn't bust me in front of a cop.

"Audrey told me a bit about his school," I said, racing onward to reach more truthful ground. "It's got state-of-the-art everything, Mom. Oil sheiks send their kids there. If it's safe enough for *them*, then it's probably a good place for me to wait for this misunderstanding to blow over."

My mom turned her big warm brown eyes on the detective in a way that was heartbreakingly fragile. That hint of vulnerability in her trembling lower lip had probably gotten her out of more than a few speeding tickets.

"What do you think, Luke?" My mom asked, as if his opinion was the only one that mattered.

His chest puffed up self-importantly. "I think your daughter should cooperate with the police."

"I *am* cooperating!"

They both ignored me.

"Emptor Academy is certainly more secure than her current public school, right?"

"We believe a professional killer wants to find your daughter, Vera. That's not going to magically disappear overnight. So let us know when Emmy is ready to come clean with the police." He pulled out a business card of his own, scribbling a quick addition in blue ink before handing it over to my mom. "That's my number. Feel free to call anytime."

"Oh, I'll be sure to do that." My mom never loosened her grip on the back of my shirt as she propelled me forward to the exit, pausing only to share one last lingering smile with the detective. She didn't speak a word to me as we walked past the seating area where I'd spoken to Sebastian, or when we crossed the threshold entirely and headed straight toward the nearest subway station.

I didn't know if this was one of her acting techniques or if she was honestly at a loss for words, but either way her silent treatment was a whole lot more effective than anything Detective Dumbass had tried in the interrogation room.

"I'm sorry I didn't tell you yesterday," I said, when I couldn't take the silence anymore. "I thought it was an *accident*. I didn't want you to worry about it."

"We'll talk about this at home, Emmy." Her lips were pressed together so tightly they looked like a single thin line slashing across her face.

"I didn't think—"

"That's right," she snapped, whirling me around to face her. "You didn't *think*, Emmy. I am your *mother*."

That last part came out like a dangerous life sentence.

"I know, I just—"

"It is *my* job to keep you safe. My job. So don't you *dare* start keeping secrets from me for my own good. It doesn't work that way."

Well, that was a first. It had been working *exactly* that way for as long as I could remember. Oh sure, none of the assholes my mom brought home had ever been violent. And if she'd noticed any of them looking at me for even a millisecond longer than she thought they should've been, she kicked them to the curb. But that didn't mean I hadn't learned not to rock the boat. I was the one who monitored her self-esteem, because when she hit rock bottom she binged on self-help books and began coating the mirrors with daily affirmations like, *You are a strong and powerful woman.*

Sometimes protecting her feelings meant keeping secrets.

Which is why she didn't know that Henri had stolen money from my piggy bank, or that Kristoff had threatened to make the tooth fairy rot every last molar in my mouth if I ever mentioned watching him try on her high heels. I probably would have forgotten the incident entirely if I hadn't found his threat so terrifying. My mom thought it was adorable that her new boyfriend had inspired her little preschooler to be such a diligent brusher.

I'd grown accustomed to the small secrets. They didn't even feel like secrets anymore. Instead they were a string of unspoken factoids that I didn't expect anyone to notice. Still, there was something about the way she said, "I am your *mother*" that had me struggling to bite back a sharp retort. To ask why she cared so much about a stupid accident when she couldn't be bothered to protect me on a daily basis. I dug a nail into my forefinger to prevent the words from escaping, to keep those old scars tightly boxed with the rest of my baggage. She might believe that it was her job to keep me safe, but it hadn't actually worked like that in a long time.

She did her best.

She always did her best.

It just sucked that all those good intentions disintegrated around the men in her life.

"I'm sorry, Mom." I choked out. "You're right. It won't happen again."

She pulled me in for a tight hug, and I mentally added, *because even if Detective Dumbass is right about some psycho Starbucks killer, I'm going to keep him far away from you.*

That's *my* job.

CHAPTER 8

Audrey and Ben were sitting on my bed, waiting for me when I arrived home.

It shouldn't have come as a surprise since I'd given them both a spare key to the apartment right after my mom had broken up with Felix and decided to change the lock. I'd asked her to make a couple extra copies, just to be safe. I hadn't mentioned that the safety feature had nothing to do with locking myself out and everything to do with my friends' ability to get in.

"Um, hi," I said lamely, as Audrey glanced up from her phone and Ben set down his chemistry textbook.

I quickly shut the door. The longer my mom had to calm down in private, the better. She had maintained an iron grip on my jacket the entire time we rode the subway home, like I was a little kid who required a leash at Disneyland. I hadn't protested because I could tell that my mom needed to cling, craved the physical closeness, because it meant that her baby was safe. Still, it would've been a whole lot harder to fill Audrey and Ben in on the events of the day with my mom breathing down my neck—literally.

"It's about time!" Audrey lurched upright on the bed and shot me her best glare of annoyance, which wasn't particularly fierce. If anything, she looked constipated. "We've been waiting and waiting, but did you call? Nooooo!"

Ordinarily, I would have laughed at the way Audrey had unknowingly imitated her Jewish grandmother who lived up to the nagging cliché with her weekly phone calls: "I haven't heard from you in ages. But do you call me? Noooo! I could be dead for all you know!"

Too bad I wasn't in a laughing mood. Not when I had to find a way to pack my life into a suitcase. I scanned my bedroom, unsure what to take with me to Empty Academy.

"I was a little preoccupied at the police precinct," I pointed out. As far as excuses go, it was a damn good one. "And I did send you guys a text."

"One!" Audrey scrunched up her nose in disgust. "And all it said was, *Fine here. Fill you in later.*"

"Well, I *was* fine and I'm with you guys now. So I'd say that my text was very informative."

I did my best to ignore the irritated look Ben and Audrey traded by tugging out my battered suitcase from the back of my closet.

"So what did the cops say when you handed over the Slate?" Ben asked. Apparently it was his turn to grill me for information.

"Nothing."

"Nothing because they were so shocked that you'd been withholding evidence?"

"Nothing because I didn't hand it over," I admitted, yanking my suitcase across the room. Two very strong hands deliberately settling over mine made my every muscle freeze. It was a stupid reaction. Ben touched me all the time. It was no big deal. We had spent thousands of movie nights curled up on a couch together, watching lame action movies. I'd even fallen asleep on his shoulder once. I still remembered lurching upright with a massive crick in my neck, meeting Ben's incredibly warm hazel eyes, and then glancing down to see a drool spot staining his sleeve that he could have only gotten from me.

His touch shouldn't have unnerved me now, but somehow it did.

"You need to go back to the station, Emmy." Ben spoke calmly, as if he expected me to jackrabbit out of my own skin.

"I can't." The words emerged hoarsely from the back of my throat. "You don't understand, the cops won't listen to me!"

Ben moved even closer, forcing me to look up and meet his eyes. Those hazel depths weren't soft now. They looked fierce and, well, kind of pissed off.

"Did you try talking to them?" he demanded. "Most people are better at listening when someone actually speaks!"

I crossed my arms. "Thanks for the lecture, Ben. It's so great that even though *you* weren't in the interrogation room you know exactly how it happened. That's quite a skill you've been hiding. Very impressive."

It took all my self-control not to yell, *Shut up. Stop expecting me to be more than I am.* According to my mom's relationship manuals, true love makes you want to become the best possible version of yourself. Too bad my best self appeared to have gone into hiding and the scared-out-of-my-mind self couldn't seem to live up to any of Ben's expectations.

"What did the cops say to you, Emmy?" Audrey asked.

"They think that someone targeted me at the Starbucks." It was getting easier and easier to say the impossible. By the end of the week, I could probably shake hands with a stranger and say, *Hi, I'm Emmy Danvers. There's a crazy killer who wants me dead. Nice to meet you.* "They think I'm involved in the old man's death."

"You *are* involved in something." Ben tried to lower his voice, but I could still feel the anger vibrating in it. "And you're keeping everyone else out."

"He's got a point, Em."

Guilt gnawed at me, but their words didn't change the situation. It was still safer for me to keep my big mouth shut. At least until the panic bubbling inside of me was reduced to a nervous simmer.

Unfortunately, there was still one detail I had to share with them.

"The dead guy told me to warn my dad. So if I'm the target, then *he* is at the heart of it."

"Jesus, Em." Ben sank down to the foot of my bed, rubbing one hand over the back of his neck. "I thought you'd moved past this. Colin Firth isn't your father. There isn't a big choreographed group dance number in your future. Real life doesn't work that way."

I instantly felt like an idiot and wished they would take their sarcastic comments, and worse, their pitying looks, and just shove it. Go analyze someone else for a change.

"I looked for him, Em." Audrey hugged her knees to her chest, probably because she knew I'd become claustrophobic if she wrapped her arms around me. "I ran a thorough search for Daniel Danvers. I even expanded it to include Danny, Dan, Denny, and Dennis Danvers, just in case he's been using a nickname. I came up empty."

"The dead guy said his name was Morgan." I couldn't resist pointing out, before amending myself. "Actually, he said that Morgan would know what to do, but that's pretty much the same thing, right?"

"This would be the same dead guy who stole your drink then handed you a Slate? Yeah, you should *definitely* follow his advice. He doesn't sound mentally unhinged at all," Ben snorted. "Seriously, Em, hand it over to the cops and then turn the whole thing into a great college admission's essay."

I stubbornly ignored Ben's advice. "We never looked for a Morgan Danvers."

"We also never looked for a Morgan Denvers or a Morgan Danningham; should we start looking for your dad in that needle stack of needles, too?" Ben demanded. "Best case scenario: your dad's first name really is Morgan, which means he lied to your mom about his name before he left her. Remind me again why you want to find this asshole?"

"Maybe he had a good reason." The excuses I'd dreamed up a billion times came spilling out. "Maybe he thought he was putting my mom at risk, or someone was after him, or he needed to help somebody in trouble."

"If any of that is true," Audrey said softly, "then don't you think that's one more reason to keep your distance, Em?"

Probably.

If I saw it laid out as a multiple choice question, it would probably have looked something like this: A sixteen-year-old girl is delivered a cryptic warning in a coffee shop. She can either:

(a) Tell the police.
(b) Tell her mom.
(c) Accept a stranger's invitation to attend a private academy while she futilely searches for a father who might not want to be found.

The correct answer should have been obvious. Ben and Audrey had no trouble selecting the most practical solution. Except I couldn't shake the feeling that option C was my best bet.

I needed to find my dad. Maybe he wasn't any better than Pierre the thief, or Kristoff the tooth-fairy terrorist, or Felix the scumbag, but he couldn't be much worse. I mean, yeah, theoretically it was possible. Maybe he *was* a murderer or a gangbanger or a stodgy accountant who enjoyed reporting people to the IRS. But the man that my mom had described—the one who had said that he believed in the beauty of her dreams—sounded wonderful.

He sounded like the kind of person who could help me become *more*. And if he was a disappointment, well, then at least I'd know for sure. It would be one less thing to spend my time imagining.

"You guys don't have to support it," I said. "But this is happening. I'm going to track down my dad. I'm going to follow some crazy dead guy's advice, because if I don't I'm going to hate myself for taking the coward's way out." I unzipped the suitcase and began tossing in the shirts that lined my dresser drawer. "You're both welcome to say 'I told you so' when . . . *if* this whole thing blows up horribly in my face."

Ben glared at me. "Are you ser—"

"Okay, Em," Audrey cut in smoothly. "You know we'll always have your back. But that's going to be a whole lot harder if you flee the country."

"I'm going to Emptor Academy. I've got a scholarship there."

That left Audrey at a complete lack for words. Too bad Ben wasn't similarly shocked into silence.

"Since *when*?!"

"Since Sebastian St. James showed up at the police precinct and offered it to me. I guess the dead guy is his grandpa and—"

"Well, isn't that cozy. His grandpa dies and suddenly Sebastian St. Jerk's first thought is to offer *you* a scholarship? Come on, Emmy. Please tell me you're not going to take him up on this."

"You guys don't have to support this," I repeated.

"So we're either the assholes who don't support your decision or we're the assholes who let you stroll into danger alone," Ben snarled. "That's fan-freaking-tastic. I feel better already!"

I continued throwing shirts into the suitcase, unable to come up with a response that wouldn't annoy both of us further.

"Why don't we, uh, try to set up some ground rules?" Audrey suggested, looking nervously from Ben to me. "Emmy has to keep us updated with regular calls. No leaving the country without advanced notice. That sort of thing."

I nodded slowly. "I can handle that."

"How about handing over the Slate to the police so that they can do their *job*? That seems like a great ground rule to me."

"If I can't find a solid lead on my dad within the next—" I paused to consider a good time frame. Ben was right when he said that knowing my dad's real first name wouldn't necessarily make him any easier to track down, "four months then I'll turn in the Slate."

Ben didn't look appeased, but he seemed to know it was the best promise he'd be able to weasel out of me.

"You have to agree to one more thing," Ben said, and I braced myself for an impossible demand. "Steer clear of that Sebastian guy. He sounds twisted."

I laughed in disbelief at the intensity in his face. "Oh, that won't be a problem. I plan to give him a very wide berth."

As wide as possible, unless I had to dig into his past to figure out my own.

CHAPTER 9

My lack of sentimentality made it a whole lot easier to pack.

I tossed in the clothes that I wore nearly every day (a few pairs of jeans, a handful of shirts with writing puns on them, some sweatshirts, and sneakers) and then, because I figured Emptor Academy was the kind of place where I might have to dress up in an attempt to blend in, I added a few dresses for good measure.

There were a few framed photos on my dresser that I protected by wrapping them in a spare sweatshirt. The first picture was from elementary school, me happily dangling from the monkey bars above Audrey, both of us sporting enormous gap-toothed grins. The next was a classic birthday party picture where I concentrated on blowing out the candles of my homemade cake. My favorite showed me as a bald red-faced newborn in my mom's arms. She looked so young in that photo, partly because she was wearing a pink loose-knit sweater and partly because she'd been captured with tendrils of her hair dancing in an invisible breeze.

She'd been alone, and scared to death, and she'd done her best by me.

Out of habit, I added a small photo album I'd hijacked years ago to the pile and tugged at the suitcase until I was able to yank the zipper closed. My hand rested on top of the hard plastic shell for a moment as I debated unpacking the photo album. Leaving the apartment with the only photographic evidence of my dad's existence felt *wrong*. My mom didn't have any good snapshots of his face because he'd insisted on taking all the photos. Still, I had spent hours flipping through the album from their time together in a pathetic attempt to understand him a little better. I'd spent over a decade trying to analyze those pictures before I realized I was simply driving myself insane and stopped.

Still, the album was undeniable proof that once upon a time my parents had done stupid touristy things together. There were a whole series of shots of my mom rocking a classic Marilyn Monroe pose with her hands on her hips and her lips puckered in a teasing kiss with the Hollywood sign looming in the background. He'd documented over twenty of their dates, everything from the Griffith Observatory and Grauman's Chinese Theatre to window shopping along Rodeo Drive and strolling down Venice Beach.

The last two photos were ones my mom had taken. All I could determine with any degree of certainty from the first photo was that my dad's broad shoulders looked well-built and strong as he walked down a street lined with palm trees. The second image was a bit more informative. My mom had taken a super close up photo of his left eye that revealed every fleck of golden brown in an otherwise green iris. I'd nearly hacked both photos into a million pieces more times than I wanted to admit.

I hated them. Loathed that the image of my father walking away was the closest we'd probably ever get. The only reason I hadn't ripped the photos into confetti was because some stupid part of me thought I might need them someday. That I'd be walking past the lions at the New York Public Library and identify a total stranger as my father with the briefest of eye contact. Then he'd sweep me into his arms in a cinematic embrace that deserved swelling orchestral music. All the photos had actually accomplished was making me wonder if his right eye was lighter than the left, if my own moss-green irises were a faithful copy of that color.

I wiped the palms of my hands on my jeans and turned to face Audrey and Ben who were hovering by the bed. They hadn't assisted me with the packing, which unfortunately left them with nothing to do but obsess over my future.

"Are you sure you don't want me to call Nasir?" Audrey asked for what had to be the hundredth time. "He might be able to help you, y'know, get settled in or something."

"If *you* want to call him, go for it. But I don't need you to contact your ex-boyfriend for me. I can look out for myself."

"Yeah, you've been doing a killer job so far," Ben countered. I ignored him.

"Your call, Audrey," I said. "I'm still willing to yell at Nasir for you. Trash his dorm room. You just say the word."

"No. That's—no. It's fine."

Yeah, I seriously doubted that whatever happened between Audrey and Nasir qualified as "fine," but Audrey clearly wasn't ready to talk about it. Part of me knew that I shouldn't push—that she'd share when she was ready—but the temptation to pry had never been stronger.

"Are you sure? I could, uh, give him the cut direct!"

Ben stared at me as if I'd just provided proof that I'd lost my mind and needed to be institutionalized for my own good.

"You know, like in Regency times when they'd pointedly ignore someone with a cold shoulder? I could do that!"

Audrey smacked her forehead against her hand. "You've been binging on historical romances again, haven't you, Emmy?"

"Maybe," I said, noncommittally.

Ben looked revolted. "Christ, Emmy. You're going to get yourself killed and your last words will be, 'But that would work in a romance novel.'"

"Will you look at the time?" I mimed checking a watch on my bare right wrist, "I'm all packed up and I've got somewhere to go."

Ben grabbed my suitcase and hauled it off my bed and onto the floor without another word. He'd wheel it out of the apartment complex, even if the elevator was broken and that meant hauling it down three flights of stairs. He'd complain, but he'd do it. Even now when he wanted to yell that it was a spectacularly bad idea to rely on a scholarship from Sebastian St. James, he'd only get extra snarky if I insinuated that I didn't need him to maneuver the monstrosity on wheels.

"Emmy, I've been doing some research on this school," my mom said as I swung open my bedroom door. She blinked at Ben and Audrey, but didn't say anything about their unannounced presence, probably because their comings and goings no longer came as much of a surprise to her. "Did you know that they have an Olympic-sized swimming pool?"

No, but it didn't come as a shock.

"Uh, that's great."

Thanks for the update, Mom, but I'm going to be a little preoccupied searching for my long-lost father to swim laps probably wouldn't have gone over well. Not exactly the response she wanted to hear from me.

"They also have a rock climbing wall, a fencing instructor, and an observation deck for anyone interested in astrology!" Her toffee-colored eyes widened as she pointed to the heavily smudged screen of our ancient computer. "This place is incredible! It's like a summer camp."

The door to my mom's bedroom jerked open, smacking against the wall with a disconcerting slam, and revealing an irritated Viktor. "Why so noisy out here?" he demanded in his thick Russian accent.

My mom visibly withdrew into herself. "Sorry, sweetie."

I gritted my teeth to stop from pointing out that for a guy who didn't pay rent he sure liked playing king of the castle.

"I'm leaving, Vik," I refused to flinch as his eyes narrowed in distaste at the nickname.

His bushy eyebrows furrowed as he took in the golden-haired boy holding my suitcase and Audrey's small feminine palm resting reassuringly on my arm.

"You are moving in with him," Viktor jerked his head at Ben, unconcerned with his own inability to remember my best friend's name. "This is good. You stay there. Keep out of trouble."

His utter lack of concern for my well-being didn't bother me in the slightest. It meant I didn't have to fake more than passing civility myself.

"Well, thanks, Vik. That's real sweet of you."

My mom winced. "It really is for the best, honey. You're going to love it there."

No more tears, Emmy, I ordered myself. *Lock it down. There's no point in wishing that she cared less about him and more about me. She can't help the way she's wired. Smile, nod, and walk out the door with your dignity intact.*

I almost crumbled when she pulled me into another hug.

"I'll see you later, Mom," I managed to say around the lump in my throat before I followed Ben and Audrey out the door. It was easier to breathe with a wall separating me from Viktor, easier to pretend that he didn't exist at all.

Easier to keep my frayed emotions tightly knitted together.

"Are you okay?" Audrey asked gently.

"Fine. Great. Let's go."

The longer we stood by the door the more likely it was that Mrs. Sampson would peek her head out into the hall and feel obliged to give her two cents. She'd probably see the suitcase and make some snide comment about the homeless youth population and how I'd fit right in.

Ben's face was remote and impassive, the way his expression always became when I showed up at his door needing a place to crash for the night. He'd gotten an extra mattress that he stored under his bed for me years ago. I kept waiting for his parents to protest, to point out that it wasn't right for me to spend so much unsupervised time in their son's bedroom now that we'd reached the age where hormones supposedly ruled our every decision, but they'd never objected.

I had no intention of ever darkening the door to Ben's apartment until this mess was cleared up. Just the thought of any of this craziness seeping further into my friends' lives was enough to have me marching briskly toward the elevators. Toward Empty Academy.

"It's going to be fine, guys." The lie slid smoothly off my tongue. "I'll text you when I get there."

"And you're sure you'll be safe at Emptor?" Audrey sounded so skeptical I had to laugh.

"Of course I'll be fine, Aud. What's the worst those snobs could do to me? Blind me with all their argyle? Crush me with the weight of their egos? I think I can handle it."

Ben didn't release his hold on my suitcase until we reached the front of the building. "If the argyle becomes too much for you—"

He didn't need to finish the sentence. I knew what he was offering.

"Then I'll stun them with a scathing indictment of their fashion choices." I almost sounded like my usual snarky self as I smiled up at him. "They'll be defenseless in the face of my wit."

"Wit, huh?" Ben didn't look impressed.

"Oh yeah. Sarcasm is always the best defense."

"Well, if you need something a bit stronger, I know somebody who would *love* to test his swing with a baseball bat on a moving target."

The image of Ben's little brother Cameron screwing up his face in concentration while he aimed to knock Sebastian St. James right in the kneecap had my weak smile turning into a full-fledged grin. "I'll keep that in mind."

"And you'll text us later tonight, right?" Audrey cut in. "No more of this *I don't want to bother you guys* bullshit, Emmy."

I nodded. "Promise."

A sleek-looking black Town Car pulled up to the curb and an enormous man who looked like he shared genetics with a granite boulder stepped out of the driver's side door and surveyed the three of us with a calm air of detachment.

"Emmy Danvers?"

"That's, uh . . . me," I gulped, suddenly wishing that I had insisted on transporting myself to the stupid school. I really hoped I wasn't making some deranged psychopath's job a million times easier by sliding into the backseat of this car. Not that the competitive-weightlifter-turned-chauffeur seemed to notice my nerves. He smoothly deposited my suitcase into the trunk with a single hand, his eyes scanning our surroundings the whole time.

"Holy crap," Audrey murmured. "If this were a romance novel—"

"I'm pretty sure that's supposed to be my line."

Audrey continued as if I hadn't spoken. "He'd be the dragon who guards the castle."

It absolutely wasn't the right time to explain the difference between fairytales and romance novels, so I merely nodded. Then I wrapped my arms around her for a quick hug before turning to Ben. My breath caught in my throat.

His eyes were unbearably intense as they raked over my face. I'd never been any good at keeping secrets and Ben didn't appear to have any trouble reading my fear.

"Em—" he whispered and the rest of the world disappeared. It was pathetic, but my name on his lips had my heart pounding outrageously hard. I was too afraid of screwing up the moment to speak, so I waited silently for him to continue.

I love you. I'll miss you. Promise that you'll come back to me.

I'm only a phone call away.
"Don't do anything stupid."
Too late.

CHAPTER 10

Either the enormous driver was under orders to be taciturn or he preferred keeping to himself, but the ride was a quiet one. He didn't ask if I wanted to make any stops before heading to Emptor Academy. He didn't recommend any detours or pry into my personal life, and I found myself wishing that he would provide a distraction. My imagination was spinning through worse-case scenarios and his silence wasn't exactly helping.

"So how long have you worked for the school?"

No answer.

"Do you like your job?"

He grunted. It wasn't much, but I chose to see it as progress.

"I've always wondered what it would be like to be a chauffeur," I lied. It wasn't a sexy profession for a hero. At least not when compared with a billionaire Brazilian corporate tycoon, for example. "I suppose the hours can be pretty unpredictable. Do you get to pick and choose your clients or—"

"I'm not a chauffeur."

Four whole words. I could hardly believe that I'd gotten so much out of him, although I was willing to bet that he'd only spoken to make me shut up.

Ben could've warned him against trying that technique with me.

"So, um . . . are you a butler? Wait, that isn't right. Butlers open doors and stuff. You're a bodyguard, right?" Now *that* was a job fit for a romance novel. "Do you usually work for moguls and, y'know, oil tycoon types?"

He snorted but otherwise didn't bother with a response. Still, I thought I caught a smile lurking on his craggy face. My mom told me once to never underestimate the power of asking someone else about their life experiences. She said it was the fastest way to make a friend and break an enemy, so I decided to press on.

"Do you have a favorite tough guy phrase?"

That one actually got him to briefly meet my gaze with a glance in the rearview mirror. "A what?"

"A tough guy phrase. *Go ahead, make my day,*" I said with all the menace I could muster. "Or maybe, *I killed the president of Paraguay with a fork.*"

He shook his head. "The president of Chile. And it wasn't with a fork."

"No, I'm pretty sure I got the line right. My mom is a big John Cusack fan so I was practically raised on *Grosse Pointe Blank.*"

His smile widened and I caught a white flash of teeth. "I'm not talking about a movie."

That did the trick. I didn't say another word as he maneuvered skillfully through traffic and headed toward upstate New York. I was no longer sure I was much safer sitting in that car than I had been in that stupid coffee shop, but short of yanking open the door and taking a flying leap I wasn't going to be making a getaway.

Watching the scenery change outside the window was my only distraction, so I rolled down the window to feel the wind rush across the back of my hand as we merged onto the Bronx River Parkway. I tried not to be creeped out by the way the bare branches of trees loomed overhead with their lengthening shadows.

"Nearly there," the driver-who-might-also-be-a-murderer said needlessly. I knew we weren't far from Emptor Academy. I'd been distracted by Audrey the night of Sebastian's party, but I still recognized the enormous metal gates. Funny how being fingerprinted at a security checkpoint tends to stay with a girl.

"Are you ever scared?" I blurted out in what must have sounded like a crazy non sequitur.

"Of Emptor Academy? No."

"No, I meant . . ." I couldn't find the right words so I decided to wing it. "You're obviously strong and, y'know, tough. No one-liners required. So I was just wondering if anything scares you."

He didn't reply immediately, but he didn't seem annoyed with me for asking. His silence felt thoughtful, as if he had no intention of giving a statement that he didn't fully support. As if anything he said should be worth repeating at his funeral.

"Fear is a matter of control."

That told me nothing. "You seem pretty athletic. Actually, you look like you could bench press a mountain. So is that a no?"

He smiled as he pulled up to the gatehouse. "Only a fool believes that physical strength equals control."

"That's a yes then?"

"I'll get back to you on that one."

That's what I got for letting my curiosity get the best of me; a menacing hulk of a man with a well-trimmed goatee now intended to keep me updated on his philosophy of fear.

"You're going to be fingerprinted here, Miss Danvers."

"Emmy." I leaned out of the window so that I could do whatever the security guys at the gate needed. "My friends call me Emmy."

If he wanted to get back to me about, well, anything, really, it meant we were already more than passing acquaintances. That's the way I saw it anyway.

He grunted. "My associates call me Force."

"Force? As in, force equals mass times acceleration?" I asked, as a guard held out a Slate, indicating where he wanted me to place my fingers.

"Thumb here," the stranger ordered. "Now your left hand."

"Force as in force," he said calmly as I pressed my fingers against the smooth cool surface of the Slate. The machine beeped and I braced myself for an interrogation.

"It appears you're already in our system, Miss Danvers. You came here a few months ago with a guest pass."

I wouldn't have been surprised to hear him rattle off details about my one previous visit.

Emmy Danvers—Sixteen years old. Accompanied guest Audrey Weinstein. She accused Sebastian St. James of committing a crime, embarrassed herself horribly, and left shortly thereafter with her friend.

Her presence is undesired for any and all future events.

If seen, remove from the premises immediately.

Apparently the security guard hadn't gotten that memo because he snapped a photo with the Slate, temporarily blinding me with the flash, and then reentered the guard shack so he could return with an ID card made from a hard, durable plastic material, which he handed me. I half expected Force to inform me that it was the latest in military technology. Instead, he remained silent. Introducing himself must have been more than enough verbal stimulation for my not-a-chauffeur, since he didn't say a word as the gate opened and the car approached the elaborate mansion standing before us.

Unfortunately for him, my nerves hadn't settled.

"Do a lot of people try to make puns out of your name?"

"No."

Oh good, we were back to one word answers.

"Nobody ever called you Isaac Newton?"

He parked right in front of the austere brick building with its dark crimson shutters and opened my passenger side door before removing my suitcase. "Do I look like a Newton to you?"

"Not really," I admitted, honestly. "A Newton probably wears horn-rimmed glasses and enjoys, I dunno, stamp collecting or something."

"There you have it."

"Maybe he could be your alter-ego, though?" I suggested. "Your version of Clark Kent? You can be Force half the time and then Newton when you're in the mood to watch reality TV or something."

"I'll keep that in mind."

I shouldered my backpack. "Will you really?"

"No."

I nearly laughed, but I wasn't entirely certain Force was joking with me and he didn't look like he'd appreciate people snickering at his expense. In fact, he looked fully capable of removing any offender's tongue with a pair of pliers.

The thought made me shiver. I quickly zipped up my sweatshirt to ward off the bitter chill of my own paranoia.

"Good, you're here. Thanks for babysitting her, Force."

I swiveled around so quickly I nearly face-planted on the gravel driveway. Sebastian was standing outside the manor house with the confidence of a guy who thought he owned the place. I bit my bottom lip as I remembered that he probably *did* own it now that his grandfather was dead.

I wasn't even remotely ready to bring up that topic yet, so instead I went on the defensive.

"He wasn't babysitting me."

"Sure, he wasn't," Sebastian said too easily for his agreement to be genuine. "Are you ready for the tour? I don't have all day."

"Yes, sir." I snapped an ironic salute. "Right away, sir."

"I like the sound of that."

He would.

"Let's move. Now."

I took the suitcase handle from Force and tried my best to smile up at the large man as I pulled it toward the fancy wrought iron archway. "Thanks for the ride, Newton."

Force's laugh sounded more like a rough bark as he climbed back into the Town Car and drove off, leaving me with just my suitcase and Sebastian for company.

Between the two, I suspected Sebastian's personal baggage was a whole lot heavier than my luggage.

"Newton?" Sebastian asked.

"We bonded."

Sebastian looked skeptical, but didn't come right out and call me a liar. Instead, he swiped his keycard next to the entrance and waited for the green light to flash before tugging it open. I noticed that his chivalry didn't extend to offering to help me lug my belongings inside. His etiquette instructor really needed to teach a refresher course on the basics of polite behavior.

"That door is to President Gilcrest's office. You'll want to see him tomorrow and make the transfer official." I nodded, but Sebastian didn't appear to notice since he was already moving down the hallway. I had to scurry to keep up with him. "Straight down this hallway is the lounge for visiting lecturers. There's a bathroom to the left."

"Great." I headed toward the restroom, but he kept walking straight out the back door, apparently unable to linger any longer in the stately building.

Somebody wasn't going to be winning any awards as the world's greatest tour guide.

"The sports complex is over there," he pointed across a small green lawn at a building that looked way too formal to house an Olympic-sized pool. "Dance classes are mandatory, but you'll have the option of taking rock climbing or fencing for your other credit."

I already knew that I wanted to be as far away as humanly possible from anyone whose idea of a good time was to poke and prod at an opponent with a long piece of metal.

"I heard there was a pool."

Sebastian smiled. "That swim class is already full, but you're welcome to use it in your free time. Although I'm not sure we have water wings."

I glared at him. "I'm not three, thanks."

"Yeah, but you look so sinkable."

I pointed at a different, yet equally formidable-looking building to change the subject. "What's that?"

"The boys' dorm. Curfew is set for midnight. It's taken very seriously here."

I snorted. "Yeah, like *you* care about making curfew. I bet it has never stopped you once."

Sebastian smiled. "You're right, I don't care. You probably will, though. Early to bed, early to rise, makes a goody two-shoes healthy, not-so-wealthy, and boring. I think I got that right."

My suitcase hit a crack in the cobblestones and went lurching forward. "Look, I get it. You can barely tolerate me. Message received. The feeling is mutual. Why don't you point me in the direction of my dorm and we'll call it a night?"

Sebastian didn't slow his pace, and I had to yank hard at my suitcase in order to catch up. "I can tolerate you. Besides if I leave now, you won't get to ask me that question of yours."

"Whether or not you were dropped on your head as a baby? Yeah, I was willing to leave that unasked. I think the answer is fairly obvious."

If anything, my insult only amused him even more. "And here I thought you wanted to know more about my grandpa. Y'know, the guy who allegedly *died* for you."

That brought me up short. I stared at Sebastian, but I couldn't break through his poker face. If he was upset or angry or grief-stricken, then he concealed it masterfully. Although there was something about the way he said the word *died* that sounded too dismissive. As if he thought it warranted air quotes so that it couldn't be taken too seriously.

"I'm, uh, sorry for your loss?" If he'd seemed broken up about it, I would have tried to be a bit more sympathetic. Understanding, maybe?

Instead, I just felt confused.

He shrugged. "That's a little premature, don't you think?"

I'm pretty sure there isn't a required time lapse after someone dies before you should offer your condolences. So no, I don't see anything premature about it. I swallowed hard and tried to find a more tactful response.

"I don't follow. Premature *how* exactly?"

"Well," Sebastian said as if the answer should be obvious. As if I were asking, *What's two plus two, Sebastian?* "We both know that he's not dead."

CHAPTER 11

"Are you sure?"

The question felt ridiculous even as I asked it. Still, I didn't think there was all that much ambiguity when it came to life and death. You were either breathing, or you weren't. And last time I had checked (aka when he was lying right on top of me) the coffee thief didn't have a *pulse*.

"The, uh, medical examiner told you he was alive?" I continued, unable to believe that Detective Dumbass had so blatantly lied when he confirmed the old man was deceased. "Is he in a coma or something?"

I wanted Sebastian to say yes for so many reasons, some of which were purely selfish. If he woke up from a coma, he'd be able to explain himself. To tell me why anyone would want me dead—why he had handed me his Slate—what my dad had to do with any of it. If he was still alive, maybe the memory of that last shuddering breath wouldn't haunt me forever. There was also a stupidly sentimental part of me that wondered if I owed the coffee thief my life.

That was one debt I'd never be able to repay.

"Or something."

I crossed my arms and glared at Sebastian. "Okay, you win. I don't understand your cryptic clues. So here's a novel idea: why don't you just tell me if your grandfather is dead or alive?!"

"It's more complicated than that, Emmy. Although I suppose someone with such a black-and-white view of morality might have trouble comprehending the shades of grey between them." I nearly snarled a retort, but Sebastian wasn't finished. "My grandfather is legally dead. A body, which may or may not be his, was delivered to the morgue. As far as the world is concerned, Frederick St. James no longer exists."

Frederick. I swallowed hard. Somehow it was harder to breathe now that I knew the dead man's name. It was easier to think of him as my coffee thief or Sebastian's grandfather, but he'd been a man named Frederick St. James.

And the past tense was the key part of that sentence.

"So he's dead." It wasn't a question, but a gut-wrenching statement of fact. I felt like an idiot for imagining him in a hospital somewhere being spoon-fed green Jell-O.

"He *appears* to be dead."

"But if the homicide detective *and* the medical examiner both believe that—"

"It's cute," Sebastian said. "Your faith in humanity is downright adorable, but since it's also going to get you killed, I'm going to fill you in on a little secret. Adults aren't smarter, or nicer, or stronger, or less screwed up than teenagers—they're simply excellent liars. They lie to themselves every single day as they wake up for work. They hide their fears and anxieties behind polite smiles and small talk. They dole out platitudes and vague generalizations, and if anyone has the nerve to call them on their bullshit, they say, 'What do you know? You're in *high school*. Talk to me when you're older,' because that's safer than looking at their own lives."

"I—"

Sebastian continued to steamroll right over me. "Consider this your second lesson: Never trust an adult. They see what they want to see, and most of the time they are lying to themselves."

"Have you ever considered that *you* might be the one deceiving yourself, Sebastian?" The words felt hot in my mouth. Hot and sour and steeped in bitterness, the kind of honesty that hurts more than it helps. "Did it ever occur to you that this isn't some kind of grand conspiracy? Your grandfather died. Yesterday. Right on top of me." I shuddered at the memory. "He tackled me to the ground and, look, I'm very sorry for your loss, but that doesn't make him any less dead."

Sebastian's lips tightened into a hard, thin line. "My grandfather has cheated death more times than I can count. He's been tracked by the best of the best of the *best*. He wasn't murdered inside that Starbucks."

"Let me get this straight: You think your grandfather was too tough to die?"

Sebastian nodded. "That's right."

"The guy had to be in his eighties!"

"We celebrated his eighty-seventh birthday in Rome six months ago."

"Of course you did," I tried not to sneer, but *seriously*? How rich do you have to be to celebrate birthdays overseas? "Did you notice him slowing down? Having trouble following conversations? Maybe confusing you with somebody else?"

Sebastian's cold expression grew even stonier.

"He was fine."

"Well, the man I met in the coffee shop wasn't fine. He wasn't remotely close to being fine. He called me *Gracie*, okay?"

Sebastian stepped back as if I'd sucker-punched him right in the gut. For the first time I watched Sebastian St. James turn speechless. If we had been discussing anything else, I would have felt a small surge of victory. A tiny jolt of triumph. Instead, I just felt sad and helpless and mean.

But if I tried to take any of it back, I would only be supporting a lie. Sebastian would keep right on believing that his grandfather was still alive. I knew enough about holding out hope for a statistical improbability to last me a lifetime. I wouldn't wish that kind of pain on my worst enemy.

Even when a self-absorbed jackass was standing right in front of me.

"He—you—" Sebastian's pale blue eyes darkened and a chill ran up my spine. He didn't seem like a devil-may-care rich kid now. He looked more like a killer whose patience was nearing the end of its rope. "What else did he say to you?"

"N-nothing!" I sputtered, trying to recall any other detail that might satisfy him and coming up empty. "Who's Gracie anyway? Is that your mom?"

"It's none of your business."

I laughed. I couldn't help it. "Seriously? Well, if I'd known *that* was an acceptable excuse I'd have used it long ago. Why don't I give it a try now? 'It's none of your business, Sebastian.' Wow. That really does make me feel better."

Sebastian didn't laugh, not that I had honestly expected him to see any humor in the situation. He didn't say a word. Instead, he prowled closer until he filled my vision, until I could see each splotch of grey that made his eyes look so icy, and then he turned and resumed walking down the pathway. As if nothing had just happened. I didn't move until he twisted around to glare back at me.

"I told you, I've got places to go and people to see. Try to keep up." He pointed to a dark silvery blob, apparently warming up to the role of tour guide. "The pigeon statue was donated five years ago from one of our alums. It's made of titanium with gold and silver accents."

"Classy pigeon."

Sebastian inclined his head. "Behind him is the Turin library, which houses an exceptional rare books collection on the third floor."

I nodded. I doubted I'd *ooh* and *ahh* over their pretentious first editions, but it might be a good place to hide out if my roommate turned out to be a high-maintenance germophobe.

"So where is your crazy-expensive computer lab?" I asked.

Sebastian raised an eyebrow. "You've done some research. I think that's the first bit of initiative you've displayed."

I snorted disdainfully. "You don't have to be Sherlock Holmes to figure out that this preppy nightmare wouldn't be complete without a tech center. Let me guess, it's state of the art and staffed by experts."

"Your jealousy is showing, Emmy. You might want to work on that, now that you're attending this 'preppy nightmare,' as you so charmingly put it. The lab is actually staffed by students, many of whom have internships with Slate Industries. Emptor Academy strongly encourages students to pursue real world experience in the tech industry." He sounded like he had swallowed the academy brochure.

Audrey would have geeked out over the opportunity to challenge Emptor's biggest techies to a coding battle. Me, though? All I wanted was to be left alone. To keep my two best friends updated on Operation Find Father, or OFF for short. And then to get the hell out of there.

Of course, Ben would say that I was *off* my meds if he ever heard my ridiculous codename.

"How many pretenti—I mean," I smiled with a sugary sweetness that wasn't even remotely genuine, "how many kids go here anyway?" It was the kind of question that made me regret not scanning the website when I had the chance.

"We have two hundred students, give or take a few."

Overwhelming claustrophobia struck out of nowhere. I was accustomed to a fair amount of anonymity. Unless you were one of the rich, popular kids at my high school, it wasn't hard to fly under the radar. That was exactly how I liked it. Audrey, Ben, and I were able to say and do virtually whatever we wanted with nobody the wiser.

That was a far cry from this expensive fishbowl.

"Two hundred? For the whole school?" My mouth fell open. "So that's what, fifty kids in each grade?"

"Impressive mathematical skills, Emmy. Two hundred divided by four does equal fifty. I can hardly wait to see you multiply and subtract."

"Shut up, Sebastian." It was the first time I'd come right out and said it, and the words felt so intoxicatingly wonderful that I repeated them. "For the love of all that is holy, *shut up*."

He pointed to yet another impressive-looking building, which had probably been designed from Frank Lloyd Wright's secret schematics, but he didn't say a word.

It was galling to admit, but I'd actually kind of appreciated his running commentary. The huge brick buildings felt slightly less imposing when I could distinguish the library from the computer lab.

"You have got to be the most frustrating person in the history of the world."

His grin was one hundred percent self-assured male. "I always aim to be the best."

I chose to ignore that particular comment. "So what's that building? The etiquette hall? The music building? Is that where our trusty steeds are housed?"

"It's the girls' dorm." Sebastian didn't offer to lift my suitcase up the four stairs that separated the cobblestone pathway from the entry doors, leaving me without the satisfaction of turning up my nose at his assistance. "Enjoy room 258. Tell Kayla we're still on for tonight."

"You're not going upstairs with me?" I couldn't hide the surprise from my voice, which was stupid because I didn't even *want* him mucking up my roommate introduction. He would probably call me "the scholarship kid" and say that he'd rescued me from a life of painful mediocrity.

"Inviting me to your bedroom already, Emmy?" He glanced at his watch. "We've only had ten minutes to become reacquainted. I don't unzip for everyone, although I suppose if you ask real nicely . . ." He trailed off, letting the words hang there between us.

If Ben had said that, I would've laughed. In fact, I had trouble suppressing my amusement even knowing that Sebastian wanted to needle me into an unguarded response. To charm me into cooperation. I pretended an air of nonchalance. "And here I thought you'd never overlook an opportunity to skulk around the girls' dormitory."

"I don't need to skulk. Not when it comes to girls. You might want to hold off on making too many assumptions. Boxing me in has never ended well for anyone."

"Why? Because you'll only pick the lock?"

His smile broadened. "Something along those lines." Sebastian hadn't taken more than two steps before he swiveled, reached into his jacket pocket, and pulled out the unmistakable slim package of a Slate. "One more perk of being a student here. Everyone gets the newest model to hit the marketplace."

My jaw fell open. I couldn't accept a brand new Slate, especially not when Sebastian's own grandfather had died after slipping one of them into my pocket less than forty-eight hours ago. I had no business carrying *that* Slate around already. So accepting yet another piece of expensive equipment, courtesy of the St. James family, definitely pushed the boundaries of my moral code.

It made me feel greedy. Manipulative. Totally materialistic.

"I can't."

Sebastian didn't lower his outstretched hand. "Because you already have one of your own, right?" he scoffed. "Everyone has a Slate here, Emmy. It's standard issue. Take it."

I didn't know what to say. *Actually, yes, I do happen to have one. Your grandpa gave it to me, in fact. But thanks for that generous offer, Sebastian. You really have a talent for irritating the crap out of me.*

That would only lead to yet another interrogation.

So I reached out, my fingers grazing over the side of Sebastian's thumb as I awkwardly accepted the small package. It wasn't nearly as light as the Slate currently hiding in my suitcase, but I chalked that up to the inclusion of a charger and the inescapable weight of packaging.

"Thanks. I, uh . . . appreciate it."

Sebastian leaned forward and I felt transfixed under his intense scrutiny. It reminded me of waiting to be chosen for a basketball game, being examined by a team captain who clearly thought of you as more of a liability than an asset. "Want to know how you can repay me for it? Fill me in on the plan."

"Tell me more about your grandpa," I countered. "What was he like? What did he do? Who were his friends?"

His eyes somehow did the impossible and became even harder and more remote.

"That's what I thought."

Grabbing my suitcase, I beat a hasty retreat into the warm depths of the girls' dormitory.

CHAPTER 12

Room 258 didn't look like anything special from the hallway.

There weren't any personalized touches or name tags to distinguish one room from any of the others. If Sebastian hadn't told me which door to knock on, I would've been stuck wandering through a maze of bland wooden doors. As it was, I half expected to be on the receiving end of a prank the moment I knocked. I wouldn't put it past Sebastian to send me into the boys' dorm instead. Steering clear of the aptly nicknamed Sebastian St. Jerk was going to be a lot harder at a small school like Emptor Academy than I'd initially thought. Some contact would be unavoidable, making my promise to Ben to steer clear of Sebastian nearly impossible to keep.

I was tempted to call him and repeat my conversation with Sebastian verbatim, just in case it sparked some jealousy. In case a little danger was all he needed to realize there was more between us than mere friendship. The fizz of heat warming my cheeks had nothing to do with the temperature inside the girls' dorm. I had no trouble picturing it.

Exterior shot: Ben's apartment.
Emmy: I know you think of me as a friend, but I want more, Ben. I want to wake up tomorrow morning with you. I want to fall asleep in the safety of the crook of your arms. I want—
Ben: I want you, too. I always have.
They kiss deeply. Passionately. Exquisitely.

Every part of that sounded right to me.

It's possible I would've stood in the middle of the hallway, clutching my suitcase and fantasizing about my best friend, if the door hadn't jerked open to reveal a black girl with riotous curlicue hair and dark, almond-colored eyes. She looked perky.

Really perky.

I wasn't sure if she'd been practicing a cheerleading routine when I had knocked on the door. Her white tank top revealed sleekly toned arms that Michelle Obama would envy and there was a slight gap between where the top ended and her short skirt began that showcased a magazine cover–worthy set of abs. There was a slight sheen of sweat on her upper lip that she wiped away with the back of her hand as she shot me an enormous smile.

"You must be Emmy! I'm *so* excited you're moving in here. We are going to have the best time together. Come in, come in."

She flung open the door and I realized that it was the only part of the room that Kayla *hadn't* decorated within an inch of its life. There were pictures and posters everywhere, most of which featured gymnasts in graceful, albeit slightly unnatural looking, positions.

"Is that all you brought?" Kayla pointed at my suitcase, as if she expected it to magically expand. It didn't. "Well. That's okay! We'll go shopping together!"

A cold sweat began to trickle down my back. Kayla's mom must've had an affair with the Energizer Bunny—that was the only explanation for her undiminished enthusiasm. "Uh, that's okay. I've got everything I need."

Kayla eyed the suitcase dubiously, but didn't press the issue. "I wasn't sure if you brought bedding, so I put my extra set of sheets on your bed. Don't worry, they're clean. You're going to love them!"

I glanced at the bed and struggled to hide my immediate reaction. They were the same eye-burning neon orange color that construction workers have to wear as vests. The bed would probably glow in the dark, like some demented crime scene taped off from nosy onlookers.

"Uh, thanks." My smile felt forced on my face, but I refused to let it fade away. Kayla was obviously trying to make me feel at home. Just because I wanted her to dial down the enthusiasm by, oh, twelve notches, didn't give me the right to be a jerk. Kayla's body maintained constant motion—feet shuffling, arms flapping, hands fluttering—and I braced myself for the possibility that she never tired. That I'd fall asleep while she practiced her imitation of a whirling dervish.

I unzipped my suitcase as she pointed to a dresser decorated with stickers of energetic hedgehogs romping about with their quills at half-mast.

"I condensed my clothes into the dresser with the kittens on it." Kayla said, reaching her arms skyward then folding her body in half until her palms rested on the floor in a deep stretch. "And I have some hangers you can use for dresses or jackets or—" her voice trailed off as she straightened. "I'm talking too much, aren't I? I'm sorry. I always do this. I get excited and then suddenly I'm talking a mile a minute while people edge toward the door. It's like, *Wow, overshare much? I didn't want to know that much about you.* And then I keep going and going and—"

Going. I got the picture.

A blush spread across her cheeks, an instant giveaway that dozens of people in her past had mocked her for being so bubbly and energetic. It must have sucked.

"Oversharing works for me." Exhaustion dampened the edges of my reassuring smile, but I gave it my best shot. "I tend to be on the nosy side."

"Really?" Kayla looked like I'd promised to whisk her off to Barbados in a private jet for spring break. Something that most of the kids at Emptor Academy could probably afford to do.

"Definitely." I shoved a handful of shirts into a drawer and eyed the makeup sprawled across every available surface. Most of it was really, *really* sparkly. "Feel free to share any how-I-met-my-boyfriend stories. Or girlfriend. No judgment here."

Kayla sank to the floor and continued stretching. "Oh. My love life isn't that interesting. The closest I've come to a relationship lasted roughly, I dunno, sixteen seconds?"

"How is that even possible?"

"We kissed in an airport right after a gymnastics training program. It was kind of unexpected. Then we went our separate ways, never to cross paths again."

I eyed the effortless way she'd contorted her body.

"Gymnastics training, as in Olympic-level stuff? You can do all the flips and the handsprings and the double whatchamacallits?"

She shrugged. "Sure. I've been training since preschool, but I landed wrong, heard my knee pop, and it was goodbye Olympic tryouts. Hello Emptor Academy."

"Can't you compete for a spot next time?" I instantly wished I'd kept the question to myself. Kayla looked deflated, as if her boundless energy had been sucked right out of her.

She shook her head. "Gymnastics doesn't work that way. You have a very short window to make it. No do-overs. No take-backs. My window closed and the doors to this place opened instead."

I nodded as if that transition made perfect sense and then froze. "So are you here on a scholarship, too?"

Kayla grinned wryly. "I share my gymnastics expertise and the school pays for my bed, board, and education. It's an unorthodox arrangement, but hey, I'm not complaining. Total win-win scenario."

I wanted to ask Kayla if she'd ever been in a lose-lose situation. She was such a positive person it wasn't hard to picture her insisting that she was totally fine with an uncomfortable situation. Letting manipulative jerks like Sebastian steamroll right over her.

"This is just a stepping stone for you, right? Something you have to do until something better comes along?"

Kayla stared at me as if I'd spoken in Klingon. "Um, are you crazy? I love Emptor Academy. *Everyone* loves it here."

I shoved my jeans into the second dresser drawer. The intense way she said that last part made the school sound like a cult full of brainwashed preppy kids. It wasn't going to suck me in. Kayla might enjoy being at the mercy of the academy, one pen stroke away from being back at square one, but it was a temporary situation for me. I was merely biding my time until any potential killers trailing me lost interest.

I decided to keep that last part to myself.

"Sebastian mentioned something about seeing you tonight." I shoved clothes into the dresser and tried my best to be casual. Breezy. As if there was only mild curiosity propelling me onward. "Is it, uh, a tutoring session or something? Tumbling or fencing or—"

An entirely different kind of exercise hit me from out of nowhere.

Please don't say sex, I thought desperately. *Please, please have too much self-respect to hook up with that asshole. You seem really nice, Kayla. You deserve better. And I* never *want to find Sebastian's monogrammed sock hanging on the doorknob.*

I would never be able to fall asleep knowing that Sebastian had once been intimately acquainted with the borrowed sheets on my bed. No amount of laundry detergent could bleach out the ick factor.

"I guess you could say it's like tumbling." Kayla bit her lower lip in a cagey gesture.

"But you're not dating him or anything, right?"

So much for subtly gleaning information from my new roommate.

Kayla laughed. "I guess you really *don't* know Sebastian. He doesn't date. Not that he's a monk or anything," she lifted her arms for another stretch, "but it's never serious."

"And the two of you?"

"God no!" Kayla's nose scrunched up as she made a face. "Never. Not my type. Wait. Are you interested in him *that* way?" She clapped her hands together. "If you need a wingwoman, I totally volunteer! I can try to feel him out, see if he might have any feelings for you, and then—"

"No!" I interjected, but it was too late.

Audrey would've had no trouble explaining to Kayla that I had zero interest in becoming another notch in Sebastian's undoubtedly elaborate four-poster bed. Coming from me, though, every fervent headshake seemed like a desperate attempt to cover up my real feelings. In a way, I guess it sort of was; I didn't want Kayla to know that I already had an enemy.

Or at the very least, an irritant.

"Sebastian's a really great guy, Emmy," Kayla assured me with all the enthusiasm of an eight year old trying to convince her parents to buy a puppy. "He's a little reclusive, I guess? But he's incredibly smart and—"

"Rich?" I suggested, because describing him as "vain" or "shallow" would've sounded even bitchier.

"Well, yes," Kayla looked taken aback. "I was going to say loyal."

Kayla was obviously one of those people who saw the best in everyone. She couldn't be any more misguided about Sebastian St. James, though. Loyal guys didn't *smile* when they were informed of a death in the family. Then again, Sebastian still refused to accept that his grandfather was dead, so maybe I was reading too much into that particular reaction.

My brain felt like it was gripped in a vise that kept tightening. There had to be something I could say to get my point across, but

I couldn't seem to find the words to explain it. And I was too worn out to care. The last time I'd reached this level of exhaustion I had spent two full days obsessively studying for a math final.

"He's super loyal, actually. His friend recently went through a breakup and Sebastian couldn't have been more supportive," Kayla's voice lowered to a conspiratorial whisper. "Although I wouldn't be surprised if the IRS pays her family a visit. I admit, he can be a bit . . ."

Sociopathic, I mentally finished for her.

She bit her lower lip thoughtfully and then smiled. "Intense."

I managed another unconvincing smile. "Well don't let me interrupt your date with Mr. Intensity."

"Are you sure you don't need help settling in?"

Kayla had no idea how disconcerting it was for me to see large swaths of the wall covered in neon pink hearts. The entire space overwhelmed me with its glitz and glitter. As nice as Kayla seemed, I wanted her to leave and take the sparkle and shimmer with her. Give me some breathing room.

"I'll be fine. But thanks. I'll see you." I flopped down on the bed as if I were already settling in. "Same place, different time."

She laughed, grabbed a water bottle from her desk, and moved toward the door. "I've got a really good feeling about this, Emmy. I think we're going to make excellent roommates."

I had no intention of sticking around long enough for us to paint each other's nails and swap secrets.

Just another unspoken confession I mentally added to my list.

CHAPTER 13

Charging my Slate proved pretty anticlimactic.

I'm not sure what I expected to happen, but I wasn't expecting it to just sit there acting all normal. It should have been flashing or vibrating or doing *something* to lead me to the next step of my plan, but it remained about as responsive as a paperweight, while I became increasingly tense. The silence that had sounded so appealing only moments before grew oppressive, so I turned my full attention to the task of unpacking.

Okay, and maybe I did a little snooping.

It's not like I pawed through Kayla's underwear drawer or anything. I didn't *completely* violate her privacy, I merely studied all the photos she'd taped onto the walls. If she hadn't wanted them to be seen, then she should have removed them before my arrival.

That was my story and I was sticking to it.

Nothing stood out to me as peculiar. There were a whole bunch of photos of Kayla wearing sparkly red leotards that contrasted beautifully against her dark skin. She had a wide smile in each shot, as if she perpetually glowed with the confidence and joy of a champion. She radiated pure glee even with a bronze medal around her neck.

I might not be an actress, but my mom had practiced her entire catalog of facial expressions before any major theater audition. The polite, practiced smiles of politicians. Calculating grins that ranged from the sexpot out to stir up trouble to the vengeful look of a scorned lover hunting for revenge. We had made a game of it. All I had to do was call out a backstory and my mom would transform into the character. It was her eyes that had always communicated the most. Kayla's had seemed so guileless and open, as if her emotions were never mixed. Never jumbled. As if she could be ordered to share her personal space with a total stranger and not feel even the slightest bit possessive or territorial. In the handful of minutes we'd spent together she had offered to take me shopping and tried to set me up with one of her close friends.

I didn't trust it.

Still there was something about Kayla's easygoing smile that made me want to confide in her, even though that should've been my very *last* instinct given the circumstances. Maybe it was the way she offered friendship as easily as breathing. As if she *knew* you were going to become good friends and the matter was already settled in her mind.

I pushed away those thoughts and studied a group of photos, noting they had all been taken in front of the Emptor Academy manor house. The architecture was unmistakable, as was the sense of history that cemented each brick in place. It was a stern building; distant and unapproachable.

Kayla was giggling right in front of it with her arms draped across the shoulders of two very familiar boys. Sebastian and Nasir.

Well, wasn't *that* cozy.

I didn't see any love letters tacked anywhere, no obvious signs of past boyfriends, no red Sharpie hearts framing any faces. Maybe she'd been telling the truth about her dating fly-by in an airport, but I couldn't shake the feeling that something was off. That there had to be some ulterior motive for Sebastian to select her as my roommate. I scanned the room for something tangible, but the only consistent decorating theme was glitter. From hedgehog stickers to photos of hedge fund trust kids, the room was unapologetically girly. The swirl of bright colors and glossy textures became overwhelming. My brain went straight into visual overload and I clenched my eyes shut. Studying every inch of the cluttered bedroom was the fastest way to drive myself insane.

Ben would have oh-so-helpfully pointed out that I'd been perched on the edge of sanity for years, and considering that he didn't even know about the starring role he'd played in more than a few of my daydreams, the boy definitely had a point. I pulled out my phone, sent both my friends a quick text to let them know I'd arrived safely, then sprawled out on my new bed and debated my next move.

Technically, I could have folded all my shirts instead of shoving a crumpled heap of clothes into the dresser drawers, except no amount of folding would stop me from fixating on the two questions which had been haunting me ever since Sebastian's grandfather grabbed my drink:

Why me? which quickly dragged me straight into, *What the hell should I do now?*

I didn't feel any closer to finding definitive answers. If anything, meeting Sebastian had only confused me more. Not only did the cops think there was a killer gunning for me, but apparently the dead man's next-of-kin didn't believe his grandfather had actually died in the first place.

Oh yeah, and for some reason everyone thought *I* had some kind of secret agenda.

I should have been able to form a theory just crazy enough to explain everything. Something that would clear the situation right up, like a case of mistaken identity courtesy of an identical twin sister. Maybe I resembled Gracie Something-or-other, and since dear little Gracie had accidentally angered the mob, she had set me up to take the fall for it.

It could have been something along those lines.

Except even by Hollywood standards that was one hell of a contrived plot line. I mean, the mob? Really? Wouldn't the dead old dude have warned me about that back in Starbucks? And you'd think that they would take the time to make sure they had the right girl before they started shooting tranquilizer guns or whatever. I tried to pretend I was reading the past few days as a big budget action/adventure screenplay.

Scantily clad heroine runs for cover as the Starbucks behind her bursts into flames.
Heroine: Why are we under attack? What's going on?
Hero: Don't worry, gorgeous. I've got this whole situation under control.

Okay, clearly I'd gone way too Hollywood. That script sounded obnoxious. I shut my eyes and tried to picture a blank page.

Incredibly average heroine leaps off the bed at her fancy new school and does something.

Anything.

I lifted the Slate carefully. It wasn't fully charged, but that didn't mean I couldn't start scrolling through its contents. There was no telling what I might be able to unearth; documents detailing all of Sebastian's exploits, a separate contact list of everyone who might be carrying a grudge against the grandfather, a new book release from one of my favorite authors. All of it was theoretically possible.

A message flashed, startling me into dropping the Slate onto the neon orange bedspread. It was the kind of moment that made for great television, all dramatic and full of flair that some online troll would instantly discount as too good to be true. Intrepid heroine turns on her Slate only to find the next clue? Too easy. Too neatly packaged to be believable.

I won't stop until I find you.

I stared at the words, but had trouble making sense of them. My head felt too thick and heavy to absorb anything properly. It was like I'd become a circus car stuffed past capacity with a dozen clowns, only now I was expected to haul around the fire-eaters and sword-swallowers, too.

I won't stop until I find you.

I didn't know if the words came from the killer in the baseball cap or from somebody else entirely. If they wanted to square away an old debt or settle a new score. It could simply be a joke between friends. Maybe my personal psychopath was mentoring somebody in the delicate art of psychological warfare.

The nagging voice in my head, the one that clamored whenever I considered taking the subway late at night or made small talk with a stranger, told me that this wasn't good. This was about as far away from good as I could get.

I won't stop until I find you.

Technically, it could have been worse. The message could have read, *I won't stop until you're dead.* Although the open-ended nature of the message had its own kind of terror. Once this person tracked me down, they intended to do what, exactly?

Interrogate me? Torture me?

Apologize profusely for scaring the hell out of me and pay for an extravagant brunch to make up for it?

I seriously doubted an omelet with Gruyère cheese and artichoke hearts was what this madman had in mind. My luck had never been that good. And that was before people started tackling me in coffee shops and randomly threatening me.

The message flashed one more time before it vanished. I pressed the power button to see if the Slate had died on me, but instead of being greeted with the display interface that I had seen on the television commercials, there was only a keycode with six empty spaces.

The desire to yell, scream, and curse every bit as loudly and creatively as Detective Dumbass had done back in the police station nearly overwhelmed me.

Of course there was a password on the phone.

And *of course* my Obi-wan "Coffee-thief" Kenobi had died before passing on *that* critical bit of information. It was hard to remind myself that a senile old man couldn't be expected to think of every possible outcome, let alone his own impending death. It wasn't his fault I couldn't unlock the Slate.

Except if you're going to hand someone a piece of technology that's worth *killing* over, you should at least have the decency to mention the password.

It's just common courtesy.

If Sebastian was to be believed—which ordinarily he wasn't, but whatever—his grandfather had a reputation for staying one step ahead of axes, machetes, knives, and guns. He wouldn't be lazy when it came to picking a password. He wouldn't choose his date of birth or his favorite sports team. That'd be way too easy for someone dangerous to decode.

Just for the hell of it, I typed out my name.

EMMY translated to 3669 on the keypad so I added on two pound symbols to the end of it. EMMY##

Invalid password.

Morgan will know what to do. I decided to put it to the test, keying in the letters, and holding my breath as I waited for a reaction.

MORGAN
Invalid password.

I began mentally scrolling through my options. I could attempt a billion other permutations and hope that the Slate wasn't triggered to self-combust after a certain number of failed entries, I could ask Audrey to hack her way past the passcode, or I could say, "Screw it!" and try to catch up on sleep. Maybe then my brain wouldn't feel like a tightly packed goose down pillow.

The sound of Kayla's key unlocking our bedroom door settled it for me. Hastily shoving the Slate into my sweatshirt pocket, I jammed the charger into the tablet Sebastian had handed me.

"Oh good, you're still up!" Kayla's face was shiny with sweat, glowing from an endorphin rush that only people who exercise every day seem to experience. "I didn't want to wake you. I'm going to take a quick shower and then crash. Is there anything you need?" She didn't give me a chance to answer. "Oh look! You've already decorated your dresser! I love the personal touch." Kayla flashed me an irrepressible grin as she spotted the framed birthday photo with Audrey and Ben. "Cute boy. That explains why you're not interested in Sebastian."

I wanted to inform Kayla that even my barren wasteland of a love life was still preferable to Sebastian St. James, but I didn't see the point. She'd never believe me. It also didn't help that she'd accurately guessed about my unplatonic feelings for Ben by simply glancing at my half of the dresser. I really didn't want her broadcasting any snippets of personal info across Emptor Academy, so I tried to play it cool.

I shrugged noncommittally. "He's okay."

If anything, my caginess only made her grin widen. "I guess you won't be needing my services as a wingwoman after all."

That was one statement I was never *ever* going to contradict.

CHAPTER 14

I opened my eyes to find a concerned face hovering over me.

"Emmy?" Kayla poked my shoulder as if I were a dead fish that she was supposed to gut but could barely bring herself to touch. "I let you sleep as long as I could, but you really need to wake up."

I groaned and flopped one of my arms over my sleep-hazed eyes to block her out. I'd tossed and turned for hours, haunted by the memory of the flashing words, *I won't stop until I find you.* My ears had been pricked at attention all night, and when I'd finally managed a rocky descent into sleep, I'd been haunted by dreams of faceless blobs in baseball caps. One of them had wielded shiny pliers as he said, "Oh look, you have a cavity from all that coffee you've been drinking. Why don't I remove that tooth first?"

I barely stopped myself from running a finger over my teeth to make sure none were missing. My mouth felt painfully dry, as if I'd been chewing on cotton, but all my teeth remained where they belonged. No dental surgery occurred while I was fast asleep.

Everything was fine, just as long as I overlooked the fact that I was at Emptor Academy with an overly chipper gymnast prodding at me and a creepy message locked away on a dead man's tablet.

"Emmy?"

My arm wasn't very good at blocking the light filtering in through the large window, so I pressed a pillow over my face. A morbid part of me couldn't help thinking that smothering to death might not be a bad way to go. It would be clean. Soft. Cushioned. I could slip into an eternal slumber beyond the reach of any and all assassins.

Except I'd also be *dead*.

"You've already missed breakfast. You've got half an hour before you're supposed to meet President Gilcrest. Up and at 'em!" Kayla bounced on my mattress and I suddenly didn't care if a killer showed up, as long as he silenced her first.

"My phone alarm," I said, blearily. "It hasn't gone off."

"You probably forgot to charge it. What with all your unpacking and—"

I tuned Kayla out as she continued rattling on.

I won't stop until I find you.

The memory of those words had me jolting upright in bed. "What time is it?"

"Eight o'clock."

"And I need to meet with President Gilweed—"

"Gilcrest," Kayla corrected.

"Right. Gilcrest. Why do I need to meet him again?"

Kayla shrugged. "It's a small campus, so he makes a point of getting to know everyone. It's nothing to worry about, though. He'll ask you a few basic questions: academic strengths and weaknesses, personal ambitions, what you're hoping to get out of your time at Emptor Academy. Basic stuff like that."

Hi! I need a safe place to hide from a killer. Yeah, somehow I didn't think that answer would go over too well.

Still caught in a sleep-deprived haze, I stumbled out of my bed and headed toward my dresser. All I had to do was keep moving. Pajamas off, clothes on. I placed my trust in the ingrained muscle memory, knowing that if I slowed—or worse, stopped—I'd slide back into unconsciousness. I fumbled with the zipper of my jeans, my hands as shaky as a heroin addict jonesing for a fix. After pulling my hair into a hasty ponytail, I discreetly shoved both Slates into my backpack and headed for the door.

"Are you really going to meet him like *that*?" Kayla sounded so scandalized, I glanced down to make sure I hadn't forgotten something. It all looked normal to me: jeans and a red T-shirt peeking out from beneath my gray sweatshirt that said, Will Write for Food.

"Uh . . . yes?"

Kayla shook her head. "What about makeup? Don't you want to look good for your first day?" She realized how that sounded a second too late, and she instantly backpedaled. "Not that you look bad or anything. Just, you know . . ."

Ordinary?

Boring?

About as exciting as congealed oatmeal?

"Nobody here to impress." It was easier to say that than to admit that my attempts at makeup tended to fail disastrously. My mom hadn't passed on the makeup genes to me. I had a bizarre skill for smearing red lipstick across my teeth before I walked more than two blocks from home. It was safer for me to go without.

"You're joking, right?" Kayla's quick burst of laughter was edged with disbelief. "Have you looked around this place? Everyone here is either obscenely rich, well-connected, or outrageously talented. Oh, *or all of the above.* Your goal should be to impress *everyone.*"

It was unnerving to think about passing the children of senators, oil tycoons, and Wall Street bankers on my way to meet President Gilcrest. They could probably sue me into oblivion if I bumped into them on the narrow cobblestone pathway. But I didn't want Kayla to see how easily she'd rattled me so I kept my gaze fixed on hers.

"What about you, Kayla?"

She looked confused. "What about me?"

"Do I need to impress you?"

Her rich brown eyes danced with humor. "Absolutely. I'm *obviously* the most important person here." She reached over to her dresser and picked up a tube of something sparkly. "Want me to do your eyeliner?"

"I'll pass."

She shrugged. "Suit yourself."

I considered leaving it at that, but Kayla had already gone so far above and beyond the call of roommate duty that I paused at the door. "Hey, Kayla?"

She swiveled away from the mirror to look at me. "Yeah?"

"You've impressed me."

Her widening smile was the last thing I saw before closing the door. Then I full out sprinted down a flight of stairs, my backpack thudding against me with every step, in order to make it to my stupid "Welcome to Emptor Academy" meeting. If Kayla was right, showing up red-faced and out of breath probably wasn't any better than being five minutes late, but some obstinate part of me refused to slow down. Running was one of the few things I knew I could do.

So I gave it everything I had.

I would've done my best to sprint all the way to the manor house if a group of three girls clad in designer skirts, tights, and shoes hadn't blocked the path. I hesitated, unsure if I should walk this stretch of pathway or if I should cut across the grass and run ahead of them, when the girl in the middle tossed her long brown hair and skewered me with an irritated glare.

"Are you lost?" She demanded in a tone that sounded more like, *Are you demented?* The two girls on either side of her smirked their approval.

"I'm new." I awkwardly brushed my bangs out of my eyes. "I'm Emmy."

I was willing to play the new kid card if it would make them stop acting like I'd crawled out of a sewer before contaminating their Manolo Blahniks.

They didn't offer to give me directions or give any indication that they'd even heard me speak. Instead, their eyes raked over me in silent assessment, as if they were cataloguing my every feature for a detailed evaluation.

The tense moment was broken when the same brunette who'd spoken dismissed me with a flick of her fingers. "You're not going to last, New Girl. You should do yourself a favor and run all the way home."

O-kay. So we weren't going to be besties anytime soon. I smiled tightly as I sidestepped around them, gritting my teeth on my unspoken retort. The last thing I needed on my first day was to get into a fight with a mean girl, especially one who looked perfectly capable of delivering a well-aimed stiletto heel to the throat.

It had taken these girls exactly four seconds to figure out I wasn't Emptor Academy material. And granted, I'd reached the exact same conclusion when Sebastian had mentioned it back in the police station, but it was still rude to say it aloud on my first day.

I refused to let them see how much it bothered me.

That it made me question what I was doing there in the first place.

So I kept my mouth shut and concentrated on running across the wet lawn in my sneakers, ignoring the catcalls and laughter from behind me. My face felt flushed from both exertion and embarrassment by the time I reached the manor house. I almost wished that I'd taken Kayla's advice and spent more time on my appearance. Glittery eyeliner would never be for me, but that didn't mean I couldn't have worn something a little more formal. Something dignified, maybe. At the very least, I could have worn the collared shirt my mom insisted would be great for college interviews instead of my shapeless gray sweatshirt.

Too late now.

I tugged out my haphazard ponytail, ruthlessly finger-combing my hair into submission before knocking on the thick hardwood door with the name *Henry M. Gilcrest* written in fancy gold-plated letters.

The occupant's rich baritone voice cut over the lilting strains of classical music coming from his office. "Come in."

I swung open the door to reveal a balding man in a tweed suit that should've made him look weedy and bookish. But somehow it didn't. Maybe it was the self-confidence he exuded that allowed him to sit behind a massive mahogany desk without looking like he was overcompensating for something.

My mom once tried to classify different kinds of confidence with me. We decided there was the quiet confidence of moral conviction; the brash swaggering confidence of the drunk and disorderly; the slick self-assurance of a trial lawyer during cross-examination; and the absolute certainty that comes from sitting in a position of power.

President Gilcrest fit that last category to perfection, and it made me nervous. Edgy. His white-streaked hair and gray-shot beard made him resemble a wolf, and I didn't particularly want to find out if he hunted in packs or preferred to take down his prey alone. He smiled expectantly at me as the door closed with a *thud* that I felt more than heard.

"Ah, Miss Danvers. It's a pleasure to meet you." He stood and offered me his hand in a smooth, polite handshake. His grasp contained enough pressure to hint at unplumbed reserves of strength, making me wonder if President Gilcrest personally instructed students in the Art of the Handshake.

"Nice to meet you, sir," I lied.

"Please take a seat." He gestured to the chairs next to his desk, but didn't wait for me to comply before continuing. "I've been looking over your transcript, Emmy. Do you mind if I call you Emmy?"

"Uh, that's fine." It didn't take a genius to figure out that if I objected to anything, I would be labeled "difficult" and "uncooperative" and then every teacher would keep one eye firmly fixed on me.

"Emptor Academy has a rather unconventional learning environment. We believe in preparing our students for real-world challenges instead of standardized tests. So while I'm sure your," he glanced down at his computer screen, "Introduction to United States History class was quite introductory, we will be expecting more from you here."

I forced my cheek muscles to stay locked in a pleasant smile.

"I'm sure I can handle it." I met his eyes and tried to fake some confidence of my own. Tried to pretend that in the midst of everything else, I could totally handle adding more schoolwork to my schedule.

Because if I *didn't* convince him, I'd be tossed back into the role of killer-bait.

"And while I love your enthusiasm, I think we should have weekly meetings while you're getting up to speed." President Gilcrest lifted a hand to silence any protest. "We wouldn't want you to become overwhelmed, Emmy. It's quite common for people to find Emptor Academy an acquired taste. Let's give your palate time to adjust."

I wanted to ask him for more detail about this mysterious "we," but I wasn't sure how best to phrase it. Was there somebody else pulling the strings for me to be here—someone with the last name of St. James, perhaps—or did he just enjoy pretending to be part of the royal family?

Instead of calling him on it, I nodded agreeably. "Sure. Weekly meetings. I'm looking forward to it."

President Gilcrest's bark of laughter reverberated around the room. "A word of advice? Don't play poker with any of the students here." Then he reached out and handed me a metal key that was strung on a plain black lanyard and a printed course schedule. "This is the key to your bedroom door. Try not to lose it."

There was a sense of finality in his voice that should have prepared me for his dismissal, but it still took me by surprise. "It was a pleasure, Emmy."

It made no sense. According to Kayla, he was supposed to grill me about my academic dreams and ambitions. I felt oddly cheated by his bland, *it was a pleasure*. I bet that was his signature phrase for everything that he didn't enjoy. *Thanks for the prostate exam, doctor. It was a pleasure.*

"Don't you want to know more about who I am? Why I'm here? What I'm hoping to get out of Emptor Academy?" I blurted out before I'd made it halfway across the room. President Gilcrest glanced up from his computer, looking faintly amused at my outburst but not particularly surprised.

"Every Emptor Academy student learns that there is *always* a caveat." I caught only the barest flash of white teeth as he smiled. "Put more simply, there is an exception to every rule. Frederick St. James took quite an interest in you."

My whole body stiffened at the casual way he was referring to a dead man, as if the two men had been enjoying a rousing game of backgammon just before I'd walked in to interrupt them.

"So y-you knew him?" I asked, tripping over my own tongue in the process. "Were you close? Did he mention me? Was he—"

President Gilcrest silenced me by raising a single white eyebrow. "Anybody who claims to know Frederick St. James is grossly mistaken. He was a private man who gave little of himself to others. He mentioned your name in conversation only once, last week, and all he said was that he thought you could benefit from our tutelage."

I shoved my hands into my sweatshirt so that President Gilcrest wouldn't see them shaking. "Did he say *why?*"

"No, he didn't." President Gilcrest shifted forward. "Would you care to offer an explanation?"

I shook my head, hating the smug gleam in his eyes that told me I was already living up to his low expectations. He didn't believe I was smart enough to say anything worth hearing.

"That's what I thought. Normally a new student would not be admitted without a full background check and an even more thorough vetting process, but Mr. St. James was an exceptional man with exceptional judgement. It remains to be seen if you will become the exception to that particular rule. Now kindly shut the door on your way out."

CHAPTER 15

I spent the majority of my Theory of Economics class trying to stay awake.

No easy feat. The teacher, Mr. Bangsley, looked like Elmer Fudd in a baggy suit but spoke with a slow, soothing cadence that tugged me toward sleep. I also had absolutely nothing to contribute. The girl who had glared at me earlier, Peyton McSomething, tucked back a strand of her glossy brown hair, exposing one shimmering diamond chandelier earring before she launched into a detailed account of her growing stock portfolio.

"What should Peyton keep in mind, everyone?"

He paused to let every student in the room chorus, "If it looks too good to be true, get out."

I already wanted to get out—out of the school, out of the state, out of my *life*—and as far as I could tell there was nothing particularly good about any of it. An old man had been obsessed with me a week before his murder. A communications expert would need to spin the crap out of that in order for me to find it comforting. It was all so twisted. Especially the part about how certain Frederick St. James was that I would benefit from the tutelage here. I mean, sure, it sort of made sense. He never would have enrolled his own grandson at Emptor Academy if he didn't believe in the quality of the education. He probably thought *everyone* could benefit from a thorough working knowledge of the stock market.

That didn't explain why he had singled *me* out.

That whole conversation involved a level of forethought and planning that the old man who'd stolen my drink hadn't possessed.

He hadn't even remembered my *name* for the bulk of that interaction, let alone his opinion on a public versus a private education.

My foot tapped with nervous energy, and I instinctively began plotting another romance novel. Ben once suggested I try counting backward when I got fidgety, but my mind strayed too quickly from the numbers. So even though I told myself *not* to let my imagination go and envision Nasir as Middle Eastern royalty incapable of love ever since banishing Audr . . . ina from his life, I clung to the familiar crutch.

The playboy billionaire prince had chosen to banish quick-witted Audrina from his country—and his heart—forever.

But why? There had to be a reason for their rift. Something juicy. A love child? I instantly rejected the idea. No, what this story needed was a villain. Somebody intent on destroying all the progress Audrina was making in Khazibekustanzia with Prince Nas . . . ek. Somebody who had the ear of the star-crossed prince.

Okay, so the evil advisor Sebastard wanted to tear Prince Nasek and Audrina apart because he bore a secret grudge that would be revealed dramatically about ten pages away from the happily ever after.

I propped my chin in the palm of my hand as I considered the possibilities. Romantic jealousy made a fair amount of sense. Prince Nasek *was* an attractive man with thick black hair, smooth dark skin, and laughing eyes that had sparkled whenever he'd looked at Audrey—crap—*Audrina*, except I couldn't picture Sebastard playing for that team. Okay, I *could* imagine it, but I didn't think there was a basis for it in real life.

Then again, this was fiction after all.

A slow grin began spreading across my face as the story began coming together. Plotting was always my favorite part of the writing process because *I* was the one in control. No man ever overstayed his welcome in my storylines.

"Something amusing you, Emmy?"

Well, that was one way to wipe the smile off my face.

My head jerked up, as I instantly tried to deflect Mr. Bangsley's question.

"Uh, n-no. No. All good here," I stuttered, then turned to the silent girl next to me. "You good?" I didn't wait for her to answer. "Yep, we're good."

"Do you have any investment ideas you'd like to share?"

My mind went blank.

I glanced down at the doodles I'd drawn in my notebook. "Not so much."

Peyton raised her voice to be heard above the snickers of amusement at my expense. "Isn't the whole point of this to have *real* investors, create *real* portfolios, and make *real* money, Greg?"

I wondered if Peyton could get away with *anything*. If anyone had ever set a boundary that she couldn't bulldoze. Not that it was any of my business. The opinions of a spoiled little debutante were beneath my attention. I was going to take the moral high ground, grit my teeth, and smile through whatever taunt she intended to send my way next.

So I was caught off guard when I heard myself snarl, "You, Peyton, are an enormous pain-in-the—"

"Emmy!" Mr. Bangsley interrupted. "You should go take a walk. Get familiar with the grounds."

Get yourself under control.

I had no trouble understanding the subtext. My heart was pounding as I scooped up my backpack and moved toward the door. It was fine. Totally fine. Getting booted out of my first class was a perfectly acceptable way to start at a new school. This would in no way alter my future here.

Except, oh wait, apparently every one of these rich kids could buy my apartment building and evict my mom with their weekly allowance money.

"Thanks, Mr. Bangsley," I said pointedly. "It's been *educational*."

As far as dramatic exit lines go, I thought that one wasn't half bad. I paused in the hallway, resting my forehead against the cool brick wall, as I continued internally freaking out.

I'd just gotten thrown out of class.

That had *never* happened to me before. I turned in my assignments, I contributed to class discussions only when I was dangerously low on participation points, but otherwise, I kept my mouth shut.

Now I was causing trouble and the weirdest part was that it felt kind of *good*.

Better than good. There'd been an intense rush of power when I stared past Peyton's perfectly mascaraed lashes to the nastiness lurking in her hazel eyes and refused to keep quiet.

And here I thought I was a writer, not a fighter.

Maybe I had been able to snap at Peyton because I wasn't worried that Emptor Academy might contact my mom. I never wanted her to be stuck cleaning up my mess, not when I owed her for everything. For loving me. A psychiatrist would probably have a field day with that admission, but despite all the assurances given in parenting books, love isn't guaranteed. For every person who cares enough about you to stick around during the rough times, a dozen people will run straight to the nearest subway station. Every single one of my mom's boyfriends had treated me as either a nuisance, a pet, or a plaything that they could discard with a handful of promises to stay in touch. I'd never confronted anyone over it. Each time my mom's latest boyfriend walked out the door, they were gone for good. There was no point getting mad at the inevitable, so I hadn't. Instead I buried the anger and resentment so deep I could almost convince myself they didn't exist. Almost.

I had always assumed it would take something *huge* for me to come out swinging. Something life threatening. Something drastic. Apparently my inner fighter preferred the spectacularly inconsequential. Accuse me of being involved in a homicide?

No problem. Let a snotty stranger mock me in class? Now *that* I wouldn't tolerate.

Go figure.

The classroom door behind me opened and Sebastian joined me in the otherwise deserted hallway. "So I take it making friends isn't part of your grand plan."

"Make new friends, but keep the old. One is silver and the other gold," I recited in my most childish sing-song voice. "I'm sure you of all people will understand why I prefer the gold." I turned toward what I hoped was the nearest exit and began walking away.

"Are you ready to tell me what you're doing here, Emmy?"

The question pulled me up short.

"Tell you what," Sebastian continued, "if you fill me in on the plan, I'll buy you a first-class ticket to wherever you want to go. Paris. Rome. Istanbul. Free of charge."

If I hadn't already stopped dead in my tracks, that last comment would've done the trick.

"You have got to be kidding me," I said incredulously. "I *can't* leave! I don't know how to outrun your grandfather's creepy obsession with me, something that appears to run in the family, by the way!"

Sebastian smiled tightly. "Give me a name and I'll make sure nobody follows you. That's all I need, Emmy. We can even turn it into a game of charades. You can act it out. Ready, set—"

"*Go*," I snarled. "Leave me alone."

"We've covered this already, Emmy. You say something pithy, I say something smarter. You look like an idiot. Let's skip over that part of our routine this time."

"I'm. Not. Planning. Anything." I enunciated each word as if that might help him understand the simple concept. I was so sick of hearing the same questions. Why *you*? What happened? What will you do now? Sick of being dismissed as a liar every time I told the truth. "Go play with your money, Sebastard."

Sebastian laughed. "Well, at least the name-calling is original."

The longer he smirked at me the higher I could feel my blood pressure rise. "Don't you have a third world nation to bankrupt?"

He sighed. "And we're back in our rut."

"Whose fault is that?" I exploded. "Isn't the definition of insanity asking the same question over and over and expecting different results?"

Sebastian wasn't smiling anymore. His expression was so intense that he didn't look capable of laughter. He stalked closer. "No, Emmy. The definition of insanity is angering *me.*"

He had a point. Sebastian St. James was not the kind of guy a sane person would alienate. He was too damn rich for his own good. And yet, I wasn't sure what was crazier: that seeing his eyes flash fire didn't make me want to run for the hills, or that the whole thing was kinda hot. His disheveled dark hair and arrogant blue eyes created a response that felt coded into my DNA. That I could hold his stony gaze without feeling repulsed left no doubt that I was indeed my mother's daughter, predestined to be attracted to jerks.

Except my pulse also picked up speed around Ben, so maybe this was a temporary glitch in my system. Something I should chalk up to raging hormones or whatever the new pamphlet they were handing out in health class said it might be.

"I, uh—"

I never got a chance to finish the sentence, which was probably for the best considering that I was at a total loss for words.

"Sebastian, you're missing all the fun!" Peyton stepped into the hallway and wasted no time in draping an arm around his waist.

"Oh look," I said dryly. "Saved by the *bell.*"

There was no doubt in anyone's mind that I'd had a different "b" word in mind, but saying it aloud would've been tacky. So I gave them both a coolly distant smile before I turned and walked away.

Maybe I'd inherited more of a flair for the dramatic from my mom than I'd thought.

CHAPTER 16

My cell phone battery was completely dead.

The Slate with the password protection and the life-threatening messages, *that* I had remembered to charge. But my actual phone—the one I used to stay in touch with my friends—yeah, I had forgotten all about it.

So I was stuck grabbing the charger from my bag, plugging it into an outlet in a deserted hallway, and then waiting impatiently for my phone to come to life. The short length of the charger made me feel like a tiger prowling around the limits of its cage. Actually, that analogy gave me way too much credit. I was more like a worried labradoodle puppy.

I winced when my phone informed me it was at zero percent battery life, then became too distracted by unread text messages to feel guilty.

Audrey: How is it, Em? I want deets.
Ben: You still alive?
Audrey: Have you seen any familiar faces there?

Wow, real subtle, Audrey. You might as well just ask if I've seen Nasir. We both know that's what you really want to hear.

Ben: Cam wants to know if you're coming to his game this weekend. Are you?

I checked my watch and decided to call Ben, on the off-chance that he could duck away from P.E. to talk. It was *possible* that he'd have left his phone in his locker, but I doubted it. After only the briefest of hesitations, I began pacing a crescent moon around the outlet while I waited for him to answer.

Ben didn't waste any time with a greeting. "You okay?"

It felt so good to hear his voice that I nearly sank to the floor in relief. It was ridiculous. I'd seen him only yesterday. I'd been able to keep it together then. No crying. No trembling bottom lip. If my knees had felt weaker than usual, well, I'd blamed it on the interrogation room grilling with Detective Dumbass. Somehow every shitty moment from the day before had been easier to withstand than Ben's simple, *you okay?*

Because I wasn't okay. I was stuck at this stupid school without my best friends. An eternity spent facing-off with Peyton and her cronies again and again and again stretched before me. Nobody here—with the possible exception of Kayla—gave a shit about me.

I'd never felt so lost before. So utterly unmoored. The only ties keeping me in place were the cord attaching my phone to a power outlet and the fear that the outside world would be even crueler than Emptor Academy.

"I—" my voice cracked and I shut my eyes in embarrassment. I didn't want to be this girl. Needy. Weak. Desperate to hear the boy she liked insist that everything was going to be okay. "Sure. Fine. I, uh, miss you."

The long pause on his end of the line sent me racing toward the worst conclusions.

I miss you?

After a total of what? Twelve hours apart? That was *way* too clingy. Ben would know that something was up for sure. He'd figure out that I had a crush on him and then everything would change. He'd start being too careful around me so that he didn't accidentally lead me on. Every time we saw each other he would arrange for there to be some kind of buffer. Ben would worry that without Audrey or Cameron around I'd squeeze him to death with my emotional tentacles.

"I miss you and Audrey," I quickly amended, before he could launch into the I-think-we-work-best-as-friends talk. "The kids here are worse than you can imagine."

"So they've all got forked tongues and breathe fire?"

I laughed as my shoulder muscles finally began to loosen. "Pretty much. There's this one girl named Peyton who wears thousands of dollars worth of diamonds in her ears while she slices people to ribbons with her eyes. If I wrote her into one of my books, I'd be accused of exaggerating. She's that kind of evil."

I could hear the smile in Ben's voice when he said, "I'd still put my money on you in a fight, Em."

I was oddly touched. "Really?"

"Absolutely. That imagination of yours doesn't work the same way everyone else's does, which makes it ten times more dangerous."

The grin that spread across my face was pure mischief. "So does that mean I scare you, Ben?"

"Constantly," he drawled. "And now look what's happened? You've been abducted by a preppy gang of rich kids. Any day now you'll be wearing argyle vests and playing lacrosse."

I laughed. "You could come visit me here. Make sure that nobody comes too close with a pink sweater set and pearls." I tried to keep the desperation out of my voice. "I'm sure I could get you a guest pass or something. There's this driver named Force who might have killed the president of Chile, but if you can overlook that, he's really not too scary."

"Em." There was a note of something in Ben's voice that made me catch my breath. It felt like a warning. As if he was trying really hard not to interfere—fighting the urge to say yes and race over here and take control—and my suggestion was only making everything harder for him. Making everything worse.

"You and Audrey, of course." I felt like an idiot constantly making it an outing for two when what I craved was some alone time with him. "You could both visit. In fact, I bet you could both enroll here. My scholarship could include the two of you."

Ben laughed, but not as if he saw much humor in the situation. "I seriously doubt your scholarship is a one-size-fits-all-of-Emmy-and-her-friends type deal."

"Well, since I don't think the scholarship really exists, I don't see why I couldn't negotiate something with President Gilcrest," I said, warming to the idea. "I'll just tell him that I need you and Audrey to help with the dead guy and—"

"You told the president of your new school about the dead guy?" Ben demanded.

"He brought it up. Apparently the two of them were friends. Sort of." I tried to mentally replay the conversation, but it was hard to concentrate with Ben grumbling in my ear.

"You shouldn't be there, Emmy. Not if the president of the academy is somehow involved in this mess. You need to hand the Slate over to the cops!"

"I—"

"I'll go with you," Ben said steamrolling over any objection. "It'll take ten minutes. We'll walk into the precinct, ask to see the cops you spoke to before, and say that you were still in shock during your first questioning."

"Ben, I—"

"Then you can spend the night at my place. You don't even have to go back to your apartment, okay? My parents have missed you, and Cam wants to show you his new curveball. You can come home, Em."

Home.

It was funny, I'd called Ben's place my home-away-from-home hundreds of times, without realizing that I had it all wrong. Home was sleeping on the spare mattress that he kept ready for me underneath his bed. Home was scrambling eggs in the kitchen with his parents while Cam waged war with his plastic Transformers against his unsuspecting dinosaurs. It was knowing that I didn't have to walk on tiptoe to avoid waking the asshole du jour.

Home was with Ben.

"I got a message last night, Ben," I lowered my voice instinctively. "It said, 'I won't stop until I find you.'"

"All the more reason for you to hand it over to the police and let them stop it for you!"

I rubbed my forehead as a wave of exhaustion hit hard. It was so tempting to walk right out the door, disconnecting the phone cord in the process so I wouldn't be tied down to anything—not even this conversation with Ben.

"It said 'I won't stop until I find you,' Ben. Not 'I won't stop until I find *it*.' Whatever is going on, it's personal. It's *me*. Handing the Slate over to the cops won't make that go away."

The momentary silence that hung between us felt saturated with the weight of his exasperation. "You know that imagination of yours, Em? *This* is the kind of trouble it makes for you. You think there's something special about you, but there isn't. You're not the princess in a fairytale. You're just a girl who was in the wrong place at the wrong time and for some stupid reason has decided that she needs to stay in the *wrongness* instead of fixing it!"

I couldn't think of a single thing to say in response. Not a damn thing.

You think there's something special about you, but there isn't.

That summed up the situation between us pretty concisely.

No need for the let's-just-stay-friends talk or the it's-not-you-it's-me excuse. Ben didn't need to make his position any clearer. I'd gotten the message and it was humiliating enough to last a lifetime. I stood frozen in horror as it finally sank in that we were never, ever getting together. That after careful consideration, he'd reached the conclusion that I was nothing special.

"I've got to go," I lied.

"Emmy—"

I hung up and leaned against the wall as my whole body shook with tremors of self-loathing.

It wasn't rejection, I told myself numbly. It couldn't count as rejection if I hadn't officially put the offer out on the table. We had merely reached an understanding.

He wanted me to come home because we were friends. Buddies. Pals. Not because I was anyone special to him. My chest felt excruciatingly tight, as if I'd been sentenced to die beneath great slabs of stone during the Salem witch trials.

My phone beeped to signal that I had a new text message.

Ben: We need to talk.

Sure. Absolutely. Just as soon as the idea of pretending that everything was normal between us didn't make me want to vomit. I'd give him a call the instant I figured out how *not* to be in love with him. Considering that I'd been trying to move past this stupid one-sided crush for years, I didn't think that would be happening anytime soon.

My pride still required that I respond to his text. Otherwise he might think I was sulking or pouting or throwing a hissy fit. Or worse, he might stumble across the truth. I quickly dashed off a response and hit send before I could reconsider it.

Emmy: Later. Tell Cam that I probably won't make it.

I tried to imagine how a plucky heroine would handle this kind of rejection. Would she drown her sorrows in a pint of ice cream? Maybe. The idea definitely held appeal, but rocky road wasn't going to fix any of my problems.

I needed to hack into the Slate.

Luckily for me, I knew just who to call.

CHAPTER 17

"You want me to hack into a dead man's tablet?"

It sounded incredibly morbid when Audrey put it that way, although I couldn't dispute the facts. All I could do was try to put a more appealing spin on it.

"You love hacking!" I reminded her. "Trying to figure out an algorithm you can run and—" my mind drew a total blank, "doing all those other hack-y things."

"Hack-y things?" Audrey laughed. "Are you sure you want to be a writer? Words are not your friends, Emmy."

I shrugged, brushing that aside. "That's what keeps editors in business. Focus, Audrey. I am offering you an incredible opportunity here. A chance of a lifetime. *You* can have the first crack at hacking into a beautiful piece of state-of-the-art technology. There's no way you can pass that up!"

I didn't need to see Audrey's face to know that she was tempted. "How intricate of a password are we talking about here?"

"Six digits."

"I might have to write a program," she said thoughtfully, and I knew that I had her. Audrey attacked technological puzzles with the same enthusiasm Ben's dad reserved for the *New York Times* Crossword. For Audrey, computer hacking was self-expression, defiance, and art all wrapped together.

"No promises."

"Just give it a shot. Work your magic."

That was a mistake. Audrey was a tech wizard; Nasir, on the other hand, was an actual magician. Not even kidding. My best friend was torn up over a guy who pulled rabbits out of his hat for fun. They had met at an underground geek event where Audrey's appreciation for a good card trick had brought them together. Ever since they'd broken up, I had steered clear of anything even remotely connected to magic around her.

So, of course, I stepped right into it now.

"Uh, sure." Audrey obviously wasn't thinking about the Slate anymore. "So how is it going at Emptor Academy? Make any new friends?"

"I have, actually," I said, more than a little surprised by my own answer. "My roommate. Kayla. She's very upbeat and sparkly. You'll like her, though."

"Sounds like you're having no trouble fitting in. New school. New friends. Next you'll have a new boyfriend and no time for your old life anymore."

There was something unsettling about her tone that I couldn't pinpoint until I'd mentally replayed her words. Then it hit me: Audrey was only half-joking.

"You caught me, Audrey." I released an overly dramatic love-struck sigh. "I admit it. I've been sneaking around with Sebastian on the sly. What can I say? There's something about the way he says 'financial quarter' that makes me melt."

"*I knew it!*"

I spun around to see a triumphant Kayla thrusting her fist in the air. "I *knew* you had a thing for Sebastian!"

"Sarcasm, Kayla. That was sarcasm."

"You're with her now?" Audrey sounded startled. "I didn't realize she was right there. I'll let you go then."

"She snuck up on me." I narrowed my eyes at Kayla as I tried to do some immediate damage control. "Did I happen to mention that Kayla is part ninja, part unicorn, and completely immune to sarcasm?"

Kayla nodded. "I'm fine with that description. Although I think we both know that—"

There was no way I could maintain two conversations at once. "I've got to go, Audrey. I'll call you again soon, okay? Thanks for helping me."

"Sure. No problem," Audrey said stiffly. "Later, Em."

She disconnected first, leaving a tight knot in the pit of my stomach. In the space of twenty minutes I'd managed to strain my relationship with the two most important people in my life. I half-expected Sebastian to announce over the school intercom system that students at Emptor Academy were expected—even *encouraged*—to alienate people from their past. That this was another one of my lessons. Right up there with accepting lifelines and avoiding adults. I could hear the rough scrape of Sebastian's voice in my head. *Here's your third lesson, Emmy. Ditch anyone who holds you back from greatness.*

"You ready to go?" Kayla asked uncertainly. "I thought you might need help finding our Negotiation and Diplomacy class. Mrs. Chin is strict on tardiness, so move it or lose it."

I unplugged the charger and my cell phone beeped at me in disgust. Five percent battery life. Great. Maybe I could send one last text before it conked out on me. Then again, who was really left for me to irritate?

"Ready."

Kayla tucked her arm through mine and began leading me down the hallway like a perky guide dog. "Ex-cellent. So tell me more about your crush on Sebastian. Financial quarter, huh? Interesting. That's not how it works for most of the girls."

I couldn't pass up such a golden opportunity to do a little digging of my own.

"Really?" I said, casually. "What about Peyton?"

Kayla ground to a halt, her eyes widening into a stricken expression. "I totally forgot about Peyton. Trust me, you do *not* want to get on her bad side."

I decided against telling Kayla that her warning was delivered about three hours too late. "Is she part of Sebastian's harem then?"

Kayla snorted at the description. "Peyton doesn't share. She's bad news. Rumor has it her dad is a foreign ambassador and her mom is a stripper turned trophy wife. Then again, I've also heard that she's an amateur drag racer who made a fortune in Monaco. When it comes to Peyton avoidance is the best policy." She pursed her lips thoughtfully. "Although if you're serious about this thing with Sebastian—"

"I'm not!"

Kayla shook her head as if she didn't know why I bothered denying it. "Uh-huh. Well *hypothetically* if you were interested—"

"Like if a tragic car accident left my brain scrambled?" That didn't sound like a half bad movie premise. "If Sebastian showed up and . . . I'm sorry, Kayla. I'm still not buying it. He wouldn't visit a hospital unless it was part of a scheme to rob the terminally ill."

"Wow, that's harsh. You're really not kidding, are you?"

I shook my head. "Totally serious."

"I thought it was just your way of flirting. The two of you would irritate each other at first, but then everything would change."

"No, then we'd continue disliking each other," I corrected her. "I love a good romance as much as the next girl. Actually, I love a good romance more than a *lot* of girls, but not every boy pulling pigtails on the playground has a crush. Some of them are little jerks who grow up to be even bigger jerks because nobody told them to keep their hands to themselves."

"Oh look, we're here!" Kayla pointed to a classroom door that was a good thirty feet ahead of us. "Right on time. Follow my lead, okay? You need to make a very good first impression with Mrs. Chin."

"And if I don't?" I asked warily.

"Then you'll spend every day for the next few years trying to fix the damage."

Point taken.

"Good morning, Mrs. Chin," Kayla said warmly, giving the tiny woman with a pageboy haircut her toothiest smile. I tried to imitate the expression, but it probably looked like I had a bad case of indigestion. "This is Emmy. She's interested in joining the Speech and Debate team."

"I am?" I coughed and pretended to clear my throat as Mrs. Chin skewered me with an intense pair of jet black eyes. "I mean, *yes*, I am."

Kayla nodded her encouragement. "I think she'll be a great addition to the team."

I wasn't sure how I was supposed to respond to that obvious lie, so I stood there mutely with a fake smile plastered across my face. Internally, I began to panic. I wasn't prepared to lead a debate in front of the class. And if she asked me to recite the Gettysburg Address, I was screwed.

Fourscore and seven years ago, our fathers brought forth . . . something something . . . conceived in liberty . . . something . . . that all men are created equal.

My pulse began pounding a frantic beat.

Mrs. Chin nodded so curtly it didn't ruffle a single hair. "Welcome to Negotiation and Diplomacy, Emmy."

"Thanks. We should probably—" My voice withered under the renewed weight of Mrs. Chin's examination. Her diminutive stature didn't make her any less intimidating.

"Take our seats," Kayla finished for me, then nodded politely at Mrs. Chin before propelling us toward two vacant seats in the third row.

"Won't she hate me more when I don't join Speech and Debate?" I hissed as I pulled out my notebook and flipped to a blank page.

Kayla stared at me in confusion. "Of course you're joining. Our team is *awesome*! We've been state champions six years in a row."

Her words made me want to bang my head against the long carved wooden table that was far too regal to be called a desk. Not when there weren't any initials etched into the surface, no gum stuck to the bottom, no dents or gouges from years of neglect. It was beautiful and expensive and ridiculously impractical for a classroom. It didn't belong there.

Or rather, *I* didn't belong there.

"Let's discuss the Treaty of Versailles. What did you think of the reading, Kasdan?"

A blond-haired Slavic-looking boy with thick tortoise-shell glasses paled. "I think that it's important to weigh long-term ramifications over immediate gratification."

"What do you think, Em?" Kayla's lips barely moved. "Is that sexier than, oh I dunno, *financial quarter*?"

I bit the inside of my cheek to stifle a laugh.

"Since you're overflowing with commentary, Kayla, why don't you share your thoughts on the Fourteen Points plan?" Mrs. Chin said coldly.

I spent the rest of the class period trying to come up with a way to stay on campus without taking classes. Listening to my new classmates debate some random treaty was a total waste of time that would be much better spent figuring out why Frederick St. James had targeted me in the first place.

Except I couldn't escape the classroom without drawing more attention to myself.

"I'll help you catch up," Kayla promised when the bell finally rang. "Don't worry, okay? It's nothing you can't handle."

Sure. And I didn't stick out like a sore thumb here. Oh, and Ben's total lack of romantic feelings for me didn't hurt in the slightest. As long as we were lying, we might as well go all out.

"Ready for lunch?"

The promise of food was enough to break through the haze of self-pity.

"Yes! Yes, I am." I picked up my pace until I was half-walking, half-trotting to the nearest exit. "I want all the food. All of it. Is it a buffet or does a butler bring it out?"

Kayla laughed. "Yes, all meals are served by butlers here. We also have an extra manservant who announces our name every time we enter the banquet hall."

I really hoped she was kidding.

"What's next on your schedule?"

I glanced down at the paper that I had folded a dozen times since I'd left President Gilcrest's office.

"I have ballroom dance after lunch. Unless you can get me out of it." I pretended to bat my lashes. "Use your status as a highly valued instructor to help your roommate out?"

"Please describe me that way to Ms. Helsenberg. Please. Her expression would be priceless. She thinks I'm a joke." Kayla didn't appear overly upset by it and sounded more matter-of-fact than anything else.

"How's that possible? You're an Olympic-level athlete!"

That made her wince. "No, I'm an athlete past her prime and put out to pasture."

I pulled up short. "You can't honestly believe that."

"Drop it, Emmy."

Beneath the blue glitter rimming her long lashes, Kayla's eyes looked haunted. I tried to imagine how it would feel to be a sentence away from completing a novel, only to have my computer crash and erase everything. It must have hurt a billion times worse for Kayla to watch her team carry the Olympic torch without her.

"Whatever happened to the first rule of Emptor Academy?" I demanded.

Kayla eyed me suspiciously. "There's always a caveat?"

I shook my head. "Okay, maybe I'm thinking of the second rule."

"If it seems too good to be true, get out?" Kayla pushed open the door to the cafeteria, momentarily distracting me. Long buffet tables with silver serving platters rested on white linen tablecloths, but it was the delicious aroma saturating the air that had my stomach growling.

"This school has too many mottos."

Kayla laughed. "You haven't even heard half of them." She ticked them off on her fingers. "Never let them see you cry. Everyone's replaceable. Never unholster your weapon unless you intend to shoot."

"You guys *shoot* here?"

"Metaphorically speaking. Well, mostly. Although that rule comes up a lot at the shooting range."

I couldn't even begin to process *that* particular piece of information, so I mentally tucked it away for later. "Okay, well, Sebastian gave me this whole speech about how adults aren't always smart, but I'm pretty sure I can come up with something better. You ready for some certified Emmy Danvers wisdom?"

"Ready."

"If they make you feel bad, screw 'em." I grabbed my plate. "And never *ever* overlook a buffet."

Kayla snickered, but I barely heard her before the Slate vibrating in my pocket claimed my full attention. I had a sinking feeling that whatever message it contained wasn't going to be sparkly.

CHAPTER 18

I pretended everything was fine.

I loaded up my tray with a random assortment of food and took a seat at a nearby table while Kayla waited in line for filet mignon. Then I forced myself to take a big bite of potatoes à la something fancy before I calmly—*very* calmly—reached for the Slate that was still buzzing silently in my pocket. I didn't really need to worry about witnesses. The sight of a student staring at their Slate wouldn't come as a surprise to anyone here.

Still, it never hurt to play it cool.

That was probably another school motto that Kayla had forgotten to mention.

One glance at the screen and I couldn't play anything. I could barely breathe. There wasn't a flashing message this time. No death threats or accusations. Not so much as an obscene promise of retribution or a hint at the treatment I could expect to receive at the hands of a killer.

It wasn't even an incoming message. For a split second I thought that Frederick St. James must have set a timer on his phone to remember his prescription pills. That I would simply have to ignore this programmed notification every day at noon. I pictured myself at a lunch date with an acquiring editor from a big publishing house. *Oh, ignore my vibrating pants. It's just a dead man's reminder. Now where were we? Right. I was thinking that my heroine is attracted to her brother's best friend who just so happens to be the Navy SEAL tasked with protecting her life.*

But instead of saying, "Take two blue Advil-oxy-pentil-whatever with a glass of water" the Slate had an entirely different alert for me.

Potential Hostile within 60 ft.
Potential Hostile within 55 ft.

There was a brief pause.

Zzzzzz!
Potential Hostile within 50 ft.

I scanned the bustling cafeteria for anyone wearing a dark baseball cap, desperately hoping that my bad guy was cocky enough to try the same trick twice. It was nearly impossible to get a clear view of anything with all the students, faculty members, and kitchen staff performing an elaborate social dance as they wove around each other in their pursuit of food. President Gilcrest waved to a slim woman with a dark brown pixie cut. Mrs. Chin ladled something into a bowl and then disappeared into the crowd. I froze in my seat, caught between the urge to stand on the table and spin in a circle to narrow down the direction of the threat, and crawling under the table where I could hug my knees to my chest until the danger passed.

Zzzzz! Zzzzz! Zzzzz!
Potential Hostile within 45 ft.

My fingers felt oddly cold. Nearly frozen stiff and clumsy. The taste of fear overpowered the chunk of potato I'd barely managed to swallow. What if I dropped the Slate on the table? What if I accidentally gave myself away?

What if the Potential Hostile had already identified me and no matter what I did, it would be too little too late?

Zzzzz! Zzzt! Zzzzz! Zzzt! Zzzt! Zzzzz!

Potential Hostile within 40 ft.

"You okay, Emmy?" Kayla asked, plunking down her tray and eyeing me from across the table. My head was bowed over the Slate in my lap, but she instantly jumped to the wrong conclusion. "Ohh, you're blessing the food?" Kayla promptly pressed the palms of her hand together. "Dear Lord, thank you for the meal we are about to eat. It looks delicious. Please help me digest all of it before coaching gymnastics. I don't want heartburn."

"Uh, amen," I said, hoping that Kayla wouldn't catch me trying to memorize the faces of everyone within a 40-foot range of our table. They all blurred together into an indistinct jumble. Everyone looked so starched. Polished.

Dignified.

Nobody slouched or snickered too loudly or chugged down a soda before racing out of the cafeteria. Nobody stood out to me as being particularly memorable. No piercings, prominent tattoos, nothing that would stand out in a police lineup. As for the few faces that did look vaguely familiar, I couldn't determine if I'd passed them in the hallways or in the prime rib line, or if it was simply that they all wore a sheen of wealth like a uniform.

My fingers wrapped around the handle of my steak knife, clenching it so tightly my knuckles turned white before they began shaking. I set down the knife, hastily wiped away the thin layer of sweat coating my palm, and tried again to get a firm grip on both the knife and reality.

There had to be a way out.

I had to be missing something important. Actually, there were probably *fifty* things that I should be noticing but wasn't because of the terror swamping my system.

Maybe Frederick St. James had felt all-consuming panic when he'd told me that *they* were coming for him. For me.

For us.

If the killer attacked me now, nobody here would throw their body in front of mine. Nobody would lay their life on the line for me. Nobody would play the part of the hero.

President Gilcrest would simply escort the killer to their state-of-the-art psych ward so that they could use my tragic demise as a learning experience for the rest of the student body.

"What are you—oh. Peyton. Yeah, she's definitely intimidating."

I didn't bother glancing in the direction that Kayla was indicating with a nod of her head. A bitchy beauty queen was the least of my worries.

"Rumor has it that Sebastian gave her the whole, 'I'm not looking for a relationship' talk last week. Not that you're interested in him. You can release your death grip on the knife now."

Death grip. I fought a bubble of hysterical laughter at her terrible word choice.

"This isn't *jealousy*. I'm testing the quality of the silverware," I lied weakly.

Zzzzz! Zzzzz! Zzzzz!
Potential Hostile within 45 ft.
Zzzzz! Zzzzz! Zzzzz!
Potential Hostile within 50 ft.

My mysterious stalker was backing away. I nearly slumped in my chair in relief. The knife slipped from my clammy palm and clattered to the tray. Telltale shudders pulsed through my body.

It was okay. I was okay. For now. I shoved the Slate into my backpack, my hands shaking and my breath coming in short jerky pants.

"You okay?" Kayla asked. This time she paused between bites of pasta to examine my face. "Your eyes look really dilated."

"That's because I'm in shock. Who uses linen tablecloths? The washing bill alone has to be insane, especially on Sloppy Joe Fridays."

Kayla smiled, apparently satisfied with the topic change. "You're more likely to be served escargot than sloppy joes."

I nodded and took a huge gulp of water. Then ignoring all the table manners my mom had drilled into me, I began scarfing down everything in sight. A ravenous, unstoppable hunger clawed inside me. After all those hours I'd spent too nervous to eat, I never wanted to stop. The familiar rhythm of fork to plate to lips eased some of the fear quivering in my stomach as I crammed half-dollar-sized slices of potato—dripping with a sautéed garlic white sauce—into my mouth.

As far as last meals were concerned, this one would be hard to beat.

Knowing that Frederick St. James had gone out of his way to enroll me somewhere with a Potential Hostile was a whole lot harder to swallow than anything on my plate. I'd accepted that the old man had some weird fixation with me. Mostly. It was still unsettling, but I'd been trying to come to terms with the idea of honoring his last wishes. I'd done a pretty decent job convincing myself that he must have thought he had my best interests at heart that day in Starbucks.

Except the more I learned about the guy the less certain I became that he had died trying to protect me. Or if he had truly died in the first place.

I felt oddly bereft, as if I was mourning the loss of some distant relative that I'd never actually met. More like mourning the fantasy that I'd had a guardian angel for the past sixteen years and only realized it when he'd saved my life by sacrificing his own.

For all I knew the old man had faked the entire scene to drag me into this hell.

"You might want to slow down. Nobody will take the food away from you."

I rested my fork on the edge of my plate, only to knock back another huge swallow of water to keep my rising anxiety at bay.

The cafeteria was too busy. Too crowded. Worse still, I was sitting there totally exposed.

"I should . . . I should . . . go back to the room. Maybe take a nap or something."

Sebastian slid down in the seat right next to mine and I half-expected the Slate to start vibrating a Morse code warning over his close proximity. Sebastian wasn't a "potential" hostile, he was *downright hostile*. All of the time.

And yet the Slate remained silent.

Grandfatherly affection had to be the only reason the tablet wasn't flashing, beeping, whistling, and screeching, *Run for your life!*

"Leaving so soon, Emmy? I thought you were made of sterner stuff."

I smiled stiffly. "Your nearness turns my stomach."

Kayla bit her lip to prevent herself from pointing out that if I really cared about my digestion, I wouldn't have been inhaling my food like a starving chipmunk. A way too familiar boy sank into a vacant seat next to her and I could feel my day going even further down the toilet.

There's nothing quite like having lunch with my best friend's ex-boyfriend to make a worst case scenario a million times more uncomfortable.

"Hey, Emmy," Nasir said. "How have you been?"

"Wait a sec. How do the two of you know each other?" Kayla asked in surprise.

I suspected she'd soon be trying to investigate if I had any special feelings for Nasir. The idea of dating the same guy who left Audrey emotionally shredded made my skin crawl, so I purposefully ignored Kayla's question. The less we rehashed the past, the better.

"I'm fine." The jerk didn't deserve more than a curt two-word answer.

Nasir shifted uncomfortably in his seat. "I didn't realize you were interested in transferring here."

"I wasn't."

"Are you settling in okay or—"

I grabbed my backpack from the floor and stood up. "As much as I'm enjoying this little game of twenty questions, I've got more pressing issues."

"Right. Well. It's good to see you."

I didn't bother faking a smile. Instead, I slung my bag onto my shoulder and headed toward the exit. Nasir could flash his white-toothed grin at me until his cheeks ached; I didn't trust him. And I refused to act like old friends when Audrey was all we'd ever had in common.

I'd barely released the wide double doors of the cafeteria when a swift yank on the strap of my bag spun me around.

"What the hell was that?" Sebastian demanded. His eyes had darkened in anger to the color of slate. It felt good to see him lose his air of calm unflappability.

I didn't want to be the only one seething.

"That was me walking away. Want to see me do it again? Let go of my bag and I'll be happy to give a repeat performance."

Sebastian growled, literally *growled* at me. "I've been patient, Emmy. I've given you time—"

"*When?*"

"I've given you space—"

"*What?*"

"You've got five seconds to get your head out of your ass and apologize to Nasir. That's the last thing I'm ever going to give you."

I laughed hollowly. "You don't scare me. I have a target on my back. I can't sleep at night. I can't see my friends. Oh, and I can't eat lunch without having a *panic attack*. So there's nothing you can say that'll make me play nice with the jerk who dumped my best friend."

"Audrey broke up with Nasir!"

I stared at Sebastian in disbelief. "No way."

"I'm sure you're right. I must have misunderstood. There are so many ways to interpret, 'Audrey dumped me. It's over,'" Sebastian said sarcastically.

I had no clever retort, so I yanked my bag out of his grip and kept walking. Chin up. Eyes forward. All the while I mentally repeated one of the mottos Kayla had shared with me: *Never let them see you cry.*

Not that I would ever break down in front of Sebastian. The only people I allowed to see me fall apart were the ones I trusted to help put me back together again. But the last of the adrenaline that had surged through me from my scare in the cafeteria had fizzled out during my little speech, leaving me emotionally drained and empty. So empty.

"You can't run away forever, Emmy."

I gritted my teeth and kept right on walking. "Watch me, Sebastard."

He didn't say anything to that. He merely kept pace next to me, increasing his speed to match mine with the ease of a professional athlete. By all outside appearances, Sebastian St. James was back to his normal confident and controlled self. No more snarling. No more yelling.

It was like he had flipped a switch and become utterly impenetrable.

Silence reigned between us as we quickly passed the library, the square lawn where a few kids tossed around a Frisbee despite the chill that hung heavy in the air, and drew closer to the girls' dormitory. My room was probably the one place where he'd be forbidden to shadow me. The big stone building with its impressive arched windows and stained glass windowpanes should've beckoned me inside with its promise of safety.

Except the idea of locking the bedroom door made my throat tighten. I would suffocate inside. I'd become so immobilized by my fear of imaginary noises and the elongated shadows that I'd refuse to step outside again. Not when the outside world included Potential Hostiles and baseball cap–wearing killers.

Outside equaled exposure. Danger.

Uncertainty.

But crawling into bed and hiding beneath the covers wouldn't keep me safe. So I kept moving. I yanked my hair into yet another sloppy ponytail and focused on the rhythm of my shoes slapping against the cobblestones.

Sebastian started whistling.

It should have annoyed the hell out of me, except there was something so familiar about the tune that instead I focused on identifying it. Something about the unflaggingly chipper melody taunted me, which was probably Sebastian's goal.

He began a second rendition of the same melody, and I cracked under the weight of my own curiosity.

"What's the song?"

"It's the Army Air Corps theme, 'Wild Blue Yonder.'" Sebastian whistled a little more of it and then descended back into silence.

"Where did you learn it?"

It was a stupid question. It didn't matter where he'd heard it or why he had started whistling it. Not compared to everything else I had going on in my life.

"My grandpa taught it to me. He said he hummed it every time a mission made him nervous. Every time he lost a friend. Every time the memories became a waking nightmare." The jaunty song was at odds with the darkness of his words. "'We live in fame or go down in flames.' That was his favorite line. He said that someday

I'd find something worth lighting myself on fire for. For him, it was me."

"I'm sorry for your loss, Sebastian." I said automatically. It was a weak stock phrase, the type better left ignored in cheap grocery store sympathy cards. I'd already said it way too many times. Sebastian wasn't interested in condolences.

Especially not coming from me.

His voice hardened. "I'm prepared to set myself on fire, but first I'm going to scour the world for him. If I have to torch a few people in the process, so be it."

I wanted to scoff at his words, dismiss them as the grief-fueled threat of a kid who was all bark and no bite. But a dangerous shadow lurked in his eyes. Something harsh and steely and unforgiving.

"I don't make mistakes," Sebastian's voice was brittle. "And I won't let you screw up either, even if that means hog-tying you to a chair before extracting information. Are we clear?"

A shiver of fear snaked up my spine, but I masked it with anger swelling inside of me. The endless threats and warnings. The relentless barrage of intimidation from everyone from the cops to the school principal to the freaking *chauffeur*. And now *this*?

The mysterious Potential Hostile might've been well beyond my reach, but Sebastian certainly wasn't.

Something inside of me snapped.

"*You're not going to let me screw up?* How generous of you. Really noble. Especially when you consider that your own grandfather trusted *me* more than you. Maybe you should reevaluate which one of us is the screwup, Sebastard."

Then I sprinted back toward my dorm.

This time he made no move to follow in pursuit.

CHAPTER 19

I was beyond tardy for my dance class.

A good chunk of my delay involved waiting for the sullen girl sitting behind the help desk, chewing and snapping away on a small wad of gum, to assign me a gym locker. She had then informed me that bringing electronic devices within the sacred walls of the dance studio was strictly forbidden. By the time I'd shoved everything inside and spun the combination to lock it, I was beyond acceptable tardiness, even for a brand-new transfer student.

Still, I entered the gym with my head held high.

"New kid." The tall, broad-shouldered instructor, Ms. Helsenberg, barely spared me a glance. "You're late. Never wear jeans again. Go warm up in the corner and watch carefully."

Well, that was nice and friendly of her.

I stalked over to the corner and started doing a set of jumping jacks. My muscles were already sore from my most recent dash across campus, but if this teacher wanted to bark like a drill sergeant, I could find the energy to snap back a salute.

"Cassie! That leg kick was supposed to come a full beat earlier. Lead Mikhail, don't stand there like a lump. Peyton, point your toes. Point your toes! *Point your toes or I will break them.* Better."

Peyton's right leg flew skyward before wrapping around some boy's torso and then whipping away so quickly it was hard to believe it had ever happened. It would take a whole troupe of Cirque du Soleil performers yanking on my limbs for me to ever replicate that move.

I decided to block out that mental image with a quick round of sit-ups.

"No!" Ms. Helsenberg bellowed at me. "You're using your neck and back, not your core. Do it *right* or not at all."

I stood up, opting to stop entirely over having everyone in the class watch as she critiqued my form.

"Let's see if you can manage a waltz with Colin." Ms. Helsenberg jerked her head at a kid on the scrawny side who nearly had a halo of rusty golden curls surrounding his face. "Your hand rests on his shoulder, New Girl! No floppy arms. Everyone pulls their weight here."

Colin rolled his eyes as soon as she began working with a different couple.

"Stop breathing, New Girl!" he snapped in a pretty good imitation of our dictator. "You can do that outside my studio. I *own* you here."

I laughed. "I usually go by Emmy. So what do we do now?"

"The waltz isn't too hard." He puffed out his chest as if he were a matador about to face off with an enraged bull and surged forward. "One two three. One two th—"

I tripped over my feet, barely managing to break free of his hold without falling flat on my face.

"Sorry, I—"

"*Hopeless!* How many times must we go over this, Colin? The man *leads* with competence and command. Watch me right now."

Before I could object, my hands were placed on Ms. Helsenberg's shoulders and I was whirling across the dance floor without once glancing at my feet. My legs responded automatically and the rapid series of movements felt surprisingly *good*. Strong. Powerful.

"*This* is how you take command," Ms. Helsenberg barked. "A true leader can control even the worst partner." She stopped abruptly, dropping her hold on my waist as if the physical contact repulsed her. "That includes Noodle here."

I stepped back feeling stung. "Hey!"

"If you don't like the nickname, Noodle, then maintain tension in your arms!"

Two days of nonstop anxiety and my dance instructor's biggest complaint was that I lacked tension. I nearly burst out laughing. Ms. Helsenberg didn't have a freaking clue.

"Nasir, you take her. I'm too busy for this."

I turned around to see a vaguely apologetic Nasir moving right toward me. My ears began to burn. I'd expected that we'd run into each other again before long, at a school this small that was inevitable, but I wasn't prepared for a confrontation. Especially not with Sebastian's earlier accusation that *Audrey* was the one who ended the relationship still ringing in my ears.

"I was rude," I blurted. "Earlier. In the cafeteria. I was rude to you."

Nasir shifted uncomfortably, as if he couldn't quite believe I was speaking in full sentences to him. "Yeah. A little. But that's okay."

I shook my head. "I don't know the details and I don't need to hear them. I'm staying out of it. But I promise you this: if you ever, *ever* hurt my best friend again, I will end you."

Nasir didn't appear cowed by my threat, but his eyes momentarily flashed at the *again* I let slip. "I hurt Audrey?"

"Of course you did!"

Ms. Helsenberg stormed over toward us. "Less yapping, more dancing!"

I obediently placed one hand on Nasir's shoulder and tried to recall the steps.

"One two three. One tw—"

"Audrey broke up with *me*," Nasir said as if that settled everything. As if she couldn't possibly miss him or she never would have dumped him in the first place.

My eyes narrowed into fierce green slits. "What did you do to make her bolt?"

His face flushed and mumbled something incomprehensible.

"What was that, Nasir?"

"I said, I stole her phone."

Just like that, my arms really did become noodles as I tried to slither out of his grasp.

"You did *what?*"

"It's not as bad as it sounds."

"You *stole* Audrey's phone?"

"I only wanted to poke around on it a little," his cheeks reddened further, adding a dusky tinge to his copper skin. I could feel my own face heating, but embarrassment had nothing to do with it. A fierce tidal wave of indignation swept through me.

"That's supposed to make it *better?*" I hissed. "That's a complete violation of privacy!"

"I know."

"It's an invasion of her trust!"

"I know."

"It's completely and totally *wrong!*"

Nasir's eyes widened in mock surprise. "Really? Now that's new information, Emmy. Oh wait. No, it's not."

I jabbed his chest with my index finger. "You don't get to be snarky here! No way. Not after telling me that you tried to steal my best friend's phone."

"Can we schedule some other time for me to be snarky then? I have so many clever retorts saved up."

I shook my head. "Is this some kind of joke to you?"

"Of course it's not!" Nasir quickly repositioned my hands so that we wouldn't get yelled at by a scowling Ms. Helsenberg. "My breakup hasn't exactly been a barrel of laughs, so excuse me if I'm not interested in your post-relationship analysis. Not that I should have to explain myself since it was *my* relationship. Not yours. *Mine.*"

He had a point. Several, in fact. Except he couldn't be any more wrong.

"Audrey is the *best*," I said. "She's smart and loyal and funny and beautiful and awesome because she's Audrey. She'd do anything for her friends—no questions asked—and she's capable of forgiveness to an extent that scares me for her safety. So you can tell me to mind my own business. I don't care. When it comes to Audrey, all bets are off."

Nasir stared at me as if I'd grown a second head, but I didn't regret saying any of it. I didn't care what Nasir thought of my protective instincts. Just because Audrey had spent the past few weeks pretending to be totally over Nasir didn't mean I could slack off on my best friend duties.

"Do you really think she'd forgive me?" Nasir asked so softly I almost thought I created the moment in my head.

But no, his dark brown eyes were riveted to my face in a way that unnerved me. There had to be a class at Emptor Academy on interrogation techniques. That would explain how everyone here could rattle me with a simple stare.

"Maybe," I shrugged. "Do you deserve to be forgiven?"

He started to speak, thought better of it, and shut his mouth.

"You think it over and get back to me. Better yet, get back to *Audrey*. But if there's even the smallest chance you might maybe, possibly, potentially hurt her again? Delete her from your phone. Right now."

Ms. Helsenberg clapped her hands for attention. "Form your lines everyone."

The room parted with the girls facing their male counterparts with a few feet of distance between the pairs. I quickly sidestepped around a short girl with a tight French braid in order to put an extra few feet of space between Ms. Helsenberg and me.

"We have ten more minutes. Let's make them count, people! The Argentine Tango is a very sensual dance. It's meant to portray passion. Heat. Fire. So get out all your immature giggling right now. I won't tolerate any sloppy footwork."

No pressure, though.

"Girls curtsy. Boys bow."

I bobbed an awkward dip, as the rest of the girls sank into graceful *Pride and Prejudice*–worthy curtsies. I half expected one of the girls to say, "Why Mr. Darcy! I'd *love* to dance with you," in some ridiculous imitation of a British accent. Although given the academy's international appeal, I was equally likely to hear the clipped vowels of the genuine accent.

"Partner up," Ms. Helsenberg ordered, and I found myself paired with a large beefy kid with sweaty palms. I tried to smile up at him, but he didn't appear to notice. His eyes were locked on Peyton, whose high cheekbones held a slight flush from exertion.

She looked pristine, delicate, and gorgeously untouchable.

I didn't blame my partner for wanting to trade me. I just wished he could be a little less obvious about it, especially with Ms. Helsenberg wandering the room, correcting postures and snapping out brusque commands.

"Is she always like this?" I asked my partner nervously.

He tightened his hold on my back before answering. "Yes."

So much for bonding with the guy about to lead me backward in an unknown dance. I found myself wishing that Colin and I were still partnered together. Better yet, I imagined that Ben was there. That he'd ignored the rules and steps of the dance, moving straight toward me, drawing me close into his arms, before slowly—deliberately—pressing his lips against mine.

Ms. Helsenberg would've seen plenty of passion then.

Something hard jabbed my stomach. The swift jolt of pain was followed by the lingering ache of a forming bruise. I wanted to rub the sensitive spot, but my partner refused to release my arms as Ms. Helsenberg hissed, "Tighten your core, Noodle!"

The remaining eight minutes of class were a complete disaster. I wasn't the only person struggling with the dance moves, but she still spent the majority of her time hollering, "Noodle! I said use your left foot! Is that your left? No? Then *don't use it.*"

Out of the corner of my eye I could see Peyton eating it up.

She didn't attempt to land any barbs of her own. Instead, she floated along with her partner while she happily took in the show.

Ms. Helsenberg clapped her hands to get everyone's attention. "Girls, I want you wearing heels in next week's class. Two to three inches. Make sure you can move in them. Boys, you should all own a nice pair of loafers. Wear them. Class dismissed."

I breathed out a sigh of relief and moved toward the door.

"Noodle you stay here. I'm not done with you."

Peyton smiled in unspoken triumph as she tossed her long brown hair over her shoulder and gave me a little finger wave before letting the door snick shut behind her.

Leaving me alone with my least favorite teacher.

CHAPTER 20

"I don't appreciate being saddled with new students midway through the semester."

I wanted to point out to Ms. Helsenberg that transferring out of McKinley High School hadn't exactly been my first choice either, but I doubted she wanted to hear it.

"Dancing is an art form. It's not to be taken lightly," Ms. Helsenberg jabbed her finger in the air to underscore the point. "If you don't give me your full dedication, I *will* fail you."

She didn't exactly look heartbroken at the prospect.

"I understand." There was nothing else I could say. *I don't give a shit about your class, I have bigger things going on* didn't seem like the best way to get off on the right foot. Then again, apparently I'd been on the wrong foot throughout the class. I doubted even the fanciest footwork could change that now.

"I don't tolerate lateness, sloppiness, or weakness."

Gee, and here I thought she'd be the most accommodating of teachers.

"I'll be on time next class."

"See that you are." She eyed me suspiciously, as if I'd busted out my surliest James Dean impression instead of pledging to be an ideal student. "Emptor Academy isn't for everyone, Noodle. I don't think you fit here."

The nickname somehow stung more in private than it had in front of the class.

"I can work on that, too." I didn't wait for her to issue a dismissal. If she had any other warnings to deliver, I certainly didn't want to hear them. There was also no point in obsessing over yet another failed attempt at a good first impression. Not unless I wanted to be late for my Criminal Law class. Unfortunately my locker didn't seem to have gotten the memo that I was not to be messed with, because twenty attempts at the combination later and the damn thing still refused to open. Swearing under my breath, I decided to deal with it later and rushed out of the gymnasium.

Ms. Pierce, aka the brunette woman with the pixie cut I'd seen President Gilcrest wave to in the cafeteria, smiled without comment, as I slid into a vacant seat in her classroom. Instead of making me introduce myself to everyone, or any of that other first day crap, Ms. Pierce turned her attention to my former dance partner Colin and asked him to explain the Ruth Snyder case.

The lanky boy who had seemed so sweet when he'd joked with me earlier, grinned wickedly now. "Ruth Snyder convinced her husband to take out a blank life insurance policy so that she could cash in on his murder."

"And can you explain how the double indemnity clause works, Kayla?"

I whipped my head around, spotting my roommate at the back of the room only when she spoke up. "Mr. Snyder's life insurance policy said that if he died in a certain way they would pay twice the normal amount."

"Peyton, why don't you list some of those ways for us?"

I hadn't missed the presence of my arch-nemesis in the room. Even silent, she wasn't easily overlooked. Her eyes were also shooting daggers in my direction.

"It has to be an accident. Or at least appear accidental."

I felt my pulse start pounding. There was a creepy light in her eyes as she continued glaring at me. It began to sink in that there was no escaping Peyton's very real hostility. That Peyton might want me dead almost as much as the baseball cap killer.

Sebastian, as he stretched lazily in his seat next to Peyton, said, "Mrs. Snyder could have pulled it off if she had taken her time." I searched for some hidden jab underlying his words, only to feel like a total narcissist when I came up empty.

"Would you like to expand on that, Sebastian?" Ms. Pierce asked.

He shrugged indulgently. "She was so focused on killing her husband, she forgot to cover her tracks. The police figured it out fast. Some people can't hold up under interrogation."

I bet he was *dying* to tell the whole class that yesterday I'd nearly cracked during a police interrogation of my own. I wasn't sure if it would be harder or easier to make friends here if that became public knowledge. At least it would distract them from the fact that our income brackets didn't belong in the same sentence, or the same paragraph, for that matter. There should be an entire set of encyclopedias separating the two.

"So what gave Ruth Snyder away? Why wasn't this a perfect murder?" Ms. Pierce opened the conversation up to the whole class as her gaze slid across her students. "What did she get wrong?"

It was a chilling question. I half hoped that somebody would say that there was no such thing as a perfect murder. That taking a life—no matter the justification—was a brutal, twisted, ugly act. That at the end of the day, regardless of the method, murder was still, well, *murder.*

I kept that to myself, unwilling to let Sebastian and Peyton mock me for it.

"She said her husband died during a break-in, but the room didn't look right."

"Excellent, Kasdan." Ms. Pierce walked over to the white board and wrote, *The scene must match the story* in dark red marker. "What else?"

"The cops asked her about a pin with the initials J.G. on them, and she demanded to know why they were dragging Judd Gray into it."

Ms. Pierce nodded with satisfaction. "And why was that a mistake?"

"Because Judd Gray was her lover and he helped her plan the whole thing." Peyton didn't bother raising her hand. "You *never* mention an accomplice."

Ms. Pierce wrote those exact words on the board.

"Anything else, Peyton?"

The popular girl didn't hesitate. "You take your time and do it right. Ruth attempted to kill her husband half a dozen times before she actually succeeded. Clearly, she should have chosen one method and seen it through instead of rushing the job."

Ms. Pierce began scribbling again. *Don't rush* was soon followed by, *stick with the plan.*

I glanced around the classroom. Nobody seemed remotely surprised that we were being given killer advice—quite literally. Thinking about murder was making my stomach twist, maybe because without my Slate my Potential Hostile could be anywhere. How much space separated us now? Thirty feet? Twenty? Ten?

It could be the girl chewing on the ends of her dirty blond hair when she thought nobody was looking. It could be *anyone*. So the last thing I wanted was for my classmates to become more skilled at masking their own murderous intentions.

"Does anyone want to tell us how this case turned out?" Ms. Pierce asked, letting an expectant pause grow until she filled in the silence herself. "Ruth Snyder and her lover, Judd Gray, were electrocuted minutes apart from each other. Her ten-year-old daughter Lorraine was left an orphan without so much as an insurance check to keep her company."

Ms. Pierce turned back to the whiteboard and at the bottom of the list she wrote, *There is always fallout.* Then she circled it. The teasing note in her voice disappeared. "Even the best laid plans often involve sacrifice. When confronted by a problem, consider what you have to lose. Your pride? Your finances? Your independence? Your family? Your physical or emotional well-being? Sometimes the reward comes at too heavy a cost."

It was a good speech, but an unsettling one. I glanced over at Sebastian, wanting to gauge his reaction, but his aristocratic face revealed nothing. His stormy blue eyes remained focused on Ms. Pierce, as if he were intent on discovering any weakness within her.

It was the same expression he'd successfully unnerved me with more than once.

"Your assignment is to write an essay about a crime that you've witnessed." Ms. Pierce raised one inky black eyebrow to silence the unanimous groan. "You've all seen something. This can mean an item stolen from your dorm room or an illegal financial transaction that was splashed across the front-page news. Describe the event and then," she smiled as she let the pause build suspense, "suggest refinements."

I stared at her in disbelief. My classmates didn't need any practice getting away with crime. They could already afford to pay off anyone who got in their way. Peyton's essay would probably read like something out of a femme fatale handbook. *I'd flirt with the security guards, distracting them with my, ahem, assets, while my team carried the painting out the side door.*

Scratch that. Peyton probably wouldn't consider a measly painting worth the trouble of plotting a heist. She'd want something wearable. Designer dresses, maybe. Better yet, diamonds. That way she could prove to her daddy that she didn't need his support to get her hands on the family merchandise.

"Class dismissed! Emmy, could you please stay after?"

I braced myself for yet another lecture as everyone else filtered out of the room. Kayla shot me a supportive smile that I was coming to realize was her default expression.

This class isn't to be taken lightly. You've a lot of work ahead. I doubt you belong here.

I could've saved Ms. Pierce some time by delivering her speech for her.

"How are you holding up?"

Well, that was unexpected.

"Fine," I said automatically. It was the only answer I could give in a place like this. Anything else would be seen as a sign of weakness.

"I know this school can be a bit overwhelming." Ms. Pierce tucked a strand of jet black hair behind one slender ear. "I remember my first week here like it was yesterday. I couldn't bring myself to unpack my suitcase for four days because I was convinced they'd realize their mistake and fire me. I was a mess."

Apparently, I wasn't the only one who hadn't instantly fallen in love with Emptor Academy. Although it was hard to believe that someone who was so at ease in front of the classroom had ever felt insecure about her position. My shoulders relaxed a fraction, and I was no longer in such a rush for her to let me leave.

"What happened on the fifth day?"

Ms. Pierce pulled on the navy coat I hadn't noticed hanging on the back of her chair. "The dean invited me to lunch. He said that I was in charge of molding the most influential minds of the next generation. That my lessons would create a legacy that would outlive the both of us, as long as I stopped trembling in front of my students." She laughed self-consciously. "I thought he was full of it. But the next day I looked at the kids—*really* looked at them—and I realized he was right."

"Why are you telling me this?" I crossed my arms and braced myself for an insult. "It's pretty obvious I don't fit in here. You'll have to advance your legacy with someone else. Try Peyton. She has the trust fund for it."

Her mouth quirked into an elfish smile. "This place isn't special because the kids are rich. Don't get me wrong; money opens plenty of doors. But the truly successful students don't rely on their bank accounts to get ahead. They find something they can do better than everyone else and they act on it. Does that make sense, Emmy?"

I nodded, even though I didn't follow her logic. I hadn't so much as spoken once during her class. Unless sitting mutely in class counted as a talent, I didn't see why she would consider *me* special.

"I'm sure you'll find your bearings. Give it time, okay? This place is full of opportunities. In the meantime, I'm always here if you need to talk. My office hours are posted on the door."

Do you know anyone who might want to kill me? Apparently somebody wants me dead, and I'm not sure if Peyton is involved. Wait a sec, can paranoia be considered a special skill? Because I'm getting good at bracing myself for the worst.

It was probably best to keep all of that to myself.

"Um, thanks. I should go. Don't want to be late for my next class."

I'd nearly slipped out the door when Ms. Pierce said, "This is your last class, Emmy. Tuesday is an early release day."

I nodded like a bobblehead. "Right. I guess that means I'll go, um, release myself."

The musical sound of Ms. Pierce's low chuckle trailed me out into the hall.

Oh yeah, I was special alright.

A special kind of idiot.

CHAPTER 21

I swore at my locker after another failed attempt to open it.

The damn thing wouldn't budge, despite the fact that I'd tried the combination roughly fifteen billion times. I had even tested numbers that *rhymed* with the code I had been given, in case I'd somehow misremembered it.

My locker remained shut.

"What have we here?" It was funny how quickly a voice could be identified and detested. I glanced up to see Peyton and her sidekicks smirking at me from the locker room door. "Did someone forget their combination?"

The girl with an asymmetrical bob that looked like her hairdresser had been startled mid-snip snickered at me. "Sucks to be you."

My back stiffened. "You mean because I'm stuck here? Yeah, it does suck. Good thing this is only a temporary glitch."

Peyton scowled. The expression should have scrunched her face, like a peeved orangutan throwing a hissy fit over a banana. Instead, she looked regal in her haughtiness.

"Sebastian's grandfather warned me about you."

I hadn't seen *that* coming. Still, I pretended like this wasn't groundbreaking news, like I chatted about dead guys all the time, which wasn't all that far from the truth anymore.

"Oh yeah? What did my pal Freddie have to say?" I hoped like hell that the nickname sounded flip and sarcastic. If Peyton knew just how badly I wanted her to fill me in, she'd probably turn on the pointy tips of her designer heels and saunter away.

"He said that I shouldn't let you out of my sight."

I waited for her to continue, but she appeared satisfied leaving me with that cryptic comment. I was starting to wonder if it was against the student code of conduct to give a straightforward answer.

"That's it? He just said, 'Hey Peyton, give the New Girl my worst, will ya?'"

"He didn't trust you and neither do I." Her glare transformed into a smile that was so sugary it could put a diabetic into a coma. "He didn't have to spell out every little detail for me. We understood each other perfectly. So watch yourself, Noodle. Because. I. Am. Better. Than. You." Peyton signaled the other girls to follow her out before letting the door swing shut behind her.

I wasn't so sure about the "better than me" part, but I didn't doubt that she was fully capable of messing with my locker combination. My pulse quickened as I realized Peyton could've done a whole lot more than alter my locker code: She could have stolen my bag.

And taken my Slates with her in the process.

I didn't have the faintest idea how to go about reclaiming my personal property from her either.

Hey President Gilcrest. I'd like to report a theft. Peyton McSomething-or-other hijacked my Slate. Well, technically, it belonged to our dead mutual friend. At this point, I think that's mostly a technicality. So can you make her give it back? Oh, and who comes to mind when you hear, "Potential Hostile"? Anyone? Think it over, okay? Thanks.

Yeah, that wouldn't raise too many red flags.

I sucked in a deep breath and focused on my best course of action. The stupid combination wasn't magically going to open if I kept yelling at it. Not unless, "you inanimate bastard!" was a preprogrammed option. There was nothing to be gained by standing in front of it like an idiot. I had to track down someone with the authorization to remove the lock before I could analyze whatever damage Peyton had done during my one-on-one chat with Ms. Helsenberg. The dance instructor's tirade may have felt like it lasted an eternity, but it couldn't have been much longer than ten minutes. Fifteen at the most.

How much damage could one spoiled debutante manage in that short a timespan?

More than I wanted to consider.

Leaving the gym behind, I went in search of Kayla. If anyone knew the inner working of the girls' locker room, it was my new roommate. There also wasn't anyone else I could ask for help. Colin had smiled at me twice. That was it. And he probably would have grinned at the devil himself if the two of them were forced to waltz under the watchful eyes of Ms. Helsenberg. I hadn't exactly won over the student body. Nobody would be rushing to help the New Girl who had alienated the elite school's most influential students in less than a day.

I ached to hear Audrey and Ben tell me it would be okay. That I was letting my imagination get the best of me again. That my Slate was still safely tucked away inside my locker, making this nothing more than a minor setback. No big deal.

Except one good hard stomp was all it would take for Peyton to destroy my Slate and officially demolish any trail that could lead to my dad. And yeah, I was fully aware how pathetic that sounded. A dead man's password-protected tablet was my best shot at finding the guy who'd done nothing but fail as a parent. A man who had disappeared on my mom without bothering to scribble his goodbye on a napkin.

But I still couldn't walk away, not without wondering every day if everything would've been better if I'd only been willing to fight a little bit harder.

Trudging outside I focused on putting one foot in front of the other. The ache in my legs had only increased after being motionless for the entire duration of Ms. Pierce's class. A long soak in a bathtub began to sound like my definition of heaven. I was daydreaming about scented bubbles all the way to the girls' dormitory before I realized that no bag also meant no swipe card.

Leaving me stuck haunting the steps outside the door like a creepy lurker.

"Waiting for someone, Emmy?"

I twisted around to see Sebastian and Nasir lounging on a nearby bench, neither of them showing any hint of the fatigue weighing on me. They would both probably love the opportunity to turn up their noses at doing me a favor.

Still, desperate times called for really, *really* desperate measures.

That had to be written on a bumper sticker somewhere.

"Have either of you seen Kayla?"

Nasir shook his head. "No."

A smirk slowly spread across Sebastian's face. "Are you locked out already? That's got to be a record."

"That's me. Total record-setter." I straightened my spine, bracing myself for another confrontation. This part was going to be hard to admit. "Can I borrow a Slate?"

Nasir instinctively reached into his pocket to hand me his tablet and I steeled myself against the temptation of checking his outgoing call log. I wanted to know if he'd taken my advice about Audrey. If he'd called her. How long their conversation might have lasted. Except that would be a complete violation of his privacy, and I refused to give up the moral high ground in order to satisfy my curiosity, especially when I could always interrogate Audrey later.

Unfortunately, Sebastian chose *that* particular moment to interfere.

"Where's the Slate I gave you?" Sebastian asked. "You can't have sold it for extra cash. Nobody here needs one."

"It's—" I cut myself off quickly. Snapping at Sebastian wouldn't help defuse the awkward situation. I still knew what I wanted to say. *Great question, Sebastard. Go ask your psycho part-time girlfriend Peyton. She could tell you.*

The last thing I needed was Sebastian sticking his nose into my fight with Paydirt. I inwardly smiled at that one. The girl might have hit the genetics jackpot, but her diamonds also had the sheen of dirty money to them. She seemed like the type of girl who wouldn't object to exploiting others if it protected her own bottom line.

The nickname suited the girl to perfection.

"It's what?" Nasir asked me, breaking my quick trip to fantasy land. The great nation of Khazibekustanzia would have to wait for me to get my real life sorted out before I could give my fiction the time it deserved. "Did you break it or something?"

"It's complicated." Neither boy looked impressed with my evasiveness. "I only need to borrow it for a second. I'll give it right back."

"Here, use Sebastian's." Nasir grinned as he held out the glorified smartphone to me. I took it before either of them could reconsider, my own mouth twitching with amusement as Sebastian's hands flew automatically to his coat pockets.

"Damn, Nasir. That was good. I didn't feel a thing." There was a note of wry respect in his voice that I'd never heard before. Probably because as far as Sebastian was concerned I was nothing more than a temporary annoyance to be tolerated.

"Of course you didn't feel it." Nasir looked offended by the very suggestion that he might have screwed up a simple snatch.

"Do it again and your dancing shoes will mysteriously vanish right before class."

Having been on the receiving end of Ms. Helsenberg's undivided attention it wasn't a threat I'd take lightly, but Nasir's answering smirk didn't reveal any unease. "I wouldn't bet on it. I bought a new lock last week."

I had no idea what to make of a friendship based on privacy violations, but apparently it worked for Sebastian and Nasir. If either Ben or Audrey threatened to screw with my stuff, I would be *pissed*. If they replaced one of their locks to keep me out, I'd be offended that they felt the need to erect any extra barriers. These boys didn't seem to play by the same basic rules. If anything, the icy depths of Sebastian's eyes lit with excitement.

"What brand?"

"See for yourself."

Sebastian grinned in a very cat-that-ate-the-canary kind of way. "Fifteen minutes. Twenty on the outside. I'll even let you time me."

"Generous of you." Nasir sighed as if accepting the inevitable. "Looks like I'll be buying a new lock next week. Are you planning on using the Slate or did you just want to hold it, Emmy?"

A new plan began to form, stilling my fingers on the smooth surface of the Slate. "You're good at cracking locks?"

Sebastian shot me one of his patented *you've got to kidding me* looks and my cheeks flushed in embarrassment. Right. Of course he was good at cracking locks. He'd been using that very skill to help himself to some very expensive liquor at the party where we'd met. For a moment, all I could see was that twisted half-smile he'd given me when he'd held up the scotch—thirty-year-old Glenlivet scotch, to be specific—and offered me a tumbler.

"Right." I wanted to glance at Nasir, at the cobblestones, at *anything* other than Sebastian, but I held my gaze steady. "Great. You need to come with me. Right now."

Sebastian eyed me warily. "You plan on holding my Slate hostage if I refuse?"

I shrugged. "It gives you an incentive to help me, right?"

He turned on Nasir. "*This* is why you don't hand my stuff to crazy girls. It gives them dangerous ideas."

I tried to picture that capitalized on my tombstone. *Here lies Emmy Danvers: The Girl with Dangerous Ideas.*

Oddly enough, I liked it.

Still, I waggled the Slate temptingly in front of Sebastian. "You know you want it."

My mouth clamped shut the second it hit me how ridiculously suggestive those words sounded when spoken out loud. They couldn't have been more misleading, because I wasn't interested in flirting with Sebastian St. James.

I just wanted him to be motivated to break a few school rules for me.

That was my story and I was sticking to it.

He raised an eyebrow and examined me so intently that my cheeks turned a darker shade of red. "What do you need me to crack?"

I grimaced and said the words in a rush so I couldn't chicken out halfway through. "*Mylockerinthegirls'changingroom.*"

Nasir burst out laughing. "Oh yeah, I really screwed you over, buddy. We should all have your problems. I'll let you two work out the details."

And before I could correct whatever screwed-up idea Nasir had in his head, which was undoubtedly as far from reality as my wildest romance novel plots, he cut across the lawn toward the boys' dorm, whistling the whole way. Leaving me alone to deal with an inscrutable Sebastian. His light blue eyes gave absolutely nothing away, even as he began sauntering toward the gym.

"Hurry up, Emmy. Let's go where I've never gone before." Sebastian's smile took on a wicked bent. "Allegedly."

I had a feeling "allegedly" was his middle name.

Not that he'd ever confirm or deny it.

My sore muscles protesting each step, I hurried to catch up with Sebastian.

CHAPTER 22

"My locker is the last one on the left."

Sebastian didn't appear to be in any rush to get there. He turned a complete circle to take in the girls' locker room in all its dubious glory. Actually, it was pretty nice. McKinley High School had gone with a Pepto-Bismol pink color scheme, set off with inspirational cat posters about *never giving up* and *just holding on*. Those posters had always creeped me out. What exactly was the cat supposed to be waiting for to happen? It wasn't like there was a super sexy fireman climbing up the tree, ready to reach the troubled feline. And just how high up was any of this in the first place? Maybe the cat's fear of falling was the only thing preventing the fluff ball from scampering home.

The light blue paint in the girls' locker room at Emptor Academy didn't belong in a special Easter coloring box. It had a glossy sheen that made the space look both sophisticated and sanitary, which was really all you could ask of a changing room.

Sebastian ignored the interior design choices, focusing instead on my locker.

"Do you want me to stand guard outside?" I asked nervously.

"No need." He fiddled with the knob, listening to it, adjusting the dial, and then he yanked. My locker door swung open.

"How did you do *that*?" I demanded, impressed in spite of myself.

"Child's play. You should really upgrade this piece of crap lock."

I crossed my arms tightly across my chest. "Didn't you just tell Nasir that no lock could keep you out?"

He grinned. "I'm not the one you need to worry about breaking in. I'm the good guy here."

I nearly rolled my eyes. Even in the girls' locker room he looked entirely in his element. Completely confident. And full of bullshit.

It was exasperating.

"Okay, well, thanks for the help." I handed back the Slate that I'd been clutching in my hands, but he didn't seem to realize that was his big cue to leave. Instead, he remained right in front of my locker, making it impossible for me to open it without brushing against his athletic frame.

Not that it mattered. I was there to grab my bag and get the hell out.

My fingers connected with soggy cloth and I flinched. Someone had poured, I sniffed at my fingers for confirmation, yep, Sprite all over it.

Lovely.

"I see you're settling right in. Making new friends."

"I've got it under control, thanks." I grabbed onto one sticky bag strap before shutting the locker with a whole lot more force than I'd intended. "Let's get out of here."

"But we haven't gotten to second base yet. Don't kill the fantasy. Boy in a girls' changing room, things get heated. I press you back against the locker and we see where it goes from there."

Oh god. *Sebastard* was better than me at creating romance novel scenarios. Except he probably pictured it as the opening sequence for a porn movie. One that he'd probably enacted plenty of times with *real* Emptor Academy girls, like Peyton.

I wondered if he'd ever used that exact line or if he hadn't needed to bother with words. Maybe Sebastian could look at a girl, really *look* at her, and have her willing to go along with whatever scheme he had in mind. He had all the polished charm of a seasoned con man.

Good thing I wasn't interested in anyone other than Ben.

"Yeah, I'm going to pass." Even holding the bag away from my body to avoid the ick factor, I knew *exactly* what the abrupt tremor meant and I froze. My Slate was vibrating.

I twisted, suddenly terrified that someone was inside the locker room with us, lurking in the shower stalls, biding their time in the shadows as they waited for me to come within reach.

My hand dove into the bag, connecting with every item that *wasn't* my Slate. Wallet. Keys. School ID card.

"Emmy?"

I didn't care if I looked half-crazed as I shoved my wallet into Sebastian's hand, hissed, "No talking!" and continued searching through my bag. The world shrank to my one need: I had to know if the Potential Hostile was skulking closer to the locker room.

Sebastian didn't need to be told twice. His mouth snapped shut, but he gripped my arm and hauled me toward the light switch. He quickly flicked it off, plunging the room into darkness, before leading me into the blackest recess of the room. He moved noiselessly, making the vibrations of my phone seem deafeningly loud. I might as well have broadcasted an announcement over the PA system.

Emmy Danvers is hiding in the girls' locker room. Feel free to kill her at your earliest convenience.

My hand finally connected with the Slate and I clutched it desperately, hoping that would muffle the vibrations. To stop it from giving us away, because someone was coming.

I could feel it.

The little hairs on the back of my neck pricked up and I *knew* it was only a matter of time. Any minute now. Any second.

I tugged out the Slate, even as a small part of my brain pointed out that the exact yardage between me and the killer wouldn't matter to their bullet. Not if they shot at close range.

There was a message waiting for me on the screen.

Are you having fun yet?

No, I wasn't having fun. In fact, this was agony. Gut-clenching, teeth-chattering torture. Cruel and unusual punishment for a crime I didn't commit.

And I didn't know how to make any of it stop.

The words kept flashing at me, obscene in their gaiety. *Are you having fun yet?* As if this was a trip to Disneyland. As if the killer wanted to share a joke with me, but didn't care that *I* was the punchline.

As if he hadn't stopped laughing since our paths had crossed in the coffee shop.

"Breathe," Sebastian's voice was so soft in my ear I felt the words more than I heard them. "You're going to hyperventilate if you don't slow it down."

The same self-assuredness of his that had annoyed me earlier no longer seemed nearly as obnoxious. Maybe because while I was struggling to remain fully conscious, he had no trouble slipping into the role of a Lamaze coach. My vision started tunneling and I felt like a freaking idiot. I ought to have mastered breathing at some point in the last, oh, *sixteen years*.

Instead I was so far out of my league that not even Jules Verne could find me.

"Slow and steady," Sebastian wrapped an arm around my stomach, pulling me deeper into the shadows. "I'm right here."

I was splintering apart. Falling to pieces. Coming unraveled just like the scarf I'd attempted to knit for my mom, but which was now a moth-eaten tangle in some dark corner of my closet.

I'm getting bored.

My fingers shook as I reached out and touched the message flashing on the screen, fully aware that I was losing it. Or maybe

I'd lost it days earlier. I didn't have to imagine how Frederick St. James had felt standing in that Starbucks with me anymore. His paranoia, his fear—I could even hear his last death rattle in my own panicked wheezing.

My stomach knotted so tightly I doubled over.

Someone was stalking me, toying with me, mocking me with these snide little texts. My fear was his entertainment.

Rage swamped my vision and suddenly my trembling fingers had no trouble spelling out a message of their own.

Get a new hobby.

I pressed "send" before I could chicken out, watching the words disappear into cyberspace with a twisted rush of satisfaction. There was nothing for me to lose.

Nothing that wasn't already in jeopardy.

No amount of texting would ever make a hardened killer change his mind, so I didn't bother pleading for pity. Maybe the killer would alter his murderous timetable, attack me sooner rather than later, but I was willing to risk it. If I was trading in a few minutes of my life for the angry rush of satisfaction in texting back my tormentor, well, it was totally worth it.

Still, I shrank away from the crack of light filtering in through the bottom of the door, pressing my body more firmly against Sebastian's in the process. I had no intention of making myself an easy target. If Sebastian was caught in the crossfire with me, he couldn't say I didn't try to warn him. Mostly because the killer would probably finish him off next.

His arm tightened around my waist as we caught the sound of footsteps and the unmistakable jangling of keys moving nearer.

The Slate vibrated harder.

We need to talk.

Sebastian's hand covered my nose and mouth, stifling the hysterical laugh that tried to escape. My head rang with the muffled sound, beat with it, as if the unspoken amusement was being jackhammered into my temple. The footsteps grew louder, or at least I thought they did. I wasn't entirely certain. The blood pounding in my ears made it nearly impossible for me to distinguish fact from fiction. Echo from enemy.

Red splotches swirled across my vision, but I couldn't let my stalker get the last word while I trembled in fear. If this was the end, I wanted to fake one last act of bravado. I wanted to annoy him as much as humanly possible.

Hey, I just met you. And you seem crazy. Delete this number. Don't call me, maybe?

Step. Jangle, jangle. Step.
Pause.

My heart stuttered to a stop. All those clichés about being frozen in fear, paralyzed with doubt, numb with terror, they suddenly made way too much sense. More red splotches appeared out of nowhere, coating the darkness, as my world shrank to include only the rattle of keys and the creak of a door handle being turned.

Sebastian whirled me around so that our faces were inches away.

Then he started kissing me.
Hard.

The icy chill of a metal locker pressed flat against my lower back seared through me, and I wanted to writhe away from it. My body felt like a ceramic mug taken directly from the dishwasher and filled with ice cubes until it was a hair's breadth away from either cracking the container or melting the contents.

Sebastian's kiss felt like both.

His hands tunneled into my hair, gripping me in place, as he took total control of my lips.

I'd spent years imagining my first kiss, mapping out the most plausible scenarios. Most involved watching a movie with Ben, glancing up to see his eyes riveted on me instead of the screen. He would push aside a lock of my unruly hair, tucking it out of the way, before *finally* making his move. It would start slow and tentative, before blistering passion would wash all the hesitancy away. I'd imagined it happening a thousand different ways in a million locations, but there were a few things that stayed constant. My first kiss would be with someone who cared about me— whether or not that someone was Ben—and it would be magical.

This hurt.

It felt too good. I hated the way my fingers clutched his coat, even as my body refused to push him away. Hated that I didn't want it to end. My first kiss was a lie. It was supposed to be with someone who *loved* me, not someone who could barely tolerate me. I had spent the past sixteen years as a devout believer in perfect moments and happily ever afters, despite all evidence to the contrary, with an intensity that could only be called faith, and this was ripping all those daydreams to shreds. They hadn't come true.

Not for my mother. Not for me.

Step. Pause. Jingle. Pause.

Sebastian's mouth captured what would have otherwise been a gasp of fear, as a set of lights flicked on. I clenched my eyes shut against the sudden brightness, bracing myself for the inevitable.

There would be pain. Endless jagged waves of torment and—

"Oh, *come on.* Get a room, will you?"

Those weren't the words I'd been expecting.

Dancing hot pink and electric blue dots temporarily obscured my vision, but they faded to reveal the same sullen-faced girl who had assigned me a locker earlier that day. Her disposition hadn't improved any in the past few hours. If anything, her scowl had only curled deeper with disgust.

Her obvious disapproval would've seemed a lot more menacing if I hadn't been braced for a killer to riddle my body with bullet holes. Sometimes I wished that my imagination was a little less active. The killer didn't need to bother taunting me with his stupid text messages: I already excelled at torturing myself.

"Emmy finds me irresistible," Sebastian offered a boyish grin that had probably gotten him out of far more serious scrapes.

The glare she leveled at me was so intense I wanted to tell her to form a club with Peyton, or better yet, file a petition.

We the students of Emptor Academy, in order to form a more perfect union, do hereby propose that Emmy Danvers never grace our hallowed halls ever again.

Either that or they could call up their doting parents to see whether a sizable donation to the school could successfully ban me from the premises. President Gilcrest didn't strike me as being immune to bribery, especially if it meant discarding the scholarship kid who didn't belong here.

She ignored Sebastian's attempt at charm. "Take it somewhere else, Romeo. The girls' locker room is off limits."

Sebastian nodded as if he'd been properly chastised. "C'mon, Emmy. I'm sure we can find a different way to give you a thrill. Add some handcuffs instead."

I jabbed him in the stomach, but that didn't shut him up.

"Ouch, babe. Clearly, we need to establish safe words. Mine is *fedora*." He slung an arm across my shoulders and I fought the urge to shove him away. My skin prickled then burned with embarrassment.

The rumor mill wouldn't be content reporting a few illicit kisses, especially not with Sebastian going out of his way to pour gasoline on the flames.

My phone vibrated again with a new message.

So will you kill him or not?

If the killer was referring to Sebastian, well, he definitely made me feel homicidal enough to consider it.

CHAPTER 23

"Stop scowling, Emmy."

I glared up at Sebastian who looked entirely too self-assured as he strolled down the gym hallway in the wake of everything that had happened in the locker room. "Or what? You'll kiss me again? That's quite a threat, Sebastian. I might die of boredom."

His smile seemed forced at the edges, like he was trying to compose a thank-you note for an itchy wool sweater that he'd never wear in public or in private. "What was the very first lesson I taught you, Emmy?"

"Never wear white to a police precinct after Labor Day?" I quipped.

"Don't piss off the person throwing you a lifeline."

Oh. Right. *That* advice.

"Yeah, that doesn't work for me. My mom taught me to stay away from jerks."

Sebastian dropped his voice to a low growl. "Shut up and smile, Emmy, or you can face your text buddy all on your own. How does that sound?"

My head jerked up and I studied Sebastian's eyes, searching for any sign, no matter how slight, that he might be secretly amused. That he might be responsible for some of it. All I saw was a simmering anger that looked to be gaining in intensity.

The Slate vibrated again, but this time I didn't spare it a glance. I was a too busy making another deal with the devil.

"Do you know what's going on?" The residual fear in my system made my voice sound thready and weak even to my own ears.

"I have my suspicions."

That was more than I had. I quickly pasted a grin on my face.

"Oh Christ, you look constipated." Sebastian paused right by the doors leading out of the sports complex and onto the lawn. "Pretend I'm somebody else, okay? I don't give a shit who you imagine, but you're dying to get your hands all over him." The gruffness was back and I tried not to shiver at the huskiness in his tone.

Ben. I had to pretend he was Ben.

"Got it?"

I nodded, but didn't say a word.

"Good. Hold that thought and follow my lead." Sebastian pushed open the door before his fingers took possession of my hand. The move felt oddly out of character. If Sebastian had tried to cop a feel, well, that would've made a certain amount of sense. From everything I'd heard, the guy was a player.

But this was almost sweet.

I instantly wanted to banish the word from my vocabulary. There wasn't anything sweet about Sebastian. He was fake and manipulative, and I kept my eyes glued on the cobblestone pathways as I missed Ben with an intensity that scared me. I tried to pretend it was Ben's hand clasping mine. The two of us had our fingers interlocked. His eyes glowing with affection as he gave my hand a proprietary squeeze that went far beyond friendship. It was Ben whose breath teased my ear as he whispered, "Perfect. Almost there."

The daydream was so comforting that I eagerly embraced it. Ben murmured that he loved me, that he had *always* loved me, but that he had kept silent for years because he wasn't sure I felt the same way. *You've always been special to me, Em. Never doubt it.*

I melted inside.

Why don't we make up for lost time, Ben?

Yeah, that's what I would say.

And then I would kiss *him*.

I grinned, imagining the way heat would simmer in Ben's eyes. The death ray glares aimed at me from Peyton and her posse didn't exist. Nothing they said could hurt me. Ben loved me. Madly. Completely. Transcendently.

Sebastian pulled out his swipe card and tugged me inside the boys' dormitory without pausing to ask for my permission. Maybe I should have fought to claim a home court advantage, but the entire school belonged to Sebastian. Insisting we return to the sparkly prison I shared with Kayla would only prolong our time together. And, okay, I wanted to see for myself how somebody as obscenely wealthy as Sebastian St. James would decorate a dorm room. I doubted there would be any neon pink.

That alone would be a vast improvement.

I wasn't left speculating for long. One short, thankfully silent, elevator ride to the top floor and I was being hustled down the hallway to the last door on the left. Sebastian blocked my view so I couldn't watch him unlock the door before he shoved it open wide enough for me to enter behind him. The whole place looked like something out of a 1940s film noir with the caramel latte–colored walls and heavy oak paneling that looked dignified. Restrained.

Pretentious.

I half-expected to see a fedora perched on the head of the Maltese Falcon.

Sebastian didn't waste any time with social niceties. Instead, he flopped into a wide leather chair and raised an eyebrow.

"Why don't you shut the door and stay awhile."

It wasn't a question or a request, but a command that rankled at me even as I slid the deadbolt into place. Now that I was alone with Sebastian, *really* alone with him, it was hard to act casual.

Still, I gave it my best shot.

"So this is the lair, huh?" I skeptically eyed the enormous seascape painting that dominated one of the walls. "It was cooler in my head. There should be gargoyles, at the very least. Maybe a butler who takes your coat and says 'as master wishes' a lot."

"Sorry to disappoint."

I edged closer toward the other vacant chair, because the alternative was perching on the end of an enormous bed that never would have fit inside the room I shared with Kayla. Not that Sebastian had to worry about making room for unexpected visitors. I doubted the idea had ever crossed his mind. He'd simply toss his money around until it was someone else's problem.

Which was probably for the best. He didn't exactly play well with others.

I fidgeted uncomfortably before I forced myself to sit in the stuffed leather chair. "So about that kiss—"

"Is *that* really what you want to clear up first?" Sebastian interrupted, something grim lurking beneath his even tone. I crossed my arms to ward off the sudden chill, determined to get the awkwardness out in the open so we could both move on.

"Yeah, I do. It was kind of a big deal, don't you think?"

He raised one brow. "Not particularly."

Ouch.

I'm not sure what I was expecting. *Yes, Emmy. Holding you in my arms was the closest I'll ever come to heaven. I want you. I crave you. Kiss me again, darling.*

Not in this lifetime.

Which was fine with me, better than fine, it was fan-freaking-tastic. It saved me the trouble of explaining that I was interested in someone else. Sebastian's disinterest came as a *relief.* Neither of us were in danger of imagining that the kiss was anything more than an accidental distraction. An aberration. One stupid kiss couldn't ruin anything if the entire dynamic was built on mutual distrust and disdain. No friendship would ever be at risk with Sebastian.

Except the ease with which he dismissed the kiss stung my pride. "If it was so forgettable then why did you do it?"

"You've got to be kidding me," Sebastian said in disbelief. "You were seconds away from hyperventilating yourself into a blackout."

God, I sounded pathetic. Hyperventilating happened to wimpy, overemotional girls. I was supposed to be strong enough to take all of this in stride. I was supposed to flash a quick grin and toss out a sarcastic comeback and keep everything else locked away. It was how I'd gotten through all of my mom's disastrous relationships. Laugh through the pain and fear and hurt.

I couldn't find a wisecrack anywhere inside of me, so I settled for denial.

"I wasn't going to faint."

His low chuckle had me gritting my teeth.

"I *wasn't*," I insisted.

"Sure. You were just practicing your impression of the Leaning Tower of Pisa. That makes total sense."

"About as much sense as your plan to stick your tongue down my throat." I crossed my arms, aiming for indifference. As if his kiss hadn't affected me in the slightest.

Sebastian shrugged. "It got your breathing to even out."

He had a point, but I refused to admit that his kiss had helped defuse the situation in any way. Sebastian was obnoxious enough without that ammunition being added to his stockpile.

"Then we both agree it meant nothing."

"No argument here."

"And it won't happen again," I continued firmly.

"In the future, if I see you hyperventilating, I will sit back and enjoy the show."

Instead of pointing out, at length, the total jackassery in *that* comment, I snapped my mouth shut.

Time to change the topic of conversation.

"So you said that you might have a theory about what's going on." I rubbed at a splotch on the inside right cuff of my sweatshirt to avoid looking overeager.

He nodded. "Of course. And I'll share it right after you explain what you're doing with my grandpa's Slate."

You can't trust anyone.

Not for the first time I wished Frederick St. James had been a wee bit more specific about his Don't Trust List. How hard would it have been to say, "Except Sebastian. Oh, and Gilcrest isn't a bad sort either," before kicking the bucket?

Too hard, apparently.

If Peyton was to be believed, Frederick St. James hadn't trusted me either.

Except Peyton was the *last* person I could trust to tell me the truth.

"I didn't steal it from him, if that's what you're getting at."

Sebastian raised an eyebrow at my obvious defensiveness. I squirmed uncomfortably in the chair, my body tightening until even Ms. Helsenberg would've agreed to banish her Noodle nickname. There was something about Sebastian that brought out my worst impulses. One of his cold assessing appraisals and I was scrambling for an insult sharp enough to draw blood. I no longer simply disliked Sebastian; I hated who I became around him. I didn't trust him to look past his own self-interest. And there was a little voice in my head that insisted I was going to regret sharing *anything* with this boy. That he would toss me aside at the first opportunity. Except he was still my best lead for tracking down the mysterious Morgan. And my father. Preferably both.

I could play his game as long as the Slate stayed in my sticky backpack.

I inhaled deeply, hoping that would help me regain control. "Your grandpa gave the Slate to me right before he died."

"Before he was declared dead," Sebastian corrected. I didn't see much of a difference between the two but I didn't want another *is he dead or not* debate with Sebastian.

"Right. Exactly."

"Was this before or after he called you 'Gracie'?" Sebastian demanded.

It felt like a lifetime had passed since that day in the coffee shop. The edges of the memory already becoming worn and faded, like a page in a library book that had been handled too roughly for too many years. I tried to visualize the chain of events with Frederick St. James, saying them aloud in case Sebastian caught something I'd missed.

"First he said that someone was after him. Then he said they were after me. I think that's the right order, but I might be mixing it up. He told me to warn my dad. I nearly told him, 'y'know, sorry, but my dad isn't really in the picture—'"

"Why not?"

Sharing one meaningless kiss didn't obligate me to get all personal with the jerk, but I needed to keep the conversation on track. Sebastian didn't strike me as the kind of guy who would easily continue past an unanswered question.

"He ran out on my mom in the early days of her pregnancy. Never to be seen or heard from again."

Sebastian nodded. "What did my grandpa say next?"

"Just that Morgan would know what to do, which makes zero sense, by the way, since my dad's name was *Daniel*. Then he said some other stuff. Trust nobody. They're trying to kill me. *Again*. You know, normal small talk material."

The corners of his mouth tilted up, and for a second I thought I'd nearly made him laugh with that one. Then his aristocratic features smoothed into a stony mask that revealed nothing.

"What happened next?"

A wave of anxiety swelled inside of me that I tried to tamp down with a dismissive shrug.

"Oh, a handful of cryptic warnings, a quick case of mistaken identity, and then he was tackling me to the ground and dying on top of me."

"Allegedly."

I did my best not to roll my eyes. "Right. Allegedly. So what's your theory, Sherlock St. James? Is the butler in on it? I'm sure you have one hiding around here somewhere."

"I don't have a butler."

A genuine smile tugged at my lips at the ridiculousness of his indignation. "I thought all rich people were required to hire 'em. You should probably double-check that there isn't a butler clause attached to your trust fund. Maybe you've got one on payroll and don't even know it."

"I have no idea where you are getting this stuff, but I don't have a secret butler."

"Uh-huh," I muttered darkly. "That's what they all say."

"Please tell me you don't make a habit of questioning people about their employees." Instead of responding, I burrowed deeper into the sofa chair. My silence made Sebastian's eyes widen in disbelief. "You haven't *actually* been asking people if they have secret butlers, have you?"

"Nooo . . ."

Although now that he mentioned it, that did sound entertaining. My head slumped against the armrest as I half-heartedly covered a yawn with my hand and tried to remember why I had followed Sebastian inside. There had been a perfectly logical reason behind it, but for some reason my whole thought process evaded me now.

My brain felt like it was slowly converting to fuzz. My eyelids drooped to half-mast but struggling to stay awake was too much work. Something wasn't right. I just couldn't be sure anymore if that something was me.

"So what's your thing?" I asked, my hand flopping in a vague gesture.

"My thing?" Sebastian looked amused.

"Yeah. The thing you were going to tell me. It was very . . . thingie."

It was a true testament to my level of sleep-deprivation that the words sounded perfectly straightforward to me. "What's the thing with the thingie" said it all. There was no need for me to muddy everything up by tacking on any pesky adjectives. Or nouns. Or verbs, for that matter.

Sebastian grinned. "You want to know who I think is behind the text messages?"

I nodded sleepily.

"I am."

CHAPTER 24

"*What?!*" I nearly toppled out of the sofa chair. "You can't. That's not funny, Sebastian."

His smiled turned tight lipped. "I'm not kidding."

"You were with me. In the locker room. I'm pretty sure I would've noticed you texting, even if I was a little out of breath."

"Hyperventilating."

I threw my hands up in the air. "Whatever! You weren't texting me!"

"Not in the locker room. I have sent a few messages to my grandpa that you've probably intercepted, though."

That pulled me up short. "I won't stop until I find you," I murmured quietly. "That was *you?*"

He shrugged. "My grandpa will explain his plan eventually. It's just a matter of time before he contacts me."

It had been Sebastian. He was the reason I'd spent last night terrified, unable to tear my gaze away from the door long enough to get some sleep. I saw red.

"Guess what, Sebastian? *Dead men don't text!*" I snarled.

"Then we're both lucky that he isn't dead."

I wanted to hit him. To cause some kind of physical damage as payback for the hell that he and his precious grandfather were still putting me through. I glared at him hotly, unsurprised by the matching anger flashing in Sebastian's icy blue eyes. He didn't want to believe that his grandpa was dead, but some part of him— even if it was buried deep, deep down—had to know that I was telling the truth.

His grandpa was gone.

The fight drained out of me. From what I'd heard about Frederick St. James, I wasn't the only one living out a nightmare scenario. If it was my mom in the morgue, I'd have been uncontrollably sobbing in the fetal position into endless boxes of Kleenex. Sebastian didn't appear to have shed a tear, but he still must have felt *something*.

I fumbled to find the right words. "Your grandpa told me to take the Slate and find my dad, okay? As far as I know, that's the full extent of his plan." I crawled bonelessly back upright into the chair, toeing off my shoes, then tucking my feet underneath me. "How come I'm always the one who does the sharing?"

The set of his features seemed to soften slightly. "Practice."

"I don't like it."

"Too bad."

I nodded, closed my eyes, and tried to add Sebastian's text messages to the puzzle. All I could see was a welcoming abyss of blackness tugging at me. Beckoning me to slide into unconsciousness. "So it wasn't a threat?"

"It was a private message that you happened to read."

My arteries felt like they'd been clogged with a triple decker burger, large fries, and an enormous ice cream sundae as I mumbled, "The texts I got today, those were threats."

"Are you sure?"

Trying to reopen my eyes would've been a losing battle against gravity, so I left them closed. This wasn't the healthy kind of sleepiness that comes from a full day spent kicking butt and taking names, but a sludgy, desperate exhaustion that made it nearly impossible to function.

"No," I said honestly. "I'm not sure about any of this anymore."

"Alright, here's what I know: My grandpa wouldn't keep me in the dark without a damn good reason."

"What about the missing thirty-year-old scotch? Maybe he was mad that you helped yourself to his liquor."

"The scotch was a birthday gift." I could hear the wry smile in his voice. "This is different, which is why there's got to be some logical explanation for him to confide in *you*."

I yawned drowsily. "No offense taken. Mostly because I'm too tired to care."

He leaned forward until I could almost feel his harshly spoken words against my cheek. "There has to be something that you know, Emmy. Something that I don't."

"Romance novels are a billion-dollar-a-year industry."

I cracked open my eyes only long enough to get a glimpse of Sebastian's obvious frustration. "What does that have to do with anything?"

"It's one of the many things that I know and you don't. Want me to keep going? The Romance Writers of America was founded in 1980 and—"

"There must be something *important* that you're not telling me."

My mind sifted through a million possibilities, as my body grew increasingly warm, overheated, like an overwhelmed computer ready to crash. "Mhmmm, well, your guess is as good as mine."

"It has to be about your dad," Sebastian got up and began pacing, his tread muffled by a gorgeous Moroccan rug. "Except if there was a threat, I could've helped him neutralize it."

"How lovely for you."

Sebastian ignored me. "So why did he leave me out of it?"

He probably intended that as a rhetorical question, but my sleep-deprived brain decided to give it my best shot. "Maybe he thought you knew the bad guys? Maybe he didn't trust you? Maybe he was trying to protect you? Maybe he wanted you to focus on school, or lock picking, or knitting ugly Christmas sweaters instead."

"You can stop now."

"Okay." My agreement sounded distant, as if I'd spoken it minutes earlier but the echo had taken a little side trip and was only now getting back to me. "That's cool."

Then I pretty much conked out.

A romance novel would've made it sexy. The hero would have tucked me into bed, admiring the way my red hair fanned out luxuriously across his pillow. Then he would've spent the night standing guard over my sleeping figure. Sebastian's idea of chivalry extended only to spreading a blanket over me, probably because he didn't want me getting sick and sneezing my germs all over the place. I didn't know how he could be so cavalier about leaving a girl he barely knew in a room lined with priceless antiques, but when I jerked awake the room was deserted.

It was also pitch black.

I couldn't distinguish furniture from fantasy. It was all darkness with a side of shadows, oh yeah, and *more freaking darkness*. More than anything, I wanted to hear my mom calmly reassure me that the monsters were all in my head. That there were no pools of blood oozing out from my closet. No killers hiding in a corner waiting for the perfect moment to strike.

Except she wasn't there and I wasn't brave enough to search for a light switch. My mind half-fogged from sleep, I decided that remaining silently perched in the chair was the safest option. As long as my feet didn't touch the ground, nobody could wrap their hands around my ankle and drag me away like a limp rag doll.

A limp, terrified, *screaming-its-head-off* rag doll.

I rubbed my eyes with closed fists and fought down a rising surge of panic. I was overreacting. Everything was fine.

Gritting my teeth, I lunged for the door, running my hands across the wall, searching blindly for a light switch plate. I sagged in relief when I finally bathed the room in light.

That's when my idiocy sank in.

I was clutching the doorknob, poised to flee an empty room without my bag, after—quite literally—falling asleep on the job. Frederick St. James couldn't have picked a worse confidante if he'd tried.

I couldn't protect myself, let alone the precious Slate that his grandson had probably swiped from my bag. It wasn't like Sebastian had any moral scruples to hold himself back from engaging in some light theft. I strode across the soft Moroccan rug back to the leather chair I'd used as a makeshift bed.

A muffled vibrating came from the bag leaning haphazardly against it.

Sebastian hadn't taken it.

That realization came more as a surprise than a relief. The Slate had succeeded in freaking me out from the first moment Frederick St. James had slipped it into my coat pocket. Knowing that Sebastian was behind the *I won't stop until I find you* text didn't magically make everything better. I hadn't come any closer to unmasking the Potential Hostile or figuring out what they wanted with *me*. Something I would have forced Sebastian to discuss if I hadn't totally checked out in the chair instead. I had fallen asleep on the job. That had to set some kind of Emptor Academy record for incompetency.

There was also that last text I'd seen in the gym with Sebastian.

So will you kill him or not?

I gave myself a half-hearted pep talk as I reached inside my bag. "Okay, Emmy. It's a Slate, not a snake. It's not going to bite you."

I glanced down at the screen and instantly wished I hadn't.

Kill him or return my money.

Too bad the old man *also* hadn't given me any pointers on refunding homicidal maniacs before he died. I'd waited too long to reach my Slate and the message disappeared, leaving an empty password screen and a tight knot of fear in the pit of my stomach.

Sebastian's words from earlier that night slowly began to resurface.

"There must be something *important* that you're not telling me."

It had to be my father. No other part of my life contained anything even remotely mysterious. He was the only missing piece of the equation, and suddenly I wasn't sure I wanted the truth. I'd spent so many years clinging to the image of my dad as the handsome young man who had swept my mom off her feet with his omelets and his quick wit, and I didn't want to update that mental image. Some part of me had always known that if my father had been hero material he would have stuck around for the happily ever after instead of disappearing without leaving so much as an e-mail address behind. But replacing all those fantasies with cold hard facts? There was a good chance that by the time I reached rock bottom of this rabbit hole, my dad would resemble the villain a whole lot more than the hero.

I glared at the Slate in my hands, even as I braced myself for the inevitable.

There was only one way to find out if my dad's six-letter name matched the password.

"What have you got to lose, Emmy?" I demanded hoarsely. "Worst-case scenario, it's not the password and nothing changes. Best-case scenario," I froze, leaving the sentence unfinished. I honestly couldn't picture a satisfying best-case scenario anymore. It used to be so simple. A five-book publishing deal and a romantic dinner date with Ben that would include candlelight and slices of dark chocolate cake. Although the trappings had never been the important part. The heart of the daydream centered on Ben confessing the depths of his feelings for me because he simply couldn't contain them any longer.

Now my best-case scenario centered on not getting murdered on a toilet.

My whole body tensed as I slowly typed D-A-N-I-E-L and pressed Enter.

Invalid password.

So much for that idea. I forced myself to smile, even though there was nobody around to see it. I refused to be disappointed. This wasn't a setback, merely an opportunity to test another theory. Sure, and every time a bell rings an angel gets their wings. I reached into my bag and pulled out my beat up cell phone.

It was time to call in the cavalry.

CHAPTER 25

I'd no sooner plugged my phone into the wall than it began ringing.

There were only three possibilities: Ben, Audrey, or my mom. None of whom would be reassured if I admitted that my day had included getting kicked out of one class, yelled at during another, and having my belongings drenched in soda by a vindictive willowy brunette. Oh yeah, there was also my panic attack at lunch, my first make-out session in the girls' locker room, and a series of death threats. But you know, overlooking all of *that*, it was a totally normal first day.

Right.

I stiffened my spine and checked to see who was calling.

Ben.

He probably wanted to check up on me, make sure I wasn't withholding any more information from the police. That I hadn't landed into even deeper trouble. Although maybe he wanted to remind me that he didn't think I was special. Not that I could ever forget hearing him say those words. Sending him straight to voice mail would only postpone the inevitable. Ben would only keep calling. Keep texting. Keep poking and prodding at me.

"Hey, Ben." I could already feel my throat closing. Longing, desperation, heartbreak, the intensity made me want to curl into a tight ball, but the worst had to be the shred of hope. There's nothing quite like placing that last bit of optimism onto the conveyor belt of an emotional wood chipper. Soon there would be nothing but a mangled mess to show for it.

"Why the hell haven't you been answering your phone?"

I wondered how quickly the indignation in his voice would fade away if I told him the truth. *I can't always handle hearing you call me a friend when I want to be so much more.* Yeah, *that* would shut him up. Too bad it would also kill our friendship.

"Sorry, I fell asleep and forgot to charge my phone." I didn't mention how desperately I'd needed sleep since the Starbucks Incident. Not that Ben would have accepted that as an excuse, given my track record with the low battery exclamation point of doom signal.

"Your mom called me when you didn't answer her calls. She's been worried sick about you, Em. You can't drop off the face of the earth with no warning!"

"I. Fell. Asleep," I emphasized each word harshly. "Maybe you've heard of it? It's this trend that's really catching on. It's recommended by ten out of ten doctors."

"I thought we'd reached an agreement. You were supposed to check in each night until this *stuff* dies down."

Cameron had to be somewhere nearby. That was the only reason for Ben to be cleaning up his language. It wasn't like my delicate ears needed protecting, not when I'd grown up with a soundtrack of swearing in more languages than I cared to count.

"I'm fine."

"Great. Glad to hear it. Next time, answer your phone before midnight."

One quick glance down told me that Ben hadn't been exaggerating about the time. My digital clock read 12:14 A.M., and a pang of guilt shot straight through me.

"I should go call my mom now." It was a lame excuse, but I didn't have anything else to say to Ben. Nothing that he wanted to hear at any rate.

"She's probably asleep."

"Then I'll leave a message."

I could hear Ben release a short breath of frustration. "You can do that later. It's not like a few more minutes will change anything."

"Yeah, but—"

"Emmy, is there a reason you've been avoiding me?"

Well, crap. I hadn't expected that question from Ben, especially not over the phone. He preferred to hash things out in person so that he could get a full read on the situation. Apparently, he'd decided to bend that rule with me.

Which was too bad for him because I had no intention of spilling my guts.

"I've been a little preoccupied. You know, what with the dead guy and the new school and that other thing, what was it again? Oh right. Trying to avoid a *killer* who seems to want me dead."

Ben knew me too well to fall for my sarcastic deflection. "Things have been off with you for a while. I want to know why."

And I wanted to spend a lazy afternoon chatting with Susan Elizabeth Phillips; both of us would just have to live with the disappointment.

The door swung open, startling me into nearly dropping the phone. Sebastian strolled inside as if he owned the place, which, okay, he kind of did. But he didn't have to smirk quite so arrogantly as he eyed the way I crouched on the floor with my cell phone jammed against my right ear. My left hand balled into a fist before returning limply to my side.

"Say *something*, Emmy!"

I tried to access my most reasonable voice, the one I reserved for talking my mom out of showcasing her cleavage on sketchy first dates.

"It's complicated." I cringed at the cliché, but I couldn't risk arming Sebastian with any more insight into my personal life. It was only a matter of time before he accepted that his grandfather was gone in the most permanent way possible, and when that happened—when he finally believed what I'd been telling him all along—there was no telling how he might react.

"Now really isn't the best time to talk, Ben. I'll call you later, okay?"

Sebastian's smile widened. He made no attempt to hide the fact that he was eavesdropping on my conversation. "Wait, is this the boyfriend?"

"Mind your own business, Sebastian," I snapped automatically, before I realized with an awful sense of foreboding that I should have kept my own mouth shut. I should have ignored him and focused on ending my conversation with Ben.

There was a long damning pause on the other end of the phone. "I thought you said you were sleeping, Emmy."

"I was!"

"I guess I should've asked if you were sleeping alone." Ben spoke slowly, as if he couldn't believe his own words. As if it had never occurred to him that I might spend the night with someone— anyone—out of an impulse other than friendship. My shoulders squared at the insult. Just because *he* wasn't interested didn't mean the rest of the world had to follow suit.

"Not that it's any of *your* business, Ben, but nothing happened."

"Nothing? Well, that's not entirely true," Sebastian's voice rang out loudly enough for Ben to catch every word. Apparently causing chaos was a St. James family trait. "That kiss seemed pretty important to you."

"You kissed *him*?"

Beating my head with the phone until the screen cracked in my hand suddenly sounded far less painful than attempting to rescue this conversation.

"It's not as bad as you're thinking, Ben."

"It wasn't bad at all," Sebastian's smile widened at my obvious discomfort. "I quite enjoyed that thing you did with your tongue right before we were interrupted."

"I'm . . . this . . . it's *not* what you think," I stuttered, unable to think of anything else I could say to reassure him. Unsure why I was trying so hard in the first place. I didn't need Ben's permission to kiss someone, and I definitely didn't owe him any explanations. "Trust me."

Ben laughed hollowly in my ear. "Trust you? *Trust you?* Emmy, I don't even know who you are anymore."

Direct hit. I sucked in my breath as the pain of those words sent shockwaves through my system. I felt raw, exposed, as if my chest had been cracked open and Ben was peering inside with a scalpel saying, *"Yes, it looks like the tumor has infected everything in here. Let's close her up, everyone. There's nothing worth salvaging."*

"Come on, Ben. It's still me," I turned my back on Sebastian, needing at least the illusion of privacy.

"No, it isn't. The real Emmy would have cooperated with the police. She wouldn't be kissing some rich douchebag while her friends and family worry about her."

The unfairness of the accusation burned deep. "*You* would run to the police, Ben. Not me. Just because you don't like my choices doesn't make them any less *mine*. I've always wanted to find my dad." I raked a hand through a tangled clump of hair, yanking my scalp in the process. "And you've never even met Sebastian, so why are you acting like he broke your favorite toy?"

My anger kept me from mentioning that I happened to agree with him about Sebastian. That wasn't the point. For all he knew, Sebastian was a perfectly nice guy who had fallen head-over-heels in love with me.

"It's called *common sense*, Emmy. Most people try to avoid jackasses like him."

One glance in Sebastian's direction confirmed that he was enjoying the hell out of my conversation. He looked like he listened to people analyzing his personality on a regular basis. Maybe he had planted half a dozen listening devices in his therapist's office. It seemed like something Sebastian would do for entertainment.

"He's not always a jackass."

He winked. "Thanks for coming to my defense, sweetheart."

I glared at Sebastian in annoyance as he strengthened Ben's original point. "Although that does appear to be his default setting."

"This is what you do, Emmy," Ben lowered his voice to a quiet warning. "You build up people in your head, fall in love with the fictional version of who you want them to be, and then they crush you."

"I've never been *crushed*," I objected, even as my cheeks heated in embarrassment.

"Pierre. Henri. That German guy, Hans. Want me to keep going?"

I stiffened, but forced myself to act calm. "What about them?"

"You were suckered in just like your mom."

Usually, I could convince myself that I liked Ben's upfront approach to honesty—that I'd rather know his opinion than waste my time second guessing everything he said—but right now? Yeah, I really wished he'd kept that last bit of analysis to himself.

"I've got to go. I'll call you later."

For the second time that day, I hung up on him. Then I tried to mimic Sebastian's own casually dismissive expression to hide my hurt.

"As entertaining as your attempts at puppy love are to watch, you have more important things to focus on, like how to be of assistance to me."

"You've got that last part backwards." It wasn't exactly my wittiest comeback, but given the current state of my life, I was willing to count the absence of humiliation as a win. "You've gone through my stuff, right?"

"You think I'd lower myself to searching your belongings?" He did that annoying answering a question with a question thing.

I didn't even have to think it over. "Absolutely."

Sebastian's eyes flashed with amusement. "I'm touched, especially since you called me—what was it again?—oh right, 'not *always* a jackass.' I'm starting to think you like me."

I choked at the thought. "Not even a little. Did you make any progress with the Slate you *stole* while I was sleeping?" I put some extra bite into my tone so he'd know I wasn't joking around.

"If I had, I wouldn't be having this lovely chat with you."

No matter what I did or said some boy always seemed to be standing nearby, ready to tell me that I was wrong or naive or making an enormous mistake. I clenched my teeth.

"So you tried and failed to crack the code. That must sting, given that he was *your* grandfather. Shouldn't you have some firsthand knowledge into the inner workings of his mind?"

That wiped the smile off Sebastian's face. "My grandpa was too smart to pick something obvious. He wouldn't use his birthday, or mine, for that matter."

"That's why you were supposed to use your insight to figure it out. Wait a second," I gasped in mock surprise. "Are you telling me that you *don't* know everything? Wow. Who would've guessed? Oh, that's right. *Me.*"

"I told you, if he wanted me to have the Slate he would've handed it to me."

I dimly remembered him saying something along those lines right before the world had gone black. That was no reason for me to give an inch, though. Not when he'd made it clear that he considered me an incompetent failure ever since our interaction at the police precinct.

"Then maybe you should leave the real investigative work to me instead of worrying your pretty little head," I said.

I would have seen red if *he'd* said those words, which was probably why it felt so damn good to watch his eyes harden. Then he stretched out, lounging on his bed, his anger betrayed only by the telltale tightening of his jaw.

"Does this mean you've finally come up with a plan?" Sebastian looked skeptical, probably because for the past two days my answer had been a resounding, "I don't have the faintest idea what I'm doing, but thanks for asking."

"Actually, yes." I pulled up the most recent call log on my phone. "I'm calling in backup."

"Your backup called me a jackass right before you hung up on him. Or did I misinterpret that fascinating teen soap opera?"

I smiled tightly. "That's why it's good to have more than one best friend. Sorry, I guess I should explain. Friendship must be an unfamiliar concept to you since it doesn't involve buying or bribing loyalty."

Sebastian remained unimpressed. "This coming from the girl who made a dozen enemies on her first day."

"That's only because the people here suck."

"Sure. Keep telling yourself that."

I raised my hand over my lips in the universal shushing gesture before calling Audrey. Sebastian continued right on talking. "So you're trying to rope somebody else into solving your problems. Such a shame your boyfriend couldn't take care of it for you."

"Shut up!" I hissed.

Unfortunately my timing left something to be desired.

"Is that a new form of greeting you're trying out, Em?" Audrey asked. "I've got to say, I'm not a fan. Call me a traditionalist, but I prefer a simple hello."

I closed my eyes and instantly regretted the gesture since my nap hadn't eliminated my exhaustion. It had only sandpapered the roughest of the sleep-deprived edges.

"How's it going, Audrey?" I said obediently, as Sebastian scoffed in disgust.

"I've been better. My best friend thinks someone wants her dead, so I've started researching nearby insane asylums."

"I think they prefer the term 'mental health facilities' now."

"Yeah? Well, I'd prefer for you *not* to become an inmate—"

"Resident," I corrected.

"Whatever! You're driving me crazy, Em!"

My lecture on political correctness could wait. "I kind of need a favor."

"Did you not hear *anything* I just said?"

Mostly what I'd heard was that she needed me to grovel. "I should have called earlier. I'm sorry. Ben has already yelled at me for forgetting to charge my phone. Now is there any chance you gave that project I mentioned earlier any more thought?"

Audrey snorted. "The one where I hack a dead man's tablet? I hoped you were kidding."

"I wasn't."

"It's not too late to change your mind, like, oh say, *now* for example. Before I spend any more time on this project."

I couldn't help grinning. Audrey loved to stress the time-consuming nature of all her undertakings. I suspected it came from having a mother who could barely work a TV remote, but dismissed Audrey's passion for programming as a "little hobby." Audrey's mom had never been subtle about her desire for her oldest daughter to go into engineering or medicine. Her dad mostly stayed out of those conversations, although he quietly appreciated her ability to hack their neighbor's Netflix account so that he could watch *House of Cards*.

"Can you do it?" I asked simply. "You're kind of my last resort. So if this is beyond you, I need to figure out something else. Fast."

"You definitely need another plan."

My stomach dropped, panic seizing control of my vocal cords, right before I heard one of my favorite sounds. Audrey sighing. I *knew* I had her.

"I can give it a shot, but I'm not making any promises."

"Really?" I twirled in place on the Moroccan rug, loving the soft texture beneath my toes. "You're okay with that?"

I could practically hear Audrey's shrug in her voice. "It won't kill me to try. Probably."

I grinned. "If it makes you feel any better, nothing bad has happened since I parodied 'Call Me Maybe' for the psychopath. So either he wants nothing to do with me or he's plotting how to make it really hurt."

"Next time throw some One Direction lyrics his way," Audrey suggested sarcastically. "He doesn't know he's a psychopath and that's what makes him a psychopath. I'm sure he'll appreciate the gesture."

"I'll keep that in mind." My shoulders relaxed slightly as the easy comfort of her voice slid over me. "Can you come over here now?"

Sebastian's low, "Why am I not surprised?" filled the momentary silence.

"It's almost one in the morning."

"Yeah, I know."

"I have school tomorrow. Scratch that, I have school *today*. I need to get up in less than seven hours."

Ignoring Sebastian's knowing smirk, I concentrated on my best friend. "Look, I know it's a lot to ask, but I *need* you, Aud. So—"

"Promise me there will be coffee. Lots of it."

I made no attempt to hide my smile. "Done. I'm sending a car to pick you up right now."

Audrey's disbelief traveled through the phone. "Um, who is paying for *that*, Emmy?"

"Sebastian St. James," I announced with relish.

"Well, in that case, I'll raid the minibar."

Audrey disconnected, probably so that she could grab every piece of equipment that might theoretically come in handy, leaving me supremely aware of the fact that I was still in Sebastian's bedroom. Oh, and that the boy in question was scowling at me from his very large, very appealing bed. His high thread count sheets probably felt like a cloud of unicorn hair.

Audrey wasn't the only one who desperately needed a caffeine boost.

"Care to share what you volunteered me for?" Sebastian didn't sound particularly concerned. If anything, he seemed amused, like I was a crappy infomercial trying too hard to sell him something that he didn't want.

"You're going to ask Force to drive Audrey. Right now."

He shook his head with mock regret. "I don't do favors for Audrey Weinstein. Ever. That's nonnegotiable."

"Because she caught *your* friend stealing her phone? That makes sense."

Sebastian's eyes iced over. "I don't help people who hurt my friends."

If the situation was reversed I'd be equally protective of Audrey or Ben, but I didn't have the luxury of caring about his personal reservations. He needed to get over them. Now.

Because there was nobody *I* trusted more to have my back.

"How badly do you want to help your grandfather?" I said, bluntly. "He gave that Slate to me and I'm a package deal with Audrey. So here's my first lesson for you: Sometimes you have to work with people you don't particularly like in order to get what you want."

Sebastian's mouth twisted into the distant cousin of a smile. "Alright, Emmy. We can play this out your way—for now. Just remember, if anything goes wrong, it'll be on you."

Yeah, I didn't need any reminders on that score.

CHAPTER 26

Audrey's arrival shouldn't have felt like a big deal.

We'd seen each other at least five days a week—usually more—for the past seven *years*. Even though my math skills left a lot to be desired, I figured we had clocked in well over ten thousand hours together. So it shouldn't have felt like my birthday and Christmas and New Year's all wrapped into one explosion of awesome when a familiar black town car pulled up to the manor house and Audrey climbed out of the back seat. Except it did.

The force of my hug nearly tackled her, as she tentatively patted me on the back. "You okay, Em?"

"Never better."

"Uh-huh. Okay. Well, you're starting to cut off my oxygen—"

I laughed, releasing my stranglehold to affectionately swat at her arm. "It took you long enough. Did Force take you sightseeing or something?"

Audrey glanced apprehensively over her shoulder at the very tall, imposing figure of a man who still looked fully capable of cracking my head open like a walnut. He didn't smile at me, but his wooden expression no longer disconcerted me. Maybe because Force ranked significantly lower on the list of the people who had reason to hate me than my dance teacher.

"How's it going, Newton? Stab anyone lately?"

Audrey gasped, clutching on to my arm, and making a futile attempt to drag me away. There was no way Force could have missed Audrey's reaction, but his expression remained calm.

"Not yet. It's still on my to-do list." He nodded once at Audrey before heading off into the darkness, ostensibly to take care of whatever outranked "murder" on his agenda.

"Do you have a death wish?!" Audrey hissed the instant she thought he was out of hearing range. "*Stop. Provoking. Strangers.*"

I shrugged. "Force thinks it's funny."

"Um, are we talking about the same guy? The silent behemoth who drove me here isn't a stand-up comic. I'm not sure he even knows how to *smile*." Audrey's grip tightened. "Just because *you* think something is funny, doesn't mean you should say it!"

I wanted to point out that Force was probably sick of people tiptoeing around him, and that if he hadn't appreciated my teasing he would've put an end to it. There's no way you get the nickname "Force" without being able to kill an unwanted topic of conversation. Since he hadn't scared me witless with a death glare, I was inclined to say that we were friends.

Sharing that wouldn't make Audrey feel any better about my personal safety, so I took her advice and kept it to myself.

"C'mon, let's get you that coffee." I ushered her inside the manor house, which looked even more regal now than it had my first night. The gray stonework, the high cathedral arches, the intricate stained glass windows that were swallowed up by the darkness but which didn't need to be seen in order to be felt. The entire structure dominated with a sense of its own self-importance.

"Holy crap. This place is *insane*."

I grinned in total agreement. "The weirdest part is that everyone thinks it's totally normal for a school to be a few flying buttresses short of a Gothic church. Well, okay, Kayla appreciates the absurdity, but that's only because she's also here on a scholarship."

Audrey stiffened but her pace never slowed as we moved through the manor house. "Right. Kayla. Are we meeting up with her?"

"I think she's sleeping." I stared in amazement as the tension in Audrey's body began to ease. "Wait, are you actually *jealous* right now?"

"Don't be ridiculous," she said quickly. Too quickly. The same way she had assured me that she was fine the first time I spent the night at Ben's without her. Even knowing that her parents never would've been comfortable letting me crash on their couch in order to avoid my mom's new boyfriend, it had still made her feel excluded. As if we'd somehow shoved her out of the inner circle. It had seemed ridiculous to me, but that didn't change how it had made *her* feel.

"If there's ever a zombie apocalypse—"

"You mean *when* there's a zombie apocalypse," Audrey corrected.

I rolled my eyes. "Whatever. You'll still be the first person I call."

Audrey shook her head and laughed. "There are so many problems with that statement, I don't even know where to begin. Telecommunication will be down, for starters, and the subway system will be an all-you-can-eat zombie buffet. I love you dearly, Em, but you won't last an hour with the zombies."

"Hey!" I said indignantly. "I'm being stalked by a ninja assassin right now and I'm still alive. That's got to count for something, right?"

Audrey groaned. "No, it doesn't. This—right here—this is why people want to kill you."

I pushed open the door leading out of the manor house. It was the fastest way to reach the enormous grassy lawn that was surrounded by all the most important buildings, including the computer lab. And I wanted to actually *talk* to my best friend without disturbing Kayla in the process. Audrey didn't stop twisting and craning her neck so that she could get a good look at everything we passed. If Emptor Academy was the kind of place that gave tours to prospective students, the picturesque cobblestone pathways and manicured lawns would be a strong selling point. Except the sight of Peyton, even without her minion horde, lounging on the steps of the girls' dormitory would have sent the smartest kids scurrying for the nearest exit. I had no idea what Peyton was planning at two in the freaking morning, but I had a feeling that Sebastian was involved. Either she was going to warn me away from him or she was lurking around on his behalf. I couldn't get a read on that relationship, but if they were ever cast as the protagonists in a novel it would be the kind of story that ended tragically for everyone.

She straightened, tilting her finely pointed chin into the air when she spotted us.

I tried to act calm. "On a related note, there's a soul-sucking monster headed our way."

"Zombies don't suck souls, Emmy. They either eat people or infect them with their bite."

I didn't think my lack of zombie knowledge was our most pressing concern, especially since Peyton was sauntering toward us with malice in her eyes.

"Oh good, you've brought a friend to help you pack." Peyton gave Audrey a once-over, noting the lack of designer anything before turning back to me. "Don't let the door hit you on the way out."

Great. So apparently she was waiting on the steps to chase me away. Good times.

"Wow, okay. I take it this isn't Kayla." Audrey scanned the lawn as if expecting my roommate to pop out at any minute, which wasn't beyond the realm of possibility. "Can we skip to the part where I get coffee?"

"Absolutely. The computer lab is right this way."

Peyton stepped forward, blocking our path. "Let's clear something up first. If you screw with Sebastian, I won't hesitate to mess with your permanent file in Gilcrest's office. Got it?"

That caught Audrey's attention. "Whoa. Did I miss something?"

"Not a thing." I spoke a touch too quickly to be convincing.

"And that's *exactly* how it's going to stay," Peyton hissed.

I raised my hands in the universal "don't shoot" gesture. "Hey, I don't care about whatever weird thing you've got with Sebastian. If you have a problem, take it up with him. Just leave me out of it."

Something flashed in her eyes—anger or hurt, maybe—but whatever it was she banked it before I could get a good look. Still, for a second it made her seem almost human.

"I'm *Peyton McQueen*," she stated as if she expected me to genuflect or dip into a curtsy. "I don't have problems, only fleeting annoyances."

Instead of contradicting that obvious lie, I concentrated on pulling Audrey toward the pathway. She craned her neck for a parting view of Emptor Academy's most intimidating student. "But—"

"Don't stop moving!"

"But what did she mean about Sebast—"

I rubbed my forehead, which did nothing to abate what would undoubtedly become a full-blown migraine. "I'll explain later."

Audrey looked like she wanted to protest, but seemed to think better of it. "Fine, but you better not hold anything back, Emmy. I want details. All the details."

"I'm telling you, nothing happened."

"All. The. Details." Audrey said with such finality that I knew nothing except the sudden appearance of Benedict Cumberbatch would distract her for long.

"Oh, will you look at that! We're here." I pulled out my ID card and swiped us into the building before she could pry anything else out of me.

"Don't think that I'm—" Audrey's voice trailed off as we both entered the computer lab. It looked like an enormous truck from Slate's headquarters had driven to Emptor Academy, discovered that they had the wrong address, and decided rather than hauling it away they'd leave it for the school administration to sort out. Everything in the room was sleekly modern; red furniture provided the only pop of color to offset the chromatic gray displays. The stylized Slate logo of a book with a claw emerging from the pages extending across the room.

"I'm in heaven," Audrey finished. "Do you think anyone would notice if I moved in? I wouldn't take up too much space. I'd stay right here." She trailed her fingers lightly across a keyboard. "Hello my precious. Aren't you a sight for sleep-deprived eyes."

"I promise, I'll get you coffee." I handed her Frederick St. James's most prized possession. "Now what can you tell me about this?"

She studied it carefully, flipping it over a couple times. "It appears to be a Slate."

I stared at her. "That's all you've got?"

"Without coffee? Yes. That's all I've got."

I rolled my eyes, resigning myself to a quick trip to the cafeteria while she stared lovingly at the equipment at her fingertips. I was startled when the door swung open and I found myself looking straight into Nasir's dark brown eyes. Right behind him, like a particularly unwelcome thundercloud, stood Sebastian.

My hands automatically flew up to block their entry. "No. No way. This is a hostility-free space, which means you need to turn around and—"

"Save your breath," Sebastian's mouth quirked in amusement at his own unintentional reminder of our time together in the girls' locker room. "I already tried to talk him out of this."

"Tried and failed, apparently," I muttered, darkly. "Figures it would be the one time I actually *agree* with you."

Nasir ignored us, circumventing me with all the smoothness of a professional basketball player moving into position to take his shot.

"Hey Audrey. It's good to see you."

She smiled back politely but her posture was rigid, her hands clenched into fists, probably so that she wouldn't twirl the ring she always wore on her right index finger.

"Yeah, uh . . . you, too."

The awkwardness was so thick it was palpable, and it tasted sharp and bitter on my tongue. It was all my fault. Not their breakup, of course. I fully intended to blame Mr. Nasir "Lightfingers" Rashad for that one, but this confrontation? This was because of me.

Well, *technically* it was because of Sebastian's grandfather, but blaming a dead guy felt disrespectful. As if I were using his death to provide a convenient scapegoat. I couldn't leave the blame on a dead man's doorstep, when I'd been the one who'd begged Audrey for help. Which meant it was also my responsibility to make this incredibly uncomfortable situation for Audrey a little easier to handle.

Even if it meant admitting something aloud that I'd much rather forget.

"Sebastian kissed me in the girls' locker room."

That did the trick.

CHAPTER 27

"Does Ben know about this?"

Those were the last words I expected from Audrey, since they had nothing to do with the truth-bomb I'd just dropped. It was like clicking a link for details on the latest celebrity divorce and getting a survey about Chihuahua sweaters instead.

"Sebastian announced it when we were talking on the phone."

Audrey whistled slowly. "Holy crap. He's going to freak out. You are *never* going to hear the end of this."

Yeah, that hadn't escaped me, but it was nowhere close to the biggest problem in my life. Which was kind of funny since a few days ago my first kiss would've been *huge* news.

Now I wanted everyone to forget I'd mentioned it.

Nasir pitched his voice an octave lower in a halfway decent imitation of his friend. "Don't hand her the Slate, Nasir. There's no telling what she might try to do with it." He shook his head. "I should have known this would happen. Hell, I *did* know. I just thought what with everything else going on, you would have opted against making out with your best lead, Sebastian."

"Best lead?" Audrey repeated. "For what?"

"To find Sebastian's grandpa," Nasir glanced from Audrey to me before all of our eyes were inevitably drawn to the boy at the heart of the chaos. "That's why we're all here, right?"

Audrey stared at her ex-boyfriend as if he'd suggested they move in together and get married. "What are you talking about? Why would I be here at"—she consulted her watch—"two in the morning—*without coffee, I might add*—to find a dead man? In what alternate reality does *that* make sense?"

Nasir looked genuinely surprised by the question. "He's not dead. This is another one of his training exercises. Sebastian's grandpa comes up with the best challenges. Last year we had to take a trip to Hungary in order to steal—"

"Nothing of value," Sebastian said, shooting Nasir a dirty look.

"Right. So this year it's a coed challenge." Nasir shrugged. "He probably wanted to test our focus with a distraction."

Audrey folded her arms and glared. "A distraction. It's not like girls could *possibly* be of any real use. Oh no, we're just here for decoration." She unzipped her backpack and held it outstretched to Nasir. "I guess you should do the hacking then. We wouldn't want my ovaries making a mess of it."

"Hey, *I'm* not the bad guy here!"

"Oh really? Do the 'good guys' usually go around stealing other people's phones? I must have missed that memo. Did you hear that, Em? Turns out chivalry isn't dead. It's delinquent."

It was so stupid. The squabbling. The arguing over stuff that didn't really matter in the grand scheme of things.

And yet I felt my blood pressure skyrocket when Sebastian leaned over to me and whispered, "This is your fault."

I made no attempt to hide my skepticism. "Want to run that logic by me?"

"If you'd kept your mouth shut about the locker room, they wouldn't be squabbling right now."

I rolled my eyes. "Right. Of course. *We're* the reason it's a bad idea for Nasir and Audrey to be in the same room together." I leaned heavy on the sarcasm.

Audrey spoke right over my side conversation with Sebastian. "I don't care. I don't care about Sebastian's grandpa or a scavenger hunt or *any of it*." The finality in those last three words made it pretty damn clear that Nasir fell into that last category. "I'm here for Emmy. So if you don't mind," she waved the Slate in her hands, "business calls."

Nasir nodded, but instead of leaving the room, he silently settled in front of one of the computers. After one last moment of hesitation, Audrey pulled out a flash drive and sank into a nearby seat. Sebastian and I both jockeyed for a clear view of the screen, which ended abruptly when my elbow connected with his abs and I flinched away.

He didn't spare me a glance. Instead, he turned to Audrey. "What are you planning to do?"

"We have to figure out the password before we can get to the good stuff."

"What a brilliant deduction," Sebastian's tone dripped with condescension.

"Right, well unless you happen to know the six-character sequence your grandpa used?" She paused, as if to give him an opportunity to fill in the blanks. "No? Okay, then. We do it *my* way and run the dictionary."

"How does that work?"

Audrey's gaze never wavered from the screen. "Most people don't choose random letters or numbers for their passwords. They want something simple that they can remember when they're tired or stressed or sleep deprived." She typed some lines of code that I would never be able to follow. "Where was I?"

"Something simple," I supplied.

"Right. So they pick their dog's name or their favorite color or their high school mascot, and then they use that same password for *everything* from their bank account to their Netflix subscription. That's why your friends are always the easiest people to hack."

Nasir stared at her incredulously. "How is that any different from palming a wallet or a phone?"

"It's not," Audrey said bluntly. "That's why *I* don't hack my friends."

"But the rest of the world is fair game, right?" Nasir pressed.

"Look, I can either work or we can sit around having a fascinating philosophical discussion, but I can't do both at once."

"Work," Sebastian and I said simultaneously.

"That's what I thought." Audrey paused and then picked up the Slate. "Here's a fun fact: Most people use *password* as their password." She snorted in contempt. "And yet they pride themselves on their creativity."

"'Password' won't fit. Too many letters." Nasir pointed out.

Audrey's fierce look of determination never wavered. "It does if you take a few vowels out of it."

Everyone watched as she wrote P-S-S-W-R-D and pressed Enter.

Invalid password.

Audrey shrugged. "Or not. Alright, back to the original plan. There are over fifteen thousand six-letter words in the English language. So right now it's a numbers game."

"You want to try typing in *fifteen thousand* passwords? That'll take—"

"Forever?" Audrey nodded. "Hacking isn't for the faint of heart or the limited of time. The good news is that I won't test them manually." She gazed lovingly at the laptop in front of her. "This baby is going to do it for me." In one swift move Audrey plugged in the Slate and then went back to typing commands. "Okay," she punctuated her words with a flurry of keystrokes. "Let's. Try. This. Now."

Invalid password.

Invalid password.

Invalid password.

The whole screen instantly blackened.

It didn't power down, there was no flash of a logo before it went lights out. One second it looked fine and the next it was as dead as, for lack of a better metaphor, Sebastian's grandfather.

"What the hell did you do to it?" Sebastian's voice was low, but no less menacing for the lack of volume. If anything, the quiet restraint increased the anxiety churning in my stomach.

"Nothing!" Audrey's gaze remained glued on the screen in front of her. "I ran the program! It should have been fine!"

Sebastian reached out and jerked the cord connecting the Slate to the computer, disconnecting the device completely.

"*Hey!* That's not a good id—" Audrey's mouth fell open as the Slate sprang to life as if nothing had happened.

"You were saying?" Sebastian said coldly.

"That you should never yank out a piece of equipment!"

Sebastian didn't look even remotely chastised. "It worked."

"This time," Audrey muttered. "Next time you won't be so lucky."

Nasir glanced from his ex-girlfriend to his best friend before he apparently thought better of speaking and kept his mouth shut.

"What now?" I asked.

"Now I have to modify the program," Audrey chewed on her bottom lip. "This Slate definitely has anti-hacking software on it."

"No, *really?*" Sebastian snapped. "What was your first clue?"

Audrey glared at him. "I'm happy to trade jobs with you at any time. Just say the word and I'll act all miserable and mysterious while you do the hacking. Let's see how well you work with someone second-guessing your every move."

"Oh, are you hacking? Here I thought you were destroying everything you touch."

I felt like a preschool teacher forced to play referee. "Guys! We're all on the same team here."

Audrey laughed. "No, we're not. I'm on *your* team, Emmy. Just because the two of you swapped spit doesn't mean I have to like him. You should know that better than anyone."

My face flushed red. I knew *exactly* how it felt to make forced small talk with my mom's latest loser boyfriend because she expected me to be pleasant. Nice. Sweet. Meanwhile the guy at the other end of the table could belch, scratch his stomach, or ignore me entirely. I hated putting my best friend in a similar situation, but we couldn't afford to waste time bickering with Sebastian.

Not when our current situation put the emphasis on *dead* in deadline.

"Let's just call a truce, okay? One day. Not even a full day. We just need to set aside our personal feelings for the next three or four hours. That way we all get what we want: answers."

"Okay, Emmy. It's official. You have got to join the debate team!"

I whirled around to see a familiar face peeking through the doorway. Kayla's sparkly pink tank top quickly brightened the room. She smiled widely at everyone.

Audrey's attention snapped from the computer to me. "Debate team? Since when have you been interested in debate?"

"Well, I definitely don't feel like arguing with you right now," I hissed. "We're on the same team, remember? Same. Team."

I didn't have a whole lot of faith that repeating the mantra would make Audrey any happier with the situation, so I focused on the newcomer instead.

"How did you find me here, Kayla?"

"Sebastian texted me. He said that we were pulling an all-nighter. Why? Is this supposed to be a secret?" Kayla bounced the rest of the way inside. "Are you guys doing something illegal?"

She didn't look particularly uncomfortable with the thought; if anything, she grew more eager. "Wait, are you guys deporting somebody? Just because *you* don't like pop music doesn't mean—"

"Nobody is getting deported." I couldn't resist adding, "Not unless the authorities catch up with Nasir and Sebastian for whatever it was they did in Hungary."

"Nothing happened in Hungary," Sebastian growled at the exact same time Nasir said, "They won't."

Audrey tuned all of us out as she concentrated on the screen, lost in an endless sea of code. I wondered if my eyes took on that slightly unfocused sheen when I was writing a romance novel. And if there was any point in asking her to explain what any of the jumble meant.

"I could try to run it with a time delay," she mused aloud, more to herself than the rest of us. "That might be enough to trick the Slate into seeing them as individual attempts instead of a brute force attack."

"And risk frying it again? No. No way." Sebastian shoved the Slate into his pocket as if that were enough to end the discussion. Or maybe it was simply so that his hands would be free to knock any prying fingers away if one of us tried to reclaim it.

"Got a better idea, Sebastian?" Audrey snapped.

Goosebumps broke out on my arms, and I looked up to find Sebastian focused entirely on me.

"Yeah, I do." He took a firm hold on my shoulder blades and propelled me into a red chair, which must have been ergonomically designed to perfection. Even with Sebastard St. James looming over me, I couldn't help thinking that it'd make a great spot to read a romance.

"Emmy knows the password. He gave it to her. He must have mentioned it. She just hasn't identified it yet." Sebastian reached into my bag and pulled out my notebook and pen. "You're going to make yourself useful by writing down *everything* that he said to you. Then we'll circle all the six-letter words."

"I didn't catch many six-letter words from your grandpa, but I've got a whole bunch of four-letter ones for you, Sebastian," I said, snatching the notebook away from him.

"Don't talk. Write."

I scowled, first at Sebastian and then at the blank page, before accepting the inevitable and replaying that awful moment in my mind. A task that would've been a lot less painful with some background music instead of all the squabbling that served as my soundtrack.

"Try 'Oswald.'"

Sebastian sat upright and focused with an intensity that flustered me.

"He mentioned Oswald? What *exactly* did he say?"

"Just that he did a shitty job."

His entire posture instantly changed, relaxed. "He says that a lot."

Nasir laughed. "Remember when the three of us went to Texas and he—"

"Took us sightseeing." Sebastian finished for him. "Do you remember the part where I said I'd kick your ass if you ever mentioned it again?"

Nasir shook his head, but he seemed more amused than unnerved. "That's what keeps landing you in therapy, man. You're supposed to use your words to express your feelings, not to make idle threats."

His grim smile wasn't amused, but something must have happened between the two boys to forge their friendship—maybe in Hungary, or Houston, or right here at Emptor Academy—because Sebastian didn't glare at Nasir. Instead, he pulled out the Slate and typed in, O-S-W-A-L-D.

Everyone, including a very confused Kayla, waited in tense silence.

Invalid password.

"This is hopeless. It could be *anything*. You get that right? Your grandpa gave his Slate to *me*, which means he's crazy enough to pick a random string of numbers." My brain felt like it had been clamped in a vise. I snatched the Slate from Sebastian and headed for the door.

He followed right behind me. "Where the hell do you think you're going?"

"To get my best friend her freaking coffee!"

I wanted to run away. The overused muscles in my legs began tightening, tensing, bracing themselves for the hard impact of the cobblestones beneath my sneakers. Except running wouldn't accomplish anything. Speed didn't make a damn bit of difference on a hamster wheel.

Zipping my hoodie up higher against the early morning chill, I kept my gaze locked on the cafeteria.

"Emmy, hold up."

Oh, hell no.

I refused to adjust my stride. If I sped up it would look like I was running away. *Poor little Emmy Danvers can't hold her own with Sebastian St. James. Can't manage much of anything. Can't last more than a handful of hours before falling apart.*

Sebastian interrupted the mocking tirade playing in my head. "You're not—"

"Don't you dare finish that sentence!" I snapped. "I swear, if you so much as *think* about giving me another one of your orders, I will end you. *So leave me alone.*"

Sebastian ignored my threat. "The cafeteria closes at midnight and there's a campus security guard who starts his rounds there.

He should be headed this way within the next twenty minutes." He held out something that gleamed dully in the darkness. "If you want coffee, swipe in at the library. Third floor, third door on the left."

My fingers closed around two cold metal keys.

"Why are you giving this to me?" I raked a hand through my hair, my head pounding with the pressure of a thousand unanswered questions. "Why are you pretending to be nice? We both know it's an act. So what are you trying to weasel out of me now?"

The lamplight illuminated a flash of his white teeth as he grinned. "Coffee, for starters. I take mine black. Oh, and grab me a bagel while you're at it. Better hurry. The guard will be here soon."

Apparently I had been demoted to the role of barista/waitress/ personal assistant.

I totally should have seen it coming.

"How will you guys get past the guard?" I called out to his retreating form as he began heading back to the computer lab.

"It's not hard. We'll lock the door and turn out the lights in fifteen minutes. So feel free to take your time in the library."

He continued down the pathway again, but I wasn't quite ready for him to leave. Not when questions still bubbled under my skin like the carbonation in a shaken soda can.

"Do I want to know how you got these keys?"

He turned slightly, his face half-cast in shadows. "Nope."

That was the last thing he said before he faded into the darkness, which made the whole situation feel like a setup. A trap. Maybe I'd be surrounded by ninjas the second I swiped my ID card and entered into the main lobby of the library. Maybe Sebastian wanted to keep me away from the computer lab so that he could blackmail my best friend without any interference.

Or maybe I had become paranoid in the extreme.

That last possibility—the paranoid one—had more than a little truth to it. Standing outside the building also increased my odds of getting busted by a security guard, escorted back to the girls' dormitory, and given a lecture about respecting the curfew.

That settled it for me.

I swiped my ID card before fumbling my way inside. The lobby was a gaping black void but flicking on a light would've turned it into a beacon. No way would the security guards overlook my trespassing expedition then. Still, the darkness creeped me out. I was getting whiplash from craning my neck every time I heard a noise. It wasn't distinct, nothing as easily dismissed as a branch tapping against a windowpane.

It was infinitely more sinister, probably because it only existed in my imagination.

I forced my mind to rewrite the script. Instead of being the stupid girl in a horror story, I was a secret agent. An international woman of mystery. A dark alter ego of myself who wore little black dresses and dark red lipstick. The kind of girl who could intimidate with a narrow-eyed glare and then follow it up with a roundhouse kick.

An opposer to evil. The nemesis of bad guys everywhere.

Nemesis, I actually liked the sound of that a lot. Nemmy wouldn't stand in front of an unlocked door because she was too afraid to turn the freaking knob. She didn't waste her time on self-indulgent displays of weakness. She kept her head down and focused on the task at hand. For tonight, I was willing to let her take the lead.

My steps faltered only once as I passed the gleaming mahogany checkout desk. Empty of all life, the library looked like a ghost town. Almost as if a plague had ravaged the residents leaving only the building untouched in its wake. I breathed in the familiar scent of pages from well-loved books and forced my muscles to unclench. It went against every instinct, but I hurried past the rows and rows of books without pausing to read the spines. Audrey was stuck with Sebastian *and* Nasir until I resurfaced with the coffee, and while Kayla might be good at diffusing tension, she was way out of her league now.

There were still ten minutes before Sebastian's scheduled blackout. If I rushed, I could rejoin the others while the security guard made sure that no millionaire heirs were helping themselves to a late night feast. Shoving open the door to the stairwell, I took the steps two at a time, panting as I raced into the rare books section. A half dozen items were placed under what looked like a bulletproof display case.

Nearly there.

The Slate began to vibrate in my pocket, and just like that, Nemmy was gone. It was like she'd never existed, which *technically* she hadn't. But still. It was as if I had never imagined her in the first place. That strong kickass, I-ain't-afraid-of-no-killers persona deserted me.

My heart thudding painfully in my chest, I fished the Slate out of my pocket.

I told you I was bored. Now we're going to play a little game.

CHAPTER 28

I was so screwed.

My life didn't flash before my eyes as I scrambled toward the room Sebastian had mentioned, I didn't have any profound thought about existence or my place in the world, and I definitely didn't care if my underwear was clean. There were exactly two words running through my head, and they were *Oh, shit.*

Not *"Run, Emmy!"*

Not *"Hide, Emmy!"*

That would've been entirely too practical for someone who forgot to take the *killer* into account before stupidly storming off on her own.

I deserved to die.

Scratch that, I didn't deserve to die. I wasn't a mass murderer, or a child molester, or a corrupt accountant who'd just screwed a bunch of senior citizens out of their retirement funds. Unless I was paying for crimes from a past life, this wasn't a case of karmic retribution.

I didn't deserve to die.

And yet the only person I had to blame was myself. Ben had told me countless times to hand the Slate over to the authorities, but I'd been hell-bent on finding my own answers. I'd gambled on myself—on my nonexistent sleuthing abilities—and now I had to pay the price.

The Slate vibrated again.

Marco.

I ducked behind a bookshelf, peering frantically into the darkness. I thought the dark blob ahead of me might be a doorframe, but I had no idea how many I'd already passed, and the sharp waves of panic crashing through me didn't make it any easier to recall.

The Slate jolted in my hand with a fresh set of vibrations.

Marco.

That wasn't the only bit of information it had to share with me.

Potential Hostile within 50 ft.

My hand flew to my mouth to stifle the scream burning at my throat. It probably defied some primal instinct that believed screaming loud and long enough would send someone running to my rescue.

Except right now? The only person who would rush over was the one currently hunting me down.

Marco.

I darted forward. I wanted to cling to the books and hide amongst the hardcovers forever, but instead I plastered my back against the wooden door and tried to hide in the dark recess of the frame.

Potential Hostile within 45 ft.

My fingers fumbled in my pocket for the keys. I should have tucked the one that unlocked the lobby door into the back pocket of my jeans. Instead, I had let them clink softly against each other as I'd raced up the stairs. Now I had to test two keys on what might be the wrong door, all without giving my position away to the killer.

Because what my life really needed at this precise moment was another challenge.

My entire body shook as if I'd tripped into an ice bank. The palms of my hands would probably still have the key imprint when the medical examiner saw me at the morgue. I was clutching the sharp ridges tightly enough to draw blood, but the pain cut through some of the fear.

It sharpened everything. The warm familiar musk of books became oppressive, the silhouettes of shelving units loomed menacingly around me. The darkness began to recede as my eyes adjusted to the room, which might've been comforting if the shadows weren't my best source of protection.

Marcooo.
Potential Hostile within 43 ft.

I shoved the key blindly at the lock, expecting it to immediately resist. Instead, it slid home so sweetly I wanted to weep in relief. Apparently, there was still enough Nemmy in me to keep it together because I didn't make a sound. Maybe it was knowing, without a doubt, that these next few minutes were going to be my last. That every scare, every instinctive glance over my shoulder, every increase in my pulse, it had all been building to this moment.

Sebastian wasn't around with any of his so-called lifelines. Audrey couldn't hack me out of danger. Ben couldn't save the day by calling the cops.

It was just me.

Marco.
Potential Hostile within 38 ft.

I shut the door as quietly as I could before engaging the lock and jamming a chair underneath it for extra reinforcement. At best, it might stall him for an extra minute or two. It wouldn't stop him. Not this time. He was still coming. I began searching the area for a weapon, a distraction, a distress signal; I wasn't picky. Nothing I saw inspired much confidence.

There was a long granite-tiled countertop with a whole set of utensils in a hard plastic container, but I didn't think the killer would be impressed if I brandished the nearest piece of silverware and advised him not to fork with me. If I had even the slightest clue how to create a bomb, I totally would have used the butter knife to strip the wires on the coffeepot or something. Except realistically that seemed like a great way to electrocute myself and take care of the killer's job for him.

The cupboards were mostly empty. A few boxes of cereal, some granola bars that had probably been sitting there for the last decade. Five very stale looking bagels sat on the counter near the coffee pot, which had me hoping that I'd find a bread knife with razor sharp teeth.

Instead, I came up with a handful of spatulas, a ladle, and inexplicably, a whisk.

I continued ransacking the drawers for anything that even vaguely resembled a weapon more than, oh, say an eggbeater. A container of bleach was the closest to a chemical weapon that I could find, and it was too sludgy and crusted over to fling into my attacker's eyes. My Slate vibrated again as I grabbed a floral-etched casserole dish.

Marco.

I held my breath and stared at the screen, bracing myself for the Potential Hostile update. It reminded me of being six years old and crawling scared into my mom's bed during a lightning storm. She had held me protectively, whispering through every electric crack that the storm was God's way of putting on a show. She said that the flash of lightning that blazed in the sky was a performer making a grand entrance and the answering thunder clap was a round of angel applause.

The killer was putting on quite a show, but I wasn't going to cheer his grand finale.

Potential Hostile within 40 ft.

He was headed in the wrong direction. All I needed to do was buy enough time for the security guard to reach the library. As long as the killer didn't bust through the door within the next ten minutes, I stood a fighting chance. My fingers trembled. Flashing the lights on and off, heaving the ceramic casserole dish out the window, it might be enough to make the killer retreat. Bide his time for another chance to strike.

Unless he decided a few more dead bodies wouldn't make much of a difference.

I stared numbly at the Slate, my body locked in a terror so complete it paralyzed me. I had a freaking casserole dish, a set of keys, and a password-protected tablet. If I had paused to grab my bag before exiting the computer lab, I could have at least called Audrey for help. Hell, I could have called the *police*. But no, I'd headed straight for the door with the one piece of technology I couldn't crack to save my life.

Literally, as it turned out.

Marco!

My heart lurched, the gleam of sweat on my palms threatening my grip on the casserole dish. I still couldn't bring myself to move. To hide. To flee. To do something—*anything*—more than staring wide-eyed with horror at the door. My pulse pounded away like a jackhammer on a construction site, loud enough to be heard a mile away.

Potential Hostile within 32 ft.

He was getting closer.

The message was replaced only by the achingly familiar password screen. Sebastian's voice rang out in my head, complete with the annoyed gruffness that always seemed to simmer beneath his words. *There has to be something that you know, Emmy. Something that I don't.*

My grip on the casserole dish tightened. I knew that I didn't want to die. Not here. Not now. Not ever, truthfully, but *definitely* not like this. The fear and panic began to slow as a sense of unreality settled over me. This couldn't be happening, but since it *was*, well, then I might as well go down fighting. It was kind of amazing how quickly true desperation eliminated the fear of looking stupid. So what if my last-minute password attempts sounded ridiculous? If it didn't work, I'd be dead. There was no downside to going straight for the jugular. Just like Frederick St. James had advised back in the coffee shop.

I typed in J-U-G-L-A-R to make it fit and hit Enter.

Invalid password.

I tried to recall those first moments in Starbucks, the shock of having my drink snatched away from me. The way I'd met the icy blue eyes that Sebastian had inherited, right before I insisted that the Frappuccino was *mine*.

There had to be something I was missing. Some clue. Some signal. *Something.*

The Slate buzzed again.

Come out, come out, wherever you are.

Ignoring the words on the screen, I focused on my one memory of Frederick St. James. The kindness that had washed over his features when he had called me "Gracie."

G-R-A-C-I-E

Invalid password.

My stomach twisted and roiled as I fought back the tears pricking my eyes. There was so much more I wanted to *do* with my life. I wanted to see my name in print, to stand right next to Audrey when we tossed our graduation caps into the air, to have the kiss I'd always fantasized about with Ben. I wanted to tell him how I felt, even if it cost us our friendship. I wanted to hug my mom and trade "I love yous" with her one last time. To apologize for being defeated by a six-character riddle.

I wanted one last chance to be completely honest.

Maybe if Frederick St. James had been a little more upfront, nobody would be on the verge of gunning me down. The guy had obviously suspected somebody or else he wouldn't have created his Potential Hostile alert. A sane person would have shared that fear with friends. Family members. Colleagues. Maybe if he'd trusted *somebody* they could have come up with a loophole out of this mess.

Wasn't that supposed to be the first rule of Emptor Academy? There's always a caveat.

Potential Hostile within 20 ft.

My fingers shaking, I typed C-A-V-E-A-T onto the screen.

Nothing happened.

My legs nearly buckled in defeat, but I couldn't give up. Couldn't let this be the end. Couldn't—

A searing light burst from the Slate, blinding me as completely as a military-grade weapon designed to stun insurgents.

There was no way the killer hadn't noticed a flash, bright enough to have pink splotches dancing in front of my eyes, shining through the cracks of the door.

My last-ditch, long shot of a backup plan had given me away for good.

CHAPTER 29

Time didn't slow down for me the way it does in the movies.

If anything, it sped up.

The Slate in my hand vibrated out of control, probably trying to warn me that the Potential Hostile was closing in and that I should *get the hell out*. Unfortunately, I still couldn't see two feet in front of my face. The pink splotches began dancing with some royal blue blotches and together they produced beautiful butterfly offspring that flitted across my vision. I shoved the Slate deep into my sweatshirt pocket, vaguely grateful that it was no longer trying to burn out my eyes. The electronic blast had died as quickly as it blazed to life. Except the damage was done. The multi-colored winged creatures continued flapping in front of my eyes, making it impossible for me to see the door.

There was nothing wrong with my hearing. I couldn't mistake the splintering crack of wood as a very strong, very motivated individual delivered a series of hard kicks to the door. I twisted instinctively to face the entrance, even though I wouldn't be able to discern more than the general shape of my killer. It was almost funny, in a seriously twisted way; the killer had been a grayish blob on the security film and even meeting face to face wouldn't give me any more clarity.

Not unless he toyed with me long enough for the bright spots to fade.

The chair I had propped up against the knob must have either broken or skidded across the floor. Not that it really made a difference either way, considering that the end result was the same. The barrier was gone and I was screwed.

"Marco." The cheery voice sounded eerily familiar. I stared at the doorway, desperately trying to place it. To identify the Starbucks killer who'd been terrorizing me ever since that first day in the coffee shop.

Lime green blotches left me with only a hazy outline.

"You're supposed to say, 'Polo.'" The faceless blob chided me.

"Polo," I said, right before I launched the casserole dish out the closed window. A loud *crack* rang through the otherwise silent room, sending glass raining down onto the floor. If that didn't capture the attention of the guards, Emptor Academy seriously needed to upgrade their security system. Surely *somebody* would notice.

Although now that the casserole dish was no longer in my hands, I wanted to hit rewind and throw it at the blob that was slowly taking form in front of me instead.

"Well, that wasn't very hospitable, Emmy. It's not polite to destroy private property."

Ms. Pierce had a broad smile plastered across her delicately featured face.

Everything inside me lurched to a sudden stop. Fear was temporarily clouded by complete disbelief as I tried to make sense of the figure silhouetted in the doorway.

"But . . . you're a woman."

"Obviously someone wasn't paying close attention in class. Men aren't the only ones capable of murder." She tutted as if I'd asked for a deadline extension on an upcoming assignment. "That kind of thinking will get you killed."

"But the guy on the Starbucks security footage—"

She winked, as if sharing a private joke, and my stomach dropped a foot. "Everyone always focuses on the hat and the sweatshirt. As soon as I ditched them and added a swipe of red lipstick, I was virtually unrecognizable. The only second glances I got were from the idiots who still think women enjoy their wolf whistling."

"But why would you—"

"*Emmy*," Ms. Pierce said my name like a gentle rebuke. "Life is a gamble—and you lost. Well, technically, *I* lost, but once you hand over that Slate you've been hiding, my debt will be cleared."

"W-who holds the debt? Maybe we could work something out? I'm not opposed to vacuuming. Have I mentioned that I'm excellent at ironing clothes? Ironing. Folding. All of it."

She shook her head with mock disappointment. "This isn't that kind of debt, and trust me, you don't want to start making deals. I'm not the only one gunning for you." Ms. Pierce grinned at her own pun. "You'd have fared worse with the ones at the police precinct."

It was kind of hard to trust someone who planned on, y'know, *killing me.*

"You saw me there?" I croaked, my voice so thready I barely recognized it. "Why didn't you—" I couldn't get out the rest, my lips felt too clumsy for any of the euphemisms that sprang to mind. Why didn't you attack me? Whack me? End me?

Send me to the big coffee shop in the sky?

Ms. Pierce stepped farther into the room. "Patience isn't a virtue, Emmy. It's a skill set. If Frederick St. James hadn't rushed in to protect you, I never would have made the connection. Ironic, isn't it? That the place he thought you'd be safest only brought you closer to me." She laughed. "Fate is such a fickle bitch."

I stumbled slightly over my own feet as I backed away from her, the unmistakable sound of glass crunching underneath my sneakers filled the brief silence between us.

The security guards will notice the casserole dish on the lawn. It's just a matter of time.

Ms. Pierce didn't seem inclined to cut her lecture short, probably because it wasn't every day that she had such a rapt audience.

"I admit, I expected tracking you down would be far more time consuming, and since my employer doesn't like to be kept waiting, your stupidity has worked out for the best."

"*Hey!*" I protested. She was already getting paid to kill me, she didn't need to add insult to impending injury.

"I talked with some of your other teachers. You've made quite an impression on your first day. Very erratic behavior. Mouthing off to Mr. Bangsley, fleeing the cafeteria during lunch, and then getting caught with a boy in the girls' locker room." She shook her head in silent reproach, then threw a chair out the same window I'd shattered only minutes earlier. Fear paralyzed me. I wasn't sure if she intended to throw me out of the enormous hole or if the chair was part of some elaborate endgame she had concocted. I couldn't think clearly as larger chunks of glass skittered across the floor. "Those aren't the actions of an emotionally stable girl."

Right, because she was obviously such an expert on emotional stability.

"I tried to talk you down, of course, but you were inconsolable. You've been suffering from the worst delusions. Crippling paranoia. You even convinced yourself that someone wanted you *dead*. It's such a tragedy."

She was setting the scene. I remembered that much from her lecture on committing the perfect crime. Hearing her discuss my death so calmly had cold sweat trickling down my back.

"You're going to make it look like a suicide."

"Oh no, sweetie. You *are* going to commit suicide. Just as soon as you give me that Slate you've been hiding."

Fear zapped through me like an electric current. "What's the hurry? I'm not going anywhere. You don't want to mess it up by rushing like what's-her-name, do you?"

"Ruth Snyder." Ms. Pierce moved so swiftly that I was unprepared for her thin fingers to wrap around my arm, squeezing hard enough to bruise. "There's one pivotal difference: I don't have an obvious motive for murder. My employer requires complete discretion. Nobody will ever believe I had anything to gain by the death of a scholarship girl, especially one as staggeringly unexceptional as you. This school is full of opportunities and you've squandered every single one of them."

Something clicked inside me as Ms. Pierce began dragging me toward the shattered window.

I officially had nothing left to lose.

My scream cut the heavy silence, first like the demented croaking of a dying mongoose but gaining in strength. It was a relief to finally let out the sound that I'd been stuffing down for days—years, even—because it had never been the right place or time. Because I didn't want to make a fuss. Because nobody likes a complainer. Because good girls don't *scream*.

Well, screw that.

Ms. Pierce's smile never wavered. "Nobody is coming to save you, Emmy. Now you'll either hand me the Slate or I will take it from you. The end result will be the same."

She sounded like a teacher explaining a homework assignment, her voice filled with an unshakable sense of authority. Even as her free hand began pawing at my sweatshirt, I couldn't believe that she was the one behind all of this.

That *she* wanted me dead.

Sebastian's words from our first encounter in the police station came filtering back to me.

Adults aren't smarter, or nicer, or stronger, or less screwed up than teenagers—they're simply excellent liars.

He didn't have to convince me now. A self-satisfied grin came across Ms. Pierce's face as her palm connected with the outline of the Slate in my front pocket. It was the same look as in weight loss commercials when the "after" girl proudly holds up an empty pair of plus-sized pants. The most terrifying part wasn't that she wanted me dead; it was how sane she looked as she dragged me closer to death.

I went limp, my unexpected weight breaking through Ms. Pierce's hold and sending me crashing to the floor. Glass bit into my right side, but the adrenaline racing through my system helped me ignore the sharp slashes of pain. My legs flailed behind me, as I tried to trip her, overturn chairs between us, or even better, to connect a blow from my foot with her kneecap.

My voice was hoarse, but I didn't stop screaming, "Help! *Help me!*" through a throat that quickly felt as shredded as my side. Some distant part of my brain registered that the coppery taste in my mouth could only mean blood, but I couldn't tell if I'd bitten my tongue or split my lips or somehow managed to breathe in fine shards of glass. I wondered if the bitter acidic taste of rusty pennies would be the last thing I ever tasted. If the sickly sweet perfume of it would linger in my nostrils even when the cobblestones raced to greet me like an old friend.

My fingers splayed out on the floor, searching for any handhold that might keep her from launching me out the gaping hole in the window. Ms. Pierce tut-tutted again, then she snagged one sneaker-clad foot and yanked me across the glass-strewn hardwood floor. Thin shards of glass sliced through the denim of my jeans like an unstoppable trail of fire ants as my fingers clawed at the floor, closing around a larger piece that gouged into my hand. I gasped in pain.

Blood dripped from my palm as Ms. Pierce hauled me to my feet, never breaking eye contact. Her face dominated my field of vision, until she became the sole focus of my world. I soaked in every detail, from the clumpy mascara that she had swiped on her eyelashes earlier that day, to her winged jade-green eyeliner, to the faint trace of a white scar right above her left eye. None of it unsettled me more than the total lack of compassion in her gaze as she adjusted my sweatshirt with a few brisk movements. As if she was tidying me up for a big interview or helping me primp for a first date. I didn't realize it was possible to quake this hard with fear. I thought it was something that they showed on television as an excuse to hand the traumatized victim a blanket at the end of a procedural. The body-heaving shivers were supposed to be an excuse for the heroine to curl into the arms of her love interest.

It felt far too real to me now.

My whole body went numb as her hand slithered into my pocket, claiming the Slate for herself. I was cold. So frozen inside that I couldn't imagine ever unthawing. The only other time I'd felt this marrow-deep chill had been in the coffee shop, right after the old man had died on top of me. Trapped, scared, confused, none of that had changed. I wasn't any closer to understanding why Ms. Pierce had been hired to kill me now than I had been during my police interrogation.

The old man's warning rattled around some cold distant part of my brain.

You won't survive long in the business if you don't go for the jugular, girl. That's how I always did it.

Somehow I didn't think Frederick St. James would be particularly impressed with a tossed casserole dish and some screaming that sounded like an audition for Dead Girl #5 in a slasher movie. He'd have wanted more from me. He would have wanted me to protect the damn Slate.

Go for the jugular, girl.

I sucked in a short breath and followed a dead man's advice.

CHAPTER 30

I slashed out with the jagged piece of glass, hoping to connect with something—*anything*—except thin air.

Ms. Pierce had my wrist clamped before I'd made it even halfway to my target. Her movement was awkward, hindered by the Slate that she still clutched in her other hand. But the brutal strength of her grasp had me crying out in pain, struggling to loosen her hold on either me or the Slate. Both preferably. She merely frowned and increased the pressure. Unending waves of red-hot agony brought me to my knees as I waited for my bones to splinter then crack.

An irreverent part of my brain couldn't help pointing out that it was a damn shame I was about to die because otherwise this would've been great material for a romance novel. My hard-edged police detective could've been tortured by a cartel leader—and I could have described *exactly* how it felt to have pain slicing into each fingertip. How every nerve could scream with an ache that refused to ebb. These were the kind of details that really humanized a character, made them nice and sympathetic so that their dark moments came across as understandable reactions to past trauma instead of general jackassery.

Why *any* of that was occurring to me when I was kneeling before a killer was beyond me. I should have been thinking of something profound. Something about mortality and how love couldn't simply end with death, not when my mom would hear the echo of a whispered *I love you* every time she looked at my kindergarten art on the refrigerator. Every time she flipped through the photo album that chronicled every birthday, every first day of school, every major haircut, she'd see it in my smile. Every autumn she'd watch the leaves redden on the trees and search for one that was the exact same shade as my hair, and she'd smile quietly to herself when she spotted it.

That's what I should've been thinking in the grasp of a homicidal criminal law teacher.

Too bad my brain was still stuck on *Oh, shit.*

Ms. Pierce's scowl didn't lessen as the shard of glass slipped uselessly through my fingers, dropping to the ground. Triumph flashed in her eyes when her free hand tugged the Slate out of my pocket.

"Look at what you made me do. Bruises weren't part of the plan. I guess I can start a rumor that you got them from Sebastian. That you like it rough." She laughed wryly. "Slut-shaming is a horrible practice, but it's so wonderfully effective."

I couldn't manage anything more than a grunt of pain.

"It's been fun, Emmy." She yanked up on the wrist that was one twist away from snapping. "But it's time for you to be on your way."

There was no secret weapon tucked up my sleeve. No brilliant last-minute plan. My life was truly over, and while that scared me witless, it almost came as a relief. The burning pain that had clawed its way up my side before taking residency in my wrist, the gut-wrenching panic, all of it was about to disappear.

Oblivion was a tempting gift, even when it came at a crippling price.

Even when it meant losing everything.

Ms. Pierce stepped behind me, gripping my shoulders to propel me the few scant remaining inches between me and the window. I could feel the Slate digging into my back. She still had it tightly clutched in her right hand, unable to conceal it in her own pocket while I struggled and thrashed like a maniac.

"Jump, Emmy."

The cobblestones glinted coolly under the glow of a nearby lightpost, hypnotizing me. Maybe I'd look that remote, untouchable, when my body connected with solid ground. I wondered if anyone would leave flowers there to mark the spot, or if some groundskeeper would quickly blast away any residual bloodstain with a power washer.

"No." The word emerged as a croak as I splayed my fingers along both sides of the glass window. "I'm *not* jumping."

Ms. Pierce sighed, as if growing annoyed by my lackluster performance. Apparently, this whole murder thing was becoming tedious for her, rather like grading essays or filing income tax statements. She inhaled slowly through her nose like she was searching for divine patience while I tried to squirm away.

I couldn't break her grasp.

"Have a nice—"

My shoulders were jerked backward so abruptly that I didn't even have time to blink at the ceiling before I made contact with the hardwood floor. Hard. The pink and blue splotches that had danced before my eyes earlier flitted back once more. They drunkenly lurched across my field of vision, keeping rhythm with the slow aching throb of my head.

She'd changed her mind.

Ms. Pierce wasn't going to show me mercy—I knew better than to hope for *that*—but she must have decided a quick death was too good for me. She wasn't finished playing with me. Jerking me around. Toying with me until I would do anything, jump right out a third story window, just to make it stop.

Her face emerged out of a swirling pink haze, close enough for me to see that the eyeliner on her right lid was a smidgen too long. Close enough to see the rage simmering in the dark brown depths of her eyes. I scrambled away, bracing myself for a brand new slap of pain.

It never came.

Instead, I heard the unmistakable sound of a fist connecting with flesh. Broken gasps of agony, that weren't coming from me for a change. Every cell in my body screamed at me to *get the hell out of there.* To make a break for it. To run—not walk—out the door, down three flights of stairs, all the way back to the relative safety of the girls' dormitory or the computer lab.

I had to make someone call the cops.

Now. Right now.

Except that entire plan rested on my ability to drag myself off the floor. My left wrist couldn't support my weight, my right hand was a bloody mess, and every inch of the rest of me hurt too badly to tell if something was broken. My teeth clamped shut as I hissed through the pain to keep from crying out. Nobody appeared to be paying any attention to me.

But I'd been wrong about that before.

A disconcerting rhythm of physical contact filled the room like the bass line to a heavy metal song. I couldn't get a good look at my unexpected protector, beyond noting that he seemed to have at least an extra foot of height on Ms. Pierce. Some distant part of my brain pointed out that his enormous frame should be unforgettable. He was bulky and huge and should have been easy to identify in a police lineup. Except he was focused entirely on my homicidal teacher, which meant that he'd turned his back on me. As they struggled closer to the window the inevitable truth that someone wasn't going to make it out of the library alive jarred me out of my frozen panic. I didn't want to stick around for a swan-dive exit.

Especially because the enemy of my criminal law teacher might not be my friend.

I fled, limping my way past the broken remains of the chair I had placed under the door knob before I managed to lengthen my stride into a jerky gait. The animalistic sounds of serious fighting felt inescapable. Grunts, pained gasps, heavy breathing, the high-pitched scrape of glass beneath shoes as both combatants fought to stay standing—all of it was punctuated by the unmistakable slam of fists. I nearly slipped on some crushed glass when I risked a glance over my shoulder. Only grabbing onto the break room countertop saved me from falling on my face.

I skidded out of the room, fear churning deep inside me.

Two aisles of books to go.

One aisle.

I stumbled down the first flight of stairs, my breath coming in pants and wheezes that had me clutching onto the railing. A slick trail of blood marked my progress and my head spun sickeningly with every lurching step. Each movement sent a fresh wave of pain zipping through me. The floor pitched wildly, but I couldn't do more than sway forward, smacking right into one of the brick walls. I couldn't slow down. Couldn't do much more than absorb the pain with a gasp and stagger onward.

Ms. Pierce might be right behind me.

Given her track record, she wouldn't be preoccupied for long.

Fresh air on my sweaty skin was the closest thing to heaven I'd ever experienced, especially accompanied by the *whoosh* and *click* of the library door closing behind me. The sweet scent of cut grass almost overpowered the coppery taste of blood, but I couldn't stop to bury my nose in the lawn or kiss the cobblestones. Couldn't slow down. Couldn't pause to steady myself. I moved unsteadily past the break room chair that jutted out of the lawn like a demented modern art sculpture. I blindly weaved in a circle, searching for a campus security guard. A fellow student. At this point, even *Peyton* would have been a welcome sight.

A piercing scream reverberated in the cold night air.

My head jerked up and I watched in abject horror as a figure crashed through what little remained of the glass window. Arms windmilled in a desperate attempt to prevent the inevitable, as if that alone might counteract the pull of gravity. The sickening *crunch* of a body colliding with the cobblestones would haunt my nightmares forever.

That body was supposed to be mine.

That death had been intended for me.

And I wasn't out of the woods yet.

CHAPTER 31

Nothing makes people spring into action quite like a murder.

The security guards that were supposed to be protecting all the rich kids at Emptor Academy came barreling toward me, as if that would make a difference. As if that could erase the memory of what I'd just witnessed. As if they could whitewash the bloodstains and make everything as good as new. Pretend the darkness no longer existed.

I didn't know what to tell them.

Hey guys. Took you long enough. I'm doubled over and vomiting from relief, actually. Okay, and nausea. And pain. And adrenaline. P.S. If anyone touches me, I might puke on them. Fun fact.

I was too busy trying not to retch on my sneakers to say much of anything. I could hear them demanding backup before calling the NYPD to report a possible homicide. The words washed over me without sinking in. My body felt completely disconnected from the scene taking shape around me. The authoritative demands, the random snatches of conversation, the awkward attempts at sympathy from the security guard who'd been stuck with the unenviable job of watching me hurl; all of it sounded like a long-distance phone call with terrible reception.

I clutched the ripped denim of my jeans as my empty stomach heaved again.

Something inside me had broken. I didn't know what, exactly, but it was gone. Smashed to bits. Some frozen part of me kept repeating, *All the king's horses and all the king's men couldn't put Emmy together again.*

Just like there was no fixing the tangle of broken limbs on the lawn.

I couldn't even bring myself to provide a positive identification of the *corpse*. The security guard at my side kept asking me if I knew what happened. If I could answer their questions. If I could tell them *precisely* what I'd witnessed.

Except the only thing that terrified me more than looking into Ms. Pierce's lifeless eyes would be to discover that it hadn't been her. That my teacher had added yet another person to her body count because I hadn't been skilled enough to stop her.

Hadn't been smart enough. Brave enough. Strong enough.

A slow whistle cut off my security guard midquestion. "Somebody did a number on this lady, Joel," said another security guard who was standing over the corpse.

My knees crumbled and I collapsed onto the lawn. Pain flared brightly, then dimmed as wet blades of grass tickled my face and the world turned sideways. My Starbucks killer was dead. My Potential Hostile. My criminal law teacher.

She couldn't hurt me now.

That probably should have come as a relief, but it didn't. My blind panic refused to subside. I felt no comfort in her death. No sense of resolution. No closure. It didn't even the score or set anything to rights. There was no fixing the damage that she'd already done. Her death wouldn't bring Frederick St. James back. It wouldn't unravel the knot of terror in the pit of my stomach.

It wouldn't wipe the slate clean.

Just as there was nothing that could fix that jagged, broken part of me.

The guard hovering over me tried to inch closer to his partner. "You sure it wasn't self inflicted?"

"She didn't punch herself in the face, Joel!"

My shoulders shook uncontrollably, blades of grass poking at my cheeks like the tines of a hairbrush. I didn't want any more information. Didn't want to imagine bruises beneath the pallor of death on Ms. Pierce's delicate heart-shaped face. Didn't want to see limbs jutting out at unnatural angles. Her solemn words from that lecture in her classroom haunted me.

There is always fallout.

Nothing that involved Frederick St. James would ever come for free. Not admission to Emptor Academy and *definitely* not the Slate. Even my life came with a price tag attached to it. Saving me, killing me, there was a steep price to pay for both acts. I didn't know what the going rate of a vigilante rescue would cost me, what strings might come attached, if I'd ever be called upon to return the favor. Only one thing in the midst of all this turmoil seemed undeniable: I owed a stranger my life.

Given the way people around me kept turning up dead, I didn't want my friends to be anywhere near me when they called in my debt.

My throat burned as I struggled to pull myself together. To brace myself for all the questions the security guards were obviously dying to ask. I could think of half a dozen just off the top of my head.

What were you doing outside the library?

How were you hurt?

Did you see who killed Ms. Pierce?

What do you mean you don't know?! Who are you covering for? Or was it you? Do you understand the seriousness of this situation, young lady?

I was trembling, bruised, and too shell-shocked to cry but the cops would show no pity. As far as Detective Luke O'Brian would be concerned I was now implicated in not one but *two* homicide investigations. I wasn't going to be greeted with any high-fives or back pats in the homicide department for setting a brand-new record in my age bracket. Just a longer stay of residency in the same cold interrogation room.

I was still on my own.

My eyes slid shut. Pain continued throbbing in my head, until it felt like it might crack open. I never wanted to move. Refused to imagine standing on my own two feet when it felt so nice sprawling out on the manicured lawn. I heard approaching footsteps and flicked my eyes open only long enough to identify the security guard vest. I didn't know how many minutes I'd spent slumped motionlessly on the grass.

I didn't much care.

"Emmy?" An enormous hand reached for my shoulder. I jerked away from the touch like a feral street cat. "Easy there, kid. You're going to be okay. Your friends are on their way."

My empty laugh emerged as a hoarse rasp. It had already started. There would be no stopping the flood of *You're-going-to-be-fine*s and the *It's-all-over-now*s. Except you couldn't box up this kind of ugliness and neatly tuck it away forever.

I couldn't pretend the dead body fifteen feet away from me didn't exist. She did. Ms. Pierce was every bit as real, as undeniable, as the dried blood splattered across my fingers.

"Look at me, Emmy." The voice was gruff, commanding. I instinctively glanced up into Force's concerned brown eyes, bracing myself for another empty platitude.

"I'm here, kid."

A cold trickle of disappointment dripped through me. Force was no better than the rest of them. No better than the men in uniform who would take my statement in a matter of minutes. When the world really went to shit, Force could only offer the same meaningless words of encouragement that everyone else shelled out.

He bent down until his face was right next to mine. I jolted again, terrified by a new weight slipping into the pocket of my sweatshirt dragging it down. An electric burst of panic and pain nearly made me curl into the fetal position.

This couldn't be happening. Not again. Not when owning the Slate had left me marked for *murder*. Not when I was so completely unequipped to deal with homicidal maniacs and danger and rich kids who toyed with me for their own amusement. My painfully dry eyes scanned Force's face, catching a hint of warmth in his dark brown eyes when he nodded. Coming from him the subtle gesture was enormous. My fingers trembled as they fumbled inside my sweatshirt and brushed against the tablet I'd failed to protect only a few minutes earlier. The one I hadn't once considered when I'd decided to run for my life in a blind panic. My heart thudded to a stop as the full implication of that finally sank in.

Force had committed murder.

For me.

"Like I said, I'm here for you, kid." Force's voice was low— calm and steady—but it didn't reassure me.

"Y-you . . . you . . . you." My frozen lips refused to shape any other words. "You."

"Me." Force smiled tightly, as if he wanted to share a raunchy joke in the middle of a funeral. "You might not want to mention it to your friend. I already scare her. I have your answer now."

I stared at him blankly, unable to follow the strange conversation shift.

"In the car. I said I'd get back to you."

Right. I'd asked him about fear. That felt like a lifetime ago, back before I'd nearly plummeted through a window to my death. Back when I naively thought I'd already experienced the most terrifying event of my life. I barely managed a nod.

"Fear can paralyze a person, but it's got nothing on relief. That'll knock you flat." He gave me a final lingering once-over, evaluating every visible cut and scrape, before nodding, straightening, and walking toward the two security guards.

As if committing murder was all in a day's work for him.

"*Emmy!*" Audrey sprinted toward me as I struggled to pry myself off the lawn. "Are you okay?" She didn't give me a chance to answer before wrapping her arms around my waist. "Sebastian got a text that something happened and—please tell me you're okay."

Guilt drenched her words and I knew that she was a heartbeat away from blaming herself for letting me stumble blindly into danger.

"Never better," I croaked. "I still owe you a coffee."

She laughed, her slight frame quivering as she clung to me. "You don't owe me anything."

"Love you, Aud." An unwanted tear snaked its way down my cheek, stinging against my fresh cuts and scrapes. "Always."

It wasn't much, but I couldn't seem to manage anything more. My lower lip continued trembling as I caught glimpses of my new classmates gasping, whispering, exchanging horror-stricken stares of shock. I thought I heard muffled sobs clinging to the air, but I wasn't sure. Everything kept blurring before snapping into hyperfocus. Kayla's shimmery top sparkled in the dim light of dawn as she hovered near the sidelines, clearly unwilling to interrupt this moment with my best friend.

"I love you, too," Audrey's voice cracked. "Scare me like that again and I'll kill you myself."

I faked a weak smile. "I'm h-h-harder to kill than you might think."

She laughed without humor and continued holding me. I didn't know how much time passed. Didn't much care that I was dead weight in her arms. Couldn't bring myself to pull away from the one person I trusted here not to be secretly planning my murder.

A slight hush spread across the crowd, and I lifted my chin from Audrey's shoulder in time to watch President Gilcrest muscle his way forward. He didn't appear surprised to find the body of an employee sprawled in a bloody heap on the grass.

"What has happened here tonight is a great loss for our community," President Gilcrest announced gravely. "Rachel Pierce was a valued member of our Emptor Academy family and her absence will be deeply felt. A grief counselor will be here tomorrow to talk with anyone who wants an appointment. In the meantime, please return to your rooms." He turned his attention on me, only to frown when he caught sight of Audrey. "You're not a student here."

Audrey didn't look remotely cowed. "Nope. Best friend. Tech genius. It really depends on who you ask. I'm here to pack up Emmy's stuff and take her home."

"The police will be here shortly. In the meantime, why don't you—"

"Take care of my best friend?" Audrey suggested, resting one hand gently on the small of my back for support. "Great idea. We'll be collecting Emmy's stuff."

Then Audrey helped me stumble away, without giving him a chance to object.

CHAPTER 32

Audrey and Kayla both banned me from packing when I tossed a shimmery gold lamé top into my suitcase.

It was probably the right call. I didn't know what was hers and what was mine, and I didn't particularly care what I took with me. All that mattered was getting away from Emptor Academy alive.

Too bad I couldn't leave without talking to the police officers that were on their way.

"Emmy? *Emmy?*"

I blinked at Audrey and shook my head slightly. Whatever she'd just said to me, I hadn't caught a word of it.

"Why don't you go clean up?" She escorted me into the nearby communal bathroom, pointedly tugging open the curtain of my shower and then closing it behind me. I shrugged out of my clothes as she rambled on about her math homework in an obvious ploy to distract me from replaying the events of the last hour. Except everything she said flowed right over me in a rush of white noise, like a yoga soundtrack set for "babbling brook" or "low ocean swells."

Hot water beat down on my face, but I couldn't get warm.

My fingers shook uncontrollably. It took three attempts for me to successfully shove my sopping wet bangs out of my face, and then the adrenaline deserted me. My legs crumpled and I found myself sitting numbly on the shower floor, staring at the red smear that mingled with two strands of some other girl's hair before it swirled down the drain. A cleaning crew would arrive within a matter of hours to scrub every inch of the place.

They would ensure it returned to its pristine condition.

I wished they could scrub my soul clean in the process.

My teeth chattered so hard that I nipped the tip of my tongue and whimpered in pain.

"Are you okay in there, Em?" The curtain rustled as Audrey peeked her head inside. My body was curled into a ball, my forehead pressed against my knees as my teeth clacked together as if they were attempting a complicated tap dance routine. Audrey sucked in a horrified breath. "Stay there, okay? Stay right there!"

I couldn't have moved even if I'd wanted to disobey her. My trembling legs wouldn't support me anymore, they had officially gone on strike, leaving me huddled on the floor.

I'd finally reached a standstill.

Actually, it was more of a sitstill. I dimly wondered if *this* was what Force had meant about relief having the power to flatten me. If he'd somehow known that I would end up paralyzed on the bathroom floor, unable to feel warmth even as scalding water pounded down on my head and steam filled my lungs.

Force had predicted my personal meltdown so easily, I wondered if he saw the same weakness inside of me that Ms. Pierce—*Rachel*—had spotted. I hadn't known her name until President Gilcrest had said it aloud, and part of me wished I'd never heard it. Rachel was the sort of name that belonged to a girl who enjoyed sleepovers and horseback riding and dealt with the occasional flare-up of acne. Rachels were supposed to have close friends, maybe a soft spot for truly excellent croissants, and a penchant for bizarre baby names.

They weren't supposed to become vicious killers.

Rachel Pierce would have mocked the tears sliding down my pale cheeks. I had no trouble imagining her derisive sneer, her voice as flat and cold as the tiles at my back.

You can't expect to cry your way through life, Emmy. It doesn't work. At some point those sad little puppy eyes of yours won't be cute. And when that goes, you'll have nothing left.

A scream bubbled up in the back of my throat, but emerged as nothing more than a garbled moan. Audrey must have heard it though, because she yanked back the curtain, shut off the water, and hastily wrapped my body in a familiar neon orange comforter. The shivers, the teeth chattering, the trembling, none of it stopped, but Audrey didn't ask if I was okay. She didn't say a word. She simply lifted wet strands of hair off my neck and guided me out of the shower. Then she settled against my side, fingers laced with mine, on the tile floor of the bathroom.

Somebody religious might be able to convince themselves that the snapping of my teacher's bones, the death-rattle of Frederick St. James, every gut-wrenching, nausea-inducing moment of the past few days had happened so that I could fully appreciate this silence with Audrey. That it had all been part of some grand *higher purpose*. Except Rachel Pierce's death didn't make me want to become a better, kinder, more generous human being.

I was a cold, hollow husk of the girl I'd once been.

"Emmy?" Kayla's disembodied voice echoed from the bathroom door. "The police are here. They have some questions for you."

"Tell them that she'll be there in a minute." Audrey brushed a water-logged lump of hair away from my left eye. "I'll grab you some clean clothes, Em. You stay right here. You don't have to say a word to them, okay?"

I nodded, unsure what I could confess without making everything worse.

Sure, Ms. Pierce had killed Frederick St. James, but someone else had hired her to do it. Probably the same someone who wanted me dead.

There was no subtle way to mention any of *that* during a police interrogation.

Audrey returned with an armful of clothes, including my comfiest jeans, the same ones that she'd repeatedly insisted I needed to throw out. It was a total pity gesture. Maybe if another homicidal crazy person took a swing at me, she'd stop critiquing my sweatshirt with the obvious tear along the left cuff.

If not for the endless throbbing pain and crippling panic, it might almost be worth it.

"Do you need help getting dressed?" Audrey asked, setting the fresh set of clothes haphazardly next to the damp pile that had gotten splashed by the hot spray.

"Got it," I mumbled. I crawled over to the heap, wrapped in my soaked comforter like an ancient Egyptian who couldn't afford high quality mummification. My clumsy fingers needed four tries to fasten my bra, attempting buttons of any kind would have been beyond me. Luckily I could yank the jeans up my legs without unbuckling, unsnapping, or unzipping. The challenge was usually in keeping them perched on my hips, not in putting them on. The worn denim clung to my shower damp skin, despite the additional weight of the Slate that I removed from my dirty, blood-smeared sweatshirt. I knew I was being reckless with the Slate. That I wasn't even *pretending* to guard it. But I still felt too numb to care. Too deadened inside to touch that damn sweatshirt even a millisecond before absolutely necessary.

It was one article of clothing I would happily allow Audrey to destroy.

"Emmy?"

I was sick of hearing my own name, especially with that tentative note of uncertainty. It was like Audrey thought repeating it with a breathy question mark in her voice could stave off any further meltdowns.

"Do you need any help in there?"

"I've got it," I repeated waspishly. It took every last ounce of my determination to walk out of the bathroom, down the hallway, and into my former dorm room where the NYPD already sat waiting for me. I paused before making contact with the doorknob, mentally debating the pros and cons of fleeing back into the bathroom and refusing to leave.

Pro: I would never have to wait for the shower. Ever.
Con: I'd have to bribe someone to bring me food.
Pro: Nobody could use up all the hot water before me.
Con: The school might turn off the water just to make me come out.

It could really go either way.

I pushed the door open only to reveal Sebastian, Nasir, and Kayla sitting on the edge of my bed as my least favorite detective paced in front of them. Luke O'Brian's head jerked toward me, noting the pallor in my cheeks and the wet tendrils of hair plastered across my forehead with the most sympathetic smile in his repertoire.

"Oh good, you're here. I was getting worried. Why don't you take a seat, Miss Danvers? Do you need a blanket? Are you cold?"

I shook my head slowly in disbelief. It was a little late for the man who'd taunted me in the interrogation room to feign concern. He sounded so anxious to please, as if he'd been ordered to claim that this had all been one big misunderstanding.

"Emmy, I owe you an apology. I never thought your life was in any danger, only that you were withholding critical information from me. If I'd known, our first conversation would've gone differently."

"If you'd known what?" I asked.

His self-condemning grimace unnerved me. I didn't trust this abrupt mea culpa. It was a little too good to be true.

I didn't belong at Emptor Academy, but Mr. Bangsley's warning that if something looks too good to be true, get out, resonated inside me. So maybe I hadn't been a total failure as a student. I merely lacked certain key survival skills, like how to ward off homicidal psychopaths.

Skills I could theoretically learn here.

I sat down on the tangled sheets next to Kayla.

"That someone was targeting you, of course." His face contorted into his best attempt at sympathy. "Why don't you tell us what happened tonight, Miss Danvers? Start from the beginning."

I cleared my throat, unsure where the beginning even began anymore. Did it still start with Sebastian's grandfather in that Starbucks? Was it my enrollment at Emptor Academy? My first— and last—class taught by the woman who tried to shove me out of a window? The splintering of the library door? The desperate brawl on the floor of the break room?

The sound of Rachel Pierce's final shriek?

All of those firsts felt like they'd been smeared into an ugly stain and then tattooed into my skin.

"I wanted some fresh air," I mumbled, unwilling to mention the computer lab in case that would somehow implicate Audrey in this mess. "Ms. Pierce must have followed me."

That thought broke through my numbness, dousing me with a cold rush of fear.

"Did she offer any explanations? Any justifications?"

Instead of answering immediately, I shoved up my sweatshirt sleeves to reveal the worst of my cuts and bruises. Kayla gasped, sprang to her feet, and headed straight for the closet. She returned with an enormous first aid kit and began patching me up.

"She grabbed me."

Detective Dumbass nodded solemnly, as if he were trying to commiserate. "But did she *say* anything?"

"It all happened so fast. I tried to run, but she caught me and—" My throat constricted as Ms. Pierce's twisted smile danced tauntingly in my mind.

"And what, Miss Danvers? I can't help you if you keep withholding information."

"She said that my death was payment for a debt," I spat out the words, hating the sharp taste of fear that lingered in my mouth. "That she needed a clean slate."

I remembered the rest of what she said, but kept it to myself. She said that she wasn't alone. That the others were even worse.

I hesitated, dread pounding harder with every beat of my pulse. Earlier that night, I'd regretted not taking Ben's advice to turn the Slate over to the cops. To leave the crime solving up to the professionals. To remove myself entirely from the equation.

I could fix that mistake right now. Somehow the trail I'd taken had looped back to the original fork. The road not taken stretched out before me and maybe—just maybe—walking down it would make all the difference.

All I had to do was open my mouth and tell the truth. But warnings were racing through my head.

If it looks too good to be true, get out.

I hissed in pain as Kayla cleaned out a particularly deep cut.

You'd have fared worse with the ones at the police precinct.

Rachel Pierce had no reason to lie, which meant someone else could be biding their time, lurking beneath the protection of a badge. Ms. Pierce's employer didn't sound like the type who'd easily accept failure. If my death was significant enough to clear her debt, I doubted he'd flinch at the prospect of ordering someone else to finish the job.

Who better to ask than an officer in the NYPD?

"It sounded like she had a gambling debt. A big one," I said slowly. "Maybe it made her unstable? I really don't know."

Detective Luke swiveled on Audrey, obviously hoping she'd be the weak link in the group.

"Do you have something you'd like to share, Miss . . . ?"

"Weinstein," Audrey supplied, and his eyebrow winged up in surprise at the Jewish last name combined with her obvious Asian heritage. "I missed all the action. Emmy sounded like she'd had a rough first day, so I came to take her home. That's it."

Detective Dumbass didn't look like he believed a word of it.

I couldn't let Audrey get in trouble. Not over this. Not over *me*.

"She forced me into the library, threw the chair out the window." My voice quavered as residual fear swamped me, but at least I had recaptured the detective's attention. "I tried to fight back, I did, b-but she was so much stronger. There was glass everywhere and . . . I-I don't know what happened. She dragged me to the window. I collapsed . . . and I don't know. I fled. That's all I can tell you."

Sebastian rose to his feet. "It's been a pleasure, Detective. I'm sure you're needed over at the crime scene. We wouldn't want to keep the coroner waiting, especially now that you've taken all our statements. I think it's time for you to leave."

"I'm in no hurry." He crossed his arms in what he clearly considered a power play. The *I'm-so-sorry-this-happened-to-you* façade slipping from his face. "I still have plenty of questions."

"And you're more than welcome to ask them—later—when our lawyers are present."

At the mention of lawyers, Detective Luke looked like a shot of whiskey had gone down the wrong pipe. Then he recrossed his arms with all the confidence of a gambler with a pair of aces tucked up his sleeve.

"We've made some progress in your grandfather's murder investigation."

Sebastian said nothing, gave nothing away, as he leaned back against the headboard of my bed. The rest of us traded apprehensive looks.

"We've identified the drugs in your grandfather's system as a lethal cocktail of antidepressants and antipsychotics, including lithium, Lamictal, and Thorazine. It's unclear which medications, if any, your grandfather had a prescription for and which were involuntarily administered to him." He looked annoyed with his own words, as if he had been hoping for an excuse to snap a pair of handcuffs around Sebastian's wrists. "The Slate you described has yet to be recovered."

Sebastian didn't so much as blink. "Fascinating. If that's all—"

"We also found a scrap of paper in his pocket. Do the words *Tamam shud* mean anything to you?"

An oppressive silence filled the room as everyone eyed Sebastian. Studying him, waiting, expecting *something*.

"No," Sebastian said simply, crossing the room and swinging open the door. "But you'll be the first to know if anything comes to mind."

Detective O'Brian hovered, staring at each one of us in turn, his eyes resting on my face the longest, as if mentally cataloging my every feature for his report. Then he leaned in close and murmured, "Give your mom my best," before sauntering out.

Sebastian shut the door behind him with a lot more force than necessary.

"He's dead," Nasir whispered into the sudden silence. "He's really dead."

Sebastian glared at his best friend. "We don't know that for sure."

"*Tamam shud*, Sebastian. He wrote, *Tamam shud*." Tears welled in Nasir's eyes, and he tipped his face toward the light fixture on the ceiling to prevent them from spilling over.

Sebastian didn't have a snarky comeback. There was no sarcastic quip, no sneer, no mocking tilt to his raised eyebrows. His face looked so remote and hard. Cold. The only physical indication that he might be upset was in the way his jaw clenched.

As if he were biting back a scream of his own.

"What does *Tamam shud* mean?" Kayla asked softly.

"Those are the last two words of a poem from my grandpa's favorite book, *The Rubáiyát of Omar Khayyám*, in the original Persian." Sebastian sounded like he was delivering a rehearsed speech, a recitation of facts that he'd memorized for the occasion. There was no hint of a personal attachment. It was as if that spark of defiance, insolence, arrogance—whichever one it was that fueled him—had been cloaked in sheets of ice.

"*Tamam shud* means 'ended' or 'finished.'" His mouth twisted in a bitter imitation of a smile. "But if—*if*—he's dead, it means that I'm only getting started."

CHAPTER 33

Sebastian had zero interest in explaining that vague statement of extreme vaguery.

He hesitated only briefly at the door. "Force will escort you home in ten minutes." Then he walked away, because apparently he didn't feel the need to waste time with basic civilities like, oh, I dunno, eye contact, before disappearing from sight.

"I should probably—" Nasir didn't finish the sentence since it was obvious to everyone that he needed to keep his unpredictable best friend from doing something stupid. He nodded a quick, awkward goodbye, and left the room.

Audrey exhaled in relief the second he was gone.

"We. Are. Never. Doing. This. Again." She raked a hand through her jet black hair, then forced herself to sit up. She grabbed my suitcase and started tugging it toward the door. "Let's go, Em."

"You're really leaving then?" Kayla's eyes dulled in disappointment. "I was kind of hoping you'd change your mind. Emptor Academy isn't usually this murder-y." Her whole face lit up with enthusiasm. "Did I tell you about the guest lecturers that are coming to campus soon? There are tons of amazing opportunities for students." Her voice trailed off as I slung my bag over my aching right shoulder.

This school is full of opportunities and you've squandered every single one of them.

The echo of Ms. Pierce's words sent an unexpected flare of pain through me. It was as if my body had fallen asleep during my brief conversation with my least favorite homicide detective, and now millions of pins and needles jabbed mercilessly at my nerve endings.

I glanced out the dorm window at the silhouette of the magnificent brick buildings, the perfectly manicured lawns, and the meandering cobblestone pathways. The early morning light tinged everything gold until it gleamed like a Photoshopped screensaver. The view was wasted on me. All I could see were the broken remains of my criminal law teacher. All I could hear was her last piercing shriek. The prestige of Emptor Academy was an illusion, nothing more than a coat of cheap polish to hide the nicks and scratches. The gouges and scrapes. The scars and blood.

Now it owned a dark splintered part of my soul that I never wanted to claim.

This place wasn't my home, not yet, maybe not *ever*, but it suited the alter ego I'd imagined in the library. It beckoned her to stay with the promise of strength. Power. Control. Leaving Emptor Academy would be trading in the world I'd found at the bottom of the rabbit hole for an ordinary existence. Except if I walked out, I'd still be resigning myself to a lifetime spent checking over my shoulder for the Cheshire Cat. Fleeing from the Queen of Hearts. Pretending to ignore the specter of Nemmy crooking her little finger as she whispered that together we could become so much more.

"Just think it over, okay?" Kayla said, turning on the puppy dog eyes. "Both of you."

Audrey looked surprised at being pulled into the conversation. "Never going to happen."

"I'll consider it." I managed a weak, unconvincing smile to keep Kayla from following us down to the pathway, rattling off a thousand and one reasons to stay. Then I shut the door.

Audrey didn't say a word as we exited the manor house and slid into the sleek black Town Car waiting for us at the curb. The quiet came as a relief. My voice needed a rest as badly as my bruised body did, and I embraced the silence that settled over us. The rhythm of the car lulled me into a weird semi-trance as the outside world flashed past me. There was nothing for me to control, no schedule for me to follow, no Potential Hostile watching me from the shadows.

Frederick St. James had written it in Persian, but I had no trouble spelling it out in English.

It was *over.*

Done. Finished. Completed.

At least that's what I really wanted to convince myself, because the possibility that somebody might still be planning my murder already had me teetering on the edge of another meltdown.

Audrey cleared her throat and pointed awkwardly at the familiar apartment complex.

"I've got to go, Em. I'm sorry I couldn't—" she glanced over nervously at Force and hastily concealed the rest of her apology with a shrug. The determined point of her chin made me want to confess everything. Tell her that I *had* cracked the Slate. All on my own.

At the very least, I'd turned it into a flash-bang. That had to count for *something.*

Except I couldn't tell Audrey anything in front of Force without also explaining that he'd saved my life by shoving my teacher out of a third-story window. A discussion that was pretty much guaranteed to send me into another panic spiral. I couldn't handle any more tonight. Then again, I wasn't convinced I could keep it together tomorrow. But that was a problem for later.

So I gave her shoulder a weak shove. "Get out of here before your parents think you're having a secret affair in a Town Car."

Audrey rolled her eyes before climbing out of the backseat. "Not everyone sees the world as a romance novel, Emmy." She flashed one last warm parting smile before entering the building.

Force waited expectantly behind the wheel. "Where do you want to go now?"

I was tempted to say something ridiculous. *Drive me to Vegas, Force. Don't stop until I see the bright lights of an Elvis-themed wedding chapel.* The guy hadn't flinched at the prospect of committing murder on my behalf. Compared to that, a road trip was nothing. The two of us could gorge on all-you-can-eat buffets before parting ways so that I could watch Cirque du Soleil while Force tested his luck at the craps tables.

I dismissed the bizarre take-your-bodyguard-on-vacation daydream by rattling off a familiar address instead.

He raised an eyebrow. "You sure you don't want me to take you home, kid?"

"Positive," I lied.

Force merged with traffic so smoothly that I wondered what other skills he might have tucked up his sleeve. Getaway driver. Combat specialist. He was probably well-versed in torture techniques, both at employing and withstanding them. Probably an expert survivalist, too.

I was trying to picture Force in hand-to-paw combat with a grizzly bear as he pulled the car up to the destination I'd given him. I had my fingers resting on the handle when he finally spoke again.

"You've got my number. Don't wait so long to use it next time."

I stared at the back of his head in confusion. "What are you talking about?"

"Your text."

"I never texted you."

"Yes, you did. From the library. Have you been checked for a concussion?" Force swiveled in the driver's seat so that he could pin me with his muddy brown eyes. "What's your name?"

"Emmy Violet Danvers," I said dutifully, not about to argue with him over a nonexistent text message. "I don't think I have a concussion. Name, rank, and social security number, right? It's 548—"

Force cut me off with a low growl. "You *never* give out that information!"

"But—"

"*No exceptions!*"

"I've got it."

He continued mumbling under his breath, something about protecting kids who gave out their own damn social security numbers. He seemed to be enjoying his tirade, so I lingered in the back seat until he'd gotten it all out of his system.

It was the least I could do.

Force opened the driver's door, efficiently carrying my suitcase to the top step of the building. It was five o'clock in the morning, and he'd shoved a woman to her death only a few hours earlier, but he didn't reveal even the slightest bit of strain.

"This isn't goodbye, kid. I'll be seeing you around."

I nodded, fighting down a sudden urge to grab him. To make him promise to keep me safe. To teach me how to fight so that I could never be this afraid again. To ask if he had any regrets over what he'd done—if he secretly wished that our paths hadn't crossed. Instead, I murmured a goodbye, typed in the building code, and wheeled my suitcase inside. Every step made my shoulder throb. My side ache. My noodle arms pleaded for relief. It had never taken me this long to trudge the short distance, and I struggled not to slump against my suitcase. Not to fall asleep right out in the open where anyone could find me.

Just a little farther.

The metallic scrape of the key sliding into the lock filled me with a strange sense of inevitability. As if I couldn't possibly have died today because this was where I belonged. I fumbled open the door, navigated my way around the deserted kitchen table, and cautiously wheeled my suitcase around the squeaky patch of flooring. Then I paused to lightly rap on the last door down the short hallway.

Silence.

I tested the handle, relief swamping me when it turned beneath my bandaged palm. Then I tiptoed inside with my suitcase before easing the door shut behind me.

"Ben?" I whispered.

No response.

I could make out the basic outline of his prone body beneath a tangle of sheets and blankets. I froze, staring intently at his silhouette while part of me hoped he would roll over and send the blankets sliding to the floor. Watching him sleep was a complete violation of his privacy, but I couldn't seem to work up any real guilt over it. Desire felt a hell of a lot better than the cold panic that still gripped me.

He mumbled something incomprehensible into his pillow.

"Ben?"

"*LemmealoneCam.*" The garbled command took me a moment to unpack. Leave. Me. Alone. Cam.

I'd just been downgraded from platonic best friend to little brother status.

Great.

"It's not Cam."

"Notmakingpancakes."

I toed off my shoes and stilled, uncertain. Nemmy probably would've launched a full-blown seduction campaign only hours after a close call with death. Then again, Nemmy wouldn't sneak into a boy's bedroom while on the verge of a nervous breakdown and looking like a half-drowned rat. At the very least, she would have finger-combed her wet hair into a vague semblance of order.

I was too exhausted to fake a smile, let alone put on a whole devil-may-care persona.

So I repeated his name, louder this time, as I edged closer to the bed. "Ben."

Some part of his subconscious must have recognized the urgency in my voice, because he twisted in bed and stared up at me in confusion. "Emmy?"

"Yeah. It's me." My teeth resumed their tap dance routine as I inched closer until I was well within his reach. Not that I expected him to pull me against his body or anything.

That was pure fantasy.

"What's wrong?" Ben rubbed his eyes. "Are you okay?"

"I-I—" I couldn't seem to find the right words. Hell, I couldn't seem to find *any* words. "No. I'm not."

"What happened?" he demanded. "Did someone hurt you?"

I shook my head. "I don't . . . I need you." I sucked in a deep breath before perching on the side of his bed. "C-could you lie to me, Ben?"

He straightened, eyeing me warily, as if I'd asked to borrow his mom's credit card and passport. "Why do you want that?"

"Because you d-don't lie to me. Ever. So if you t-tell me that I'm going to be okay, I'll b-believe you." My teeth chattered so hard that saying anything else was beyond me. Every part of me shook, and not in the sexy trembling way of a heroine filled with uncontrollable lust, but like a skinny Chihuahua forced outside without a sweater.

"Lie to me," I whispered, afraid that if I closed my eyes I'd be back in the library, crawling on the glass-strewn floor, with Rachel Pierce's thin fingers wrapped around my ankle. That I'd relive the mocking jeer in her voice, her high-pitched scream, the horrific crack of broken bones. "Lie to me, please. Lie—"

"Emmy." Ben's touch was gentle, hesitant, like he was afraid I'd shatter. "You're going to be okay."

I stared blindly at the doorway that I had blocked with my suitcase. Any second now somebody would take me away. Somebody would interrogate me. Accuse me. Mock me.

Kill me.

"I'm not lying to you." Ben wrapped an arm around my waist and tugged me against him. Ignoring the tangled blanket between us, I burrowed into the warm wall of his chest. My muscles remained tense, but he didn't seem to mind. He didn't loosen his hold even when I shook with hiccuping sobs.

"It's okay, Em. Whatever happened, we'll figure it out, okay? It's going to be okay."

That was the last thing I heard before sleep claimed me.

CHAPTER 34

There was a Post-it stuck to the pillow next to mine when I woke up.

Welcome home, was written in Ben's familiar scrawl. He didn't sign it *Love, Ben* or *Always, Ben* or anything else that I could have spent hours evaluating. There was no secret message hidden inside the two simple words.

It wasn't code for *I love you madly, desperately, eternally.*

All it meant was *welcome home.*

I had enough craziness in my life without blowing a simple sticky note out of proportion.

Especially since I'd barged into his bedroom before dawn—uninvited—and immediately dissolved into a puddle of tears.

Pathetic.

I shoved my hair away from my gritty, red-rimmed eyes. I never should've crawled into Ben's bed like a five-year-old afraid of finding monsters in her closet. I should have made the mature, responsible choice and gone straight home to my mom.

Ben's parents had to be at work by now, their sons were at school, making me an interloper in an empty apartment. I was still scared witless. Last night my total lack of direction had come as a relief. Force had taken the wheel, and I'd only needed to keep it together long enough to knock on Ben's bedroom door. Technically, I began my meltdown in the apartment hallway, but whatever. I had shoved away all thoughts of the future. Except the tomorrow I'd envisioned was today and the rest of the world wasn't going to slow down just because I felt like a white-bellied fish about to be gutted.

I needed a new plan.

A nuanced survival strategy, with bullet points and checklists and a multi-pronged approach aimed at keeping me safe.

Instead, I slid out of the bed and fumbled inside my suitcase for my photo album. Maybe it was self-indulgent to hide in the pages of the past, but I didn't care. Future Emmy would just have to deal with it. I sat cross-legged on the warm bed, cocooned in blankets, flipping through pictures that I'd examined thousands of times.

My mom grinned back at me from each page, flaunting over-dramatic poses in front of dozens of Los Angeles landmarks. I tried to imagine what it would have been like to visit California as a family. I could almost feel the oppressive heat of the sun, taste the gritty layer of dust that would coat my teeth near the Hollywood sign, feel my cheek muscles tighten into a stilted smile for the camera, hear my dad insist on taking a few more shots of his girls.

It would have felt like heaven.

I flipped to the close-up photo of my dad's left eye, searching it once more for some trace of emotion—sadness, anxiety, impatience, amusement—I'd accept anything.

Nothing.

Except this time the tingly *you-are-missing-something-right-under-your-nose* feeling refused to ease. It prickled, growing in intensity, until I sat rooted with an overwhelming sense of certainty.

I was *definitely* missing something here.

Something important.

My hand automatically slid into my sweatshirt for the Slate that I'd spent the night ignoring. I hadn't wanted to think about it. I'd been an emotional trainwreck *before* Force had slipped the Slate into my pocket, and having it back had only intensified my anxiety. I'd tried. I'd done my best to get my panic under control. To keep a cool head.

Given the way I had sobbed hysterically all over Ben, I couldn't have failed any harder.

Internally cringing, I turned on the Slate.

It wasn't password-protected anymore.

Welcome Emmy Danvers looped and curled across the screen in a swirling script, knocking out my breath faster than a sucker punch in the stomach.

It really had been intended for *me*. Not Sebastian. Not President Gilcrest or Force or anybody else. Me. It was my name plastered across the home screen. I didn't doubt that Frederick St. James had found the wrong girl, but my fingers couldn't stop trembling as I clicked the inbox.

You have 438 new text messages.

I skimmed over half a dozen of them, most of which included the word *payment* before listing five-digit sums. One client in particular appeared to be growing increasingly desperate for a response judging by the excessive use of exclamation points. The names of the senders were blocked, but half a dozen of them shared Rachel Pierce's creepy mocking cadence. A chill shuddered through me.

Eeny, meeny, miny, moe.
String up a girl by her toe.
When she hollers, let her go.
Eeny, meeny, miny, moe.

A wave of panic knotted my stomach so tightly I fought back a wave of nausea.

She was dead.

Ms. Pierce had been skilled enough to hide her insanity from her Emptor Academy colleagues, but even she couldn't cheat death. Not when Force had delivered the final push. There was also one person Ms. Pierce hadn't been able to trick—not completely—and I clicked on the camera icon to see the world through the eyes of a dead man.

The first image on the screen was me.

It wasn't the most flattering of photos. My face was scrunched with annoyance, my eyebrows furrowed, as I glared at the screen of a bulky laptop, tuning out the mid-afternoon Starbucks crowd. It was strange seeing myself at the table where it all began. The girl in the photo deserved to have "BEFORE" plastered over her forehead in giant block letters. She looked blissfully ignorant of her own danger. Clueless that in a handful of minutes her world would shatter all around her.

Unprepared to be terrorized, hunted, and nearly shoved out of a third story window.

I zoomed in on my face, wanting to study the girl Frederick St. James had chosen to drag into this mess. My index finger traced the thin lines of frustration that bracketed my eyes, accidentally leaving a trail of bright green dots in my wake. Instead of fading or disappearing when I failed to give the Slate a direct command, a tiny book graphic appeared with moving black squiggles as it flashed: *Loading. Loading. Loading.*

Loading *what*, I didn't know.

The book enlarged until it consumed the whole screen before transforming into a detailed case file. In the top right corner sat my unflattering high school photo, and beneath it was a stalker's treasure trove of information.

Name: Emmy Violet Danvers
Mother: Vera Lynn Danvers, née Vera Lynn Smith
Father: Daniel Danvers
Spouse: NA
Eyes: Green
Height: 5'7"

I skimmed the rest, which included every crappy apartment building my mom and I had shared and every single report card I'd received in school. My soy allergy. A list of my favorite bands, books, and movies. There was some information that I hadn't known about myself. Apparently my stern-faced elementary school teacher Mrs. Wolff thought that I displayed great maturity.

I wasn't sure Mrs. Wolff would stand by those words if she could see me now.

There was more—so much more—but the massive amount of text made the individual sections blur together in my mind. I scrolled down the page, pausing only to read a handful of other teacher evaluations, before I found the statement that Officer McHaffrey had taken from me right outside the Starbucks. Right beneath it was the file Detective Dumbass appeared to be compiling on me, although the Slate had helpfully added the words *in-progress* on the tab.

Numbly, I scrolled back up to my basic statistics and tried to click on my dad's name. The Slate refused to link to a new page. My mom's name required only a brief loading session before it spit out all of her financials, her tax statements, her job recommendations, even the scripts with her lines as Bored Waitress #2 highlighted in yellow. They weren't even *good* lines.

Take table four, will ya? I gotta pee.

An unabridged account of her past was spread out before me, and yet the most I could find for Daniel Danvers was a copy of my birth certificate and a name-change form for my mother. She claimed to have taken his name simply because "Danvers" was better for her acting career, far more memorable than Smith. The one time I had pointed out that it made them sound married, she'd merely shrugged and said that the assumptions of strangers weren't her concern.

I had always thought it might be her way of trying to bring him back.

Not that it had worked, as evidenced by the section inside her file devoted to all her loser boyfriends.

My dry eyes burned as I forced myself to stare at the sweatshirts hanging in Ben's closet.

It was too much to take in. The names, dates, and figures merged into a tangled mess as I struggled to make sense of the information resting in my hands. To understand the full impact of everything laid out before me.

The Slate had access to information it shouldn't be capable of discovering.

Things that only law enforcement should be able to see after going through all the proper channels to obtain a warrant. Otherwise it was a total invasion of privacy that couldn't possibly be legal. It *definitely* wasn't ethical for me to be prying into other people's secrets this way.

So why had the old man given it to *me*?

For that matter, how had he even come to own it in the first place?

"Not good. Not good. *Not good,*" I mumbled to myself as I paced from the closet back to the bed. "You can't use this, Emmy. You need to make Ben's bed, grab your stuff, and resume your life as a normal, *sane* member of society. That means no checking into your mom's credit card history to satisfy your own curiosity."

My fingers yanked on a corner of the bedspread, sending the photo album toppling onto the floor with a muffled *thump*. Every muscle in my body stiffened.

There must be something important *that you're not telling me.*

I'd turned over Sebastian's comment so many times in my head that it felt as smooth as sea glass. It had sounded absurd when he'd first said it and nothing that had happened in the interval had changed my mind. If anything, the files on the tablet made it even more painfully obvious how little I knew about *anything*.

I curled into a ball on the floor, reliving those panic-fueled moments before Ms. Pierce had kicked down the door as an excruciatingly detailed set of flashbacks. The glow of the Slate's screen as I'd keyed in my Hail Mary of a password. The blinding flash that had spots of color spinning before my eyes. The extreme disorientation I'd felt right before the door exploded.

I'd assumed the Slate had been programmed to incapacitate me as revenge for all my failed attempts, but the Slate hadn't triggered any other emergency protocols. It hadn't instantly shut down in the library like it had in the computer lab for Audrey. The screen never blackened.

Instead, it had *identified* me with a retinal scan in an unlit room.

The blinding flash must have been part of the design, specifically created to compensate for the darkness of the room. A feature that had completely backfired last night. Although there was no way any tech engineers could have foreseen that particular flaw in the design, since most people went their entire lives without being stalked by homicidal private school teachers.

There must be something important *that you're not telling me.*

I could relate to the frustration behind those cold words. There was a hell of a lot that I still couldn't piece together. The Slate had identified me from the retinal scan. Okay, fine. Big deal. *Welcome Emmy Danvers* sprawled across the home screen had sort of spoken for itself.

There had to be a whole lot more to the story.

Instead of thumbing through over four hundred text messages clogging up my inbox, I clicked on the Sent folder.

Help.

I stared at the simple message, time-stamped for 3:17 A.M. with a location listed at the bottom of the message: *Emptor Academy, Library. 302L.*

I dimly remembered screaming, pleading, begging, as I scrambled away from a killer with a pixie cut. Nobody had heard me. I'd been certain at the time that my fate rested in the hands of whichever security guard happened to be making the rounds that night.

I hadn't considered the possibility that my Slate called in for backup.

My mind reeled. Why had it chosen Force? Surely he couldn't be the *only* person Frederick St. James trusted to watch his back in a brawl. Was the bodyguard/driver simply the closest preapproved person within a certain radius? What if Force had decided to put on his favorite tuxedo and catch a concert at the Kennedy Center? Whose name would the Slate have pulled out of its database *then*?

The closer I came to getting answers the more questions began stacking up.

The Slate buzzed softly in my lap as the inbox rose to 439 unread messages. Probably another frantic request from yet another mysterious texter. Another mystery to be unraveled. I was damn near drowning in them.

And *none* of it was pointing me in the direction of my dad. In fact, I was starting to think that the old man had given me the Slate as part of an exercise in futility. Judging by the lack of information in my dad's file, Frederick St. James had made zero progress tracking him down.

There must be something important *that you're not telling me.*

I reached for the photo album. Maybe it wasn't something that I knew. Maybe it was something that I *had*.

Carefully, I tugged the photo of my dad's left eye out of the protective plastic cover, trying not to leave any smudges on the edges. If the Slate could perform a retinal scan in a near pitch-black room, then there was a fighting chance it could handle *this*.

Before I could overthink myself into a tailspin, I snapped a picture.

Loading. Loading. Loading.

The book icon enlarged to reveal a face with only one familiar feature.

My father.

His hair was lighter than mine, a sandy reddish brown that looked carelessly rumpled even in his unsmiling snapshot. The basic information on the other side of his face made my stomach writhe like an angry snake struggling to get into striking position. My heart thudded too fast. My hands trembled unsteadily.

Name: David William Danverse
Hair: Brown
Eyes: Green
Height: 6'2"
Occupation: FBI agent, investigated in 2006, resigned in 2007
after being cleared of all charges.

That was preceded by a whole list of aliases that included Robert C. Redford and Lucas Rodriguez. He didn't look much like a "Rodriguez" to me, but apparently he hadn't gotten busted for it since there wasn't a record for any prison time. Of course, it was still entirely possible he was locked up in some hellhole where they didn't document their inmates. Or maybe he was sipping cappuccinos on the beach in some tiny Italian villa, reading a lengthy biography on Winston Churchill, and smiling as he watched his other *legitimate* kids frolicking in the waves.

My pulse increased into hyperspeed, like a caffeine junkie who'd just knocked back five shots of espresso.

I had found him.

It had only taken sixteen years, two untimely deaths, and my complete loss of faith in humanity, but I'd tracked down my father. The man who had walked out on my mom without a backward glance was only a phone call away. I sat on my hands in a desperate attempt to control the shaking. It didn't help though. Not when my whole body twitched with nervous energy. I'd spent over a decade daydreaming about a father-daughter reunion. I should have felt happier at the prospect of actually making it happen. The one constant in all those fantasies was that I'd *wanted* to find him. See him. Meet him.

I'd never imagined the possibility that my emotional range would ever be stunted to the point that I vacillated between panic, fear, anxiety, and an overwhelming numbness that left no room for enthusiasm. All I could think was that this information should have been my birthright. His face should have lingered over my crib for countless games of peekaboo. Nobody should have needed to *die* for me to find one lone picture of him.

Anger rose inside of me, flushing my cheeks and filling all the empty spaces inside me. I craved the heat of outrage, embracing it like a long lost friend. It made me reckless. Impulsive. Honest. I didn't claim to be an expert on law enforcement agencies, but I'd read enough romance novels to know that FBI agents weren't obligated to lie about what they did for a living. They weren't forbidden to get married or raise kids. They might not be able to discuss their cases at home, but they could say, "*Sorry, honey, work calls. I might be out of reach for a week or two*" if they had been handed a particularly big assignment.

If my dad thought his disappearing act would never come back to bite him, then he was in for one hell of a wakeup call.

I pressed the phone number before I could chicken out, holding my breath as the Slate sprang into action.

Riiiiiing.

Oh, holy shit. What was I doing?

Riiiiiing.

What was I supposed to say? "Hey asshole. Welcome to Fatherhood?"

Beeep!

"Um, hi," I said lamely, my anger deflating like a cheap grocery store balloon. "I'm looking for Dan . . . uh, *David*," I corrected myself. "This is . . ." *your long-lost daughter, your best kept secret, your least favorite person,* "Emmy Danvers."

I swallowed hard, feeling hopelessly unprepared to string complete sentences together. I ordered myself not to panic. Not yet.

"I've got a message from Frederick St. James. If he wants to hear it, he's going to have to call me back."

I didn't think a perky "Have a nice day!" would be the right note to end a cryptic message with my absentee father, so I simply disconnected and clutched at Ben's blankets with trembling fingers.

I'd done it. I had called him.

I had chosen my path, made my bed, fallen further down the rabbit hole—insert cliché here—but with that decision made, the worst had to be over. No more stumbling blind. No more hesitation. From this point on, I could face whatever conflict came my way without flinching.

Too bad, I didn't believe a word of my own lies.

"Toughen up, Emmy!" I snarled into the silence of Ben's bedroom. "You don't want people to push you around? Then you need to *fight back*."

Go for the jugular, girl.

Trust nobody.

The Slate clutched in my hand began to ring and my heart seized with a strangling panic.

Time to find out if those warnings applied to my own father.